AF872738

DON'T CROSS MO ELLERY

Outstanding Praise for

Don't Cross Mo Ellery

"A page-turning, laugh-out-loud romp of a mystery full of delightful shenanigans. I couldn't get enough of Mo Ellery!"

—Gloria Chao, *USA Today* bestselling author of *The Ex-Girlfriend Murder Club*

"*Don't Cross Mo Ellery* starts with a bang and gallops like a pack of poodles toward a major collision. Looking for a good time? Get yourself to Mo Ellery's side of the street."

—Lori Rader-Day, *USA Today* bestselling author of *Wreck Your Heart*

"Hilarious. A delightful and cleverly woven story starring an anxious, chaotic crossing guard. She may not be good with kids or with traffic, but she is the hero of the corner. A thoroughly charming read."

—Emily Austin, author of *Everyone in This Room Will Someday Be Dead*

"This batshit Chicago mystery had me laughing from page one! Mo's voice sparkles with absurd wit and loser authenticity. Don't miss it."

—Lina Chern, Mary Higgins Clark Award–winning author of *Play the Fool*

"It is impossible not to root for Mo. This book is winsome, full of heart, laugh-out-loud funny, and also—honestly?—really hot. The perfect reminder that, sometimes, rock bottom is where the fun begins. Birdie Horne is the literary conductor of the Hot Mess Express, and we should all hop aboard."

—Lillian Stone, author of *Everybody's Favorite*

"Never have I had such a blast reading about murder and crossing guards! *Don't Cross Mo Ellery* is a joyful escape that made me literally laugh out loud from the first page to the last! It's packed full of quirky, lovable characters and outlandish twists that kept me guessing until the very end. Birdie Horne is a wonder!"

—Mary Pauline Lowry, author of *Last Night Was Killer*

DON'T CROSS MO ELLERY

A NOVEL

BIRDIE HORNE

wm

WILLIAM MORROW

An Imprint of HarperCollins*Publishers*

HarperCollins books may be purchased for educational, business, or sales promotional use. For information, please email the Special Markets Department at SPsales@harpercollins.com.

hc.com

FIRST EDITION

Designed by Diahann Sturge-Campbell
Stop sign illustration © Vector DSGNR/Stock.Adobe.com

Library of Congress Cataloging-in-Publication Data

Names: Horne, Birdie author
Title: Don't cross Mo Ellery : a novel / Birdie Horne.
Other titles: Do not cross Mo Ellery
Description: First edition. | New York, NY : William Morrow, 2026. |
Identifiers: LCCN 2025053764 (print) | LCCN 2025053765 (ebook) |
ISBN 9780063473089 trade paperback | ISBN 9780063473096 ebook
Subjects: LCGFT: Humorous fiction | Detective and mystery fiction | Novels
Classification: LCC PS3608.O7627 D66 2026 (print) | LCC PS3608.O7627 (ebook)
LC record available at https://lccn.loc.gov/2025053764
LC ebook record available at https://lccn.loc.gov/2025053765

ISBN 978-0-06-347308-9

Printed in the United States of America

26 27 28 29 30 LBC 5 4 3 2 1

For our dear friend Joshua Briggs, who helped us become enemies

DON'T CROSS
MO ELLERY

CHAPTER 1

The first Chicago fire burned the city to the ground.

The *second* Chicago fire is happening right now, between my legs.

In a good way.

In a very, *very* good way.

My original plan was just to pop home for a quick birthday lunch with my boyfriend. Chris is on overnight shifts for his emergency medicine rotations, and this was the only time we could celebrate. I'm twenty-nine today, which is just a handful of panic attacks away from thirty, and I've already had two this morning thinking about it.

But I'm not panicking right now.

Nope, right now, I'm sprawled across our sleek midcentury coffee table naked, Chris is doing mind-boggling things with his mouth, and I'm fantasizing about calling in sick for the rest of the day.

Hard to believe that an hour ago, I was swearing at the copier. *Why do we even still* have *a copier??* I think, just as Chris does a tongue-twisty thing near my south pole, and I accidentally gasp, "Take that, Xerox!"

He lifts his head. "What did you say?"

God, I wish my brain would shut up *for once.* "Oh, uh . . ." I scramble for a reasonable thing to have said. "Don't stop!"

But Chris *does* stop, grins at me, then scoops one arm under my back and the other under my legs, trying to pick me up romance-novel style. It's an adorable idea, except he can't quite get the leverage right, and he slips, dropping me back on the table in more of a WWE kind of way.

Thankfully the table doesn't break. My tailbone, on the other hand, sends out a sharp stab of pain and I wince. *Bruised, broken, or some secret third thing?*

It's a good question, but I decide to shake it off for the moment, because there are more important, *immediate* things to take care of. That said, I also don't want Chris to try that particular move again—not with his current success rate—so instead I scoot across the coffee table, I hope sexily, my butt cheeks squeaking a little on the polished wood. He grabs my wrist and tugs me through our open-concept living room, over piles of hastily discarded clothes, and directly to the kitchen island.

I figure this signals sexy time is over, and tbh, I'm kinda bummed even though I guess a sandwich might be nice, but then he swings me around and bends me over the counter, where the cold granite makes me yelp.

Okay, this is a totally different kind of lunch meat scenario.

I should mention that this is *not* how we usually operate. We're *bed* sex people. Maybe once, twice a week, ever since we first got together in college, when we fell into a routine and kept it. Which is fine! Beds are comfortable, they're specially made for horizontal activities. Honestly, I don't even go for sofa sex, because (a) it's a really expensive microsuede couch his mom bought for us and (b) I worry about the cushions getting funky. People *sit* on those.

But when I got home from work and opened the door, Chris was standing right there, pitching a tent in his pajama bottoms, and before I knew it, there we were! On the coffee table! And now apparently the kitchen island!

And okay, *that* makes me think about how I literally just called our sex life "fine" and maybe twenty-nine is too young to be living that kind of life, when suddenly it's *Welcome to Dick City!* and I can't think about anything at all.

Chris grips my wrists together in one hand, pinning them behind my back, and holy smokes, what has gotten into him, this whole kitchen counter scenario is *very* hot, and I'm doing the mental acrobatics of being extremely turned on while also taking play-by-play notes of what's happening because hopefully it'll be Our New Thing. I honestly did not know sex could *be* like this! I didn't know I *liked* this! I'm having a kind of simultaneous mind-body revelation right now—everything is vibrating!

And I guess I mean that literally—because right then, when Chris lets go of my hands to grab my hips, my right arm slingshots itself across the counter.

And knocks over the terra-cotta salt bowl his aunt gave us that we never use.

Which spills a big pile of fancy salt all over the counter.

And because my brain is not functioning right, and only some glimmer of instinct is still operating, I automatically reach out, grab a handful of salt, and throw it over my left shoulder.

The way you're supposed to.

You know, so you don't have bad luck. Look, it's a good instinct.

Except at that moment, Chris is, of course, very *very* close behind me, and I guess his eyes must be open because he screams and cries, "My eyes!"

Shitballs.

"*What is this?*" Chris yells, rubbing his eyes.

"Just salt! Sorry!"

His voice is about an octave higher than usual. "You mean the *cayenne* salt?"

Who can keep track of all these fancy salts? "I didn't want bad luck!"

"So you threw it in my eyeballs?"

My brain panics, bombarding me with questions: *Why were your eyes open? You are not an eyes-open sex guy! Was I boring you? Were you thinking about work? Looking around for your phone?* But also, if this is a thing he's into now—unblinking sex—I don't want to slut shame!

"I'll get some water!" I yell instead and run to the fridge. Chris's water bottle is sitting in there, exactly where it always is. I grab it and run back to Chris, whose moans are definitely more pained than swoony now, and it's at that extremely inconvenient moment that my phone rings. It's on the edge of the island, where I dropped it whilst being consensually mauled.

I lunge over and check the number.

It's work.

"Shhh," I say solemnly to Chris, who is sort of whimpering, and then I answer as I open the drawer where we keep the dish towels. "Hello?"

"Hey," says the voice on the other end. It's Ollie, who manages the front desk. "You working remote this afternoon?"

"Yes, that is exactly right," I say confidently, as if that was my plan this whole time. "Everything okay?"

"Kendra wants you to join the Midwest Tool Warehouse meeting. They just started."

Nuts. Even though it's three months away, we're already nailing down the marketing material for their annual Black Friday sale. Kendra, my boss, owns our scrappy little agency, and she literally can't comprehend why anyone would *not* be working all the time. She works through lunch. She definitely does not have sex through lunch. So of course there's a meeting.

I would rather throw cayenne salt in my own eyeballs right now.

"Okay, sounds good!" I say, tossing the dish towel at Chris.

He still has his eyes closed, so it just smacks him in the face and falls to the ground.

"Why do you want to hurt me?" he whimpers.

"Mo? You there?" Ollie says. "Click the link I just sent and hit 'Join.'"

"Got it, got it," I say to the phone. I maneuver Chris onto one of the kitchen stools. He's got his eyes squeezed shut. "Stay strong," I whisper. "I'm going to flush it out."

He nods helplessly, and I make soothing noises so he feels taken care of.

I tip Chris's head back and grab the dish towel from the floor to hold under his cheek, while, with the other hand, I hang up the call, check my email, click the link, and hit Join. Once the call starts, I'm not totally sure how to do all this eye-flushing *and* pay attention if someone asks me a question.

I shove the phone in Chris's hand and lean over to whisper in his ear, "Video's disabled, but I'm not muted, so just hold this, okay?"

He grips the phone in response, and I'm pretty impressed with my multitasking skills.

Speaking of multitasking, I'm wondering if the sex is over, or if we can circle back to it after I get off this call.

Or during? Hmm.

"Thanks for being *prompt*, everyone," Kendra says, and I know that's a dig at me, since she had to get Ollie to track me down, but I decide not to care. The meeting wasn't on my calendar. This is fine.

"Ready?" I whisper to Chris.

He nods.

"So what are we—" Kendra starts.

I squeeze the water bottle so it flows directly into Chris's eyes. He muffles a scream, and then he whisper-whines, "*Lemon! There's lemon in this water!*"

"Lemon in water, cayenne in salt!" I whisper-hiss back. "Is *anything* what it seems in this condo?"

Meanwhile, through the phone, Kendra's getting louder: "—looking at in terms of OH. MY. GOD."

The sounds of chaos erupt on the other end of the phone, and I figure the Midwest Tool Warehouse deals must be pretty incredible this year, until I hear Kendra yell, "WHOSE PENIS IS THIS?"

I cannot believe I'm missing a meeting where somebody's showing their penis is my first thought.

As I snatch the phone back from Chris and turn the screen to face me, my brain starts putting the pieces together. Not fast enough, though.

"MO ELLERY, DID YOU COME TO THIS MEETING *NAKED*??" Kendra demands.

"Whoops, my wi-fi's going out," I say, making crackling noises with my voice like it's an old-fashioned landline.

There's another burst of chaos as I end the call.

Okay, so my video was *not* disabled.

Chris blinks his bloodshot, red-rimmed eyes at me in shock. "Did your entire office just see my penis?"

CHAPTER 2

I go straight to the bathroom, lie on the cool tile floor, and proceed to hyperventilate.

After a couple of minutes, Chris comes in, pajama bottoms back on but *sans* sexy tent, and holds up my phone. Even from down here on the floor, his eyes are inflamed and puffy and terrible. He looks like a hungover possum.

"Kendra just sent you a text. You're, um, fired."

An involuntary wail, reminiscent of a car horn, comes out of me. This is bad. This is very bad. The walls close in, my chest tightens . . .

"Honestly, you can't be *too* surprised," Chris says diplomatically. "What with all the nudity."

"I'm having a heart attack," I mumble.

"I don't think you are," he says.

"This is definitely a heart attack."

"Speaking of," he says, squatting next to me like a coach, "I've been thinking about hearts lately. As a doctor, we deal with them a lot.

Really resilient organs. Can take tons of bad stuff and still be totally fine."

"What are you talking about?" I groan.

"Do you want a paper bag to breathe into?" he asks helpfully.

This is his answer for everything. A pep talk and a paper bag. It's adorable, but it does sometimes make me worry about his future in the medical field. "Yes."

He starts to leave.

"Wait." I stop him. "Hand me my phone. I can fix this. It's not too late."

Chris hesitates. "Are you sure you don't want to give it a minute?"

"It's my dying wish."

"You're not dy—"

"*Hand me the phone.*"

From the bathroom floor, I text a truly heartfelt apology to Kendra—one of my best—adding that I've been struggling a bit with this whole birthday thing, but I can be back in the office in fifteen minutes, and I hope we can all ultimately agree that this was hilarious.

When I don't get a reply, I try Chris's approach.

Me: Or why don't I just take some time off? Let things cool down before I come back?

This time, she responds immediately.

Kendra: Are you KIDDING me? You are fired. SO fired. SO PERMANENTLY FIRED. There do not exist enough words for me to describe how fired you are. You're lucky

Midwest Tool Warehouse is run by old guys who are too embarrassed to admit they saw naked people they weren't married to.

Me: So it's a no

Kendra: IT IS A NO

By the time Chris comes back, I've flopped over and mushed my face on the tile. This is why you keep your bathroom floor clean. For these moments.

"I'm still fired," I mumble.

"Well, yeah," says Chris, holding out the paper lunch bag. "That makes sense. But if there's one thing I know about you, Mo, you're strong. When bad things happen, you dust yourself off—"

A sudden thought occurs to me, and I sit up. "We've never had sex outside the bedroom, right?"

"Not even once." Chris shakes his head. "And you must be really disappointed about that. Which I can *totally* understand. I mean, that's not the life you want, is it? Like, I'm so boring and you're so adventurous—"

"Am I?" That distracts me for a second. It's not how *I* would describe myself.

"Of course you are!"

I guess I am now? I snap my fingers. Bingo. "Chris, what if I have one of those tumors that makes you do things that are out of character? Kendra couldn't fire me then, right? That's illegal."

Chris scrunches his face up, like he's being very delicate about his answer. "I think you were just horny."

"Well, I should probably get an MRI anyway, just to be sure. Plus one of those heart attack tests," I say, standing up and immediately going weak-kneed as the realization hits. "Chris, I just got *fired.* I won't have insurance to pay for all this!"

"*Mo.*" He pulls me into a hug. "It's going to be okay."

"How can you be so sure?" I ask pathetically.

"Listen, I can't always be here to make you feel better when you freak out about nothing."

Okay, that is not fair.

Chris and I have an agreement. And the agreement is that I get to freak out about all my weird health fears whenever I want, and he gets to make me feel better. That is our deal.

He holds up the paper bag again. "This is my last lunch bag. Out of like a hundred. And I haven't been using them for lunch."

"I'm stressed out," I say. "I'm about to turn thirty."

"Next year!"

"I got *fired*. And so on."

"You had a nice birthday lunch, right?" he says.

"Other than the fact that you're the only one who ate—*heeeeeyo*!"

I'm pretty impressed with myself for coming up with a joke mid–heart attack/tumor.

"*Mo—*"

The tone of his voice is clear: not the time for jokes, got it. This is supposed to be one of those heart-to-heart relationship moments.

"Seriously, you did great," I say. "I'm not sure I needed a heart resilience lecture, but otherwise this was a terrific birthday lunch. And you take amazing care of me. I really appreciate all the lunch bags. Like my mom says—if you move in with a doctor, nothing that bad can happen to you."

Chris blinks in surprise.

"I mean, that's not *why* I moved in . . ."

"That's what you just said."

"No, that's what *my mom* said. I moved in because we've been together for ten years."

"That's . . . not a great reason either."

I can't put my finger on why, but he seems almost . . . happy when he says that?

I pause. "Are we fighting? Are you mad because I showed everybody your penis?"

"This is not about my penis," Chris says firmly. After a second, during which I suspect we are both thinking about his penis, he sighs and is quiet for a really long time.

He isn't looking at me.

Wait, what *is* this?

Oh shit, I know this Chris. This is the Chris who hates confrontation. He literally freezes and cannot speak.

Don't help him don't help him don't help—

"What are you trying to say?" I ask quietly.

Dammit, Mo.

"I just—" He freezes again. He takes a deep breath, and then he fucking says it. "I just wonder if we're together for the right reasons."

What do you *say* to that? "But we've always been together."

He runs a hand through his really nice hair and shrugs. "I hope we can be friends."

FRIENDS?

My ribs start to close in on me again. I snatch the paper bag from him, but we're both holding on too tight, and it rips before I can hyperventilate into it. I half-heartedly crumple my piece up and feel it drop from my hand. This cannot be happening.

"Can't we be together *and* be friends? Like at the same time?" My voice is going up into the stratosphere, like I've sucked on helium, like I'm the balloon that can pull us out of this mess.

He doesn't answer.

"Did you coffee table me out of *pity*?" My voice echoes off the expensive tile.

And he can't look me in the eye. He's staring intently at the sink, then at the daddy longlegs in the corner, then in the mirror for moral support. "Breakup sex is totally normal," he says in an infuriating doctor voice, as if a doctor would ever say that.

"That was not breakup sex, Chris. It's only breakup sex if BOTH PEOPLE KNOW IT'S BREAKUP SEX. Otherwise it's just sex with really shitty timing!"

"I'm sorry, Mo," he says, and I want to shove the entire roll of toilet paper in his mouth before he can finish the sentence.

But I don't.

And he does.

"I think we should . . . take a time-out."

CHRIS CAN'T BRING himself to kick me out of what is now very clearly HIS condo. He shrugs sheepishly in the direction of the nice microsuede couch we've never had sex on, as though I should consider sleeping on it, and I almost throw up.

In approximately thirty-seven seconds, I throw some clean underwear and a couple of T-shirts in a duffel bag, all while blowing through an entire box of tissues.

Chris went out so I could do this part by myself.

Before I go, I take a handful of tissues and one more look around the sleek condo his parents bought. I notice for the first time that there's hardly any trace of me here. The bathroom with classy aquamarine tiles and hip-kitsch tropical bird wallpaper. The bedroom with the memory foam king mattress I've slept on every night—the mattress that conveniently springs right back, as though I was never on it. The kitchen with every cool gadget I could possibly want, if I knew how to cook. The living room with the floor-to-ceiling windows and the tasteful, faux-industrial light fixtures that I would never have chosen.

Chris is out there somewhere, waiting for me to leave. He doesn't want me here anymore. He doesn't want me anywhere anymore. I glare at the coffee table with its streak where my butt used to be. Traitor.

I've never felt so alone.

I grab the one piece of evidence that I lived here—the photo of Chris and me from graduation ten years ago. The two of us smile for the camera, and for the first time, the thing I notice isn't how happy we look; it's that I haven't changed at all. I look exactly the same. I could still be that eighteen-year-old kid, and not in a cute way.

My straight, boring brown hair hangs to my shoulders, which always seemed like the responsible choice for a person who isn't particularly tall or short. My eyes are blue, but not the exciting, piercing variety. My boobs are shrug-worthy. My smile is crooked, in a way that says my childhood dentist was more into golf than teeth. Next to me, Chris looks goofy—a little skinny, a little scraggly, a little too earnest.

The two of us used to match, but I stayed the same while he went and got muscles and Invisalign. Now he binges YouTube videos about clothes so he knows what to wear for his body type and also I think he plucks his unibrow.

He's the main character.

I'm a flyover girlfriend.

No wonder he wants to move on.

Okay, he didn't say that *exactly*, he said a bunch of stuff about how the only constant is change but the heart is resilient (UGH), how people sometimes drift apart, how we both need to spread our wings and fly, how we're like muscles and gas transfer.

The metaphors were, frankly, relentless and sometimes confusing.

But the overall message was clear.

I stay an extra moment to run an antibacterial wipe over the coffee table. I have the sudden desire to erase every last trace of myself from this condo. That, plus it just doesn't seem sanitary to have a butt streak where you put your pizza. Not that Chris eats pizza anymore.

And doing something—doing anything, really—will keep me from spiraling about how quickly my whole life has collapsed into disaster.

Just three hours ago, I couldn't get the copier to work. Right now, I would give anything to go back in time and swear at that copier. But I don't get to have nice things anymore. Not copiers. Not Chris.

I'm losing everything, I want to howl, but it's not true; I still have Hannah, who was already my best friend before Chris and I even met. Han is my ride-or-die. And yeah, she's fancy now, an up-and-coming influencer with a whole wellness brand that actually helps people, but we've held each other's hair while puking, and nothing will ever change that.

Down on the street, I gaze up at my fancy condo life one last time. I can almost see myself waving at me from the seventh-floor window-with-skyline-view. Then my Uber driver honks, tapping his wrist, and the fantasy shatters for good.

Leaving the ashes of my former life behind, I head to Hannah's two-flat in Loganville. She bought it with her boyfriend and her other boyfriend and his girlfriend who is also her first boyfriend's girlfriend when the neighborhood was up-and-coming and something something low interest rates. The four of them are living their dreams.

When I first told my parents Hannah was in a polycule, they thought I was talking about a geometrically unusual building, and I didn't have the heart to explain that it was how some people dated these days. And honestly, it seems like a whole second job just keeping track of everyone's feelings, not to mention all the associated terminology, but it works for them and they're all awesome people and always seem happy and in love. I can't even hold on to one boyfriend, and here's Hannah with a small city of lovers happily taking care of one another in an amazing piece of real estate in a great neighborhood.

I tamp down my jealousy as I ring their doorbell. They all live in the upper apartment and rent the downstairs one to help with the mortgage, and I know for a *fact* that it's currently vacant.

When Hannah opens the door, she looks exhausted, like she's been up all night. Even worse, she kind of wedges herself in the doorway, blocking me from getting in.

"I thought we weren't meeting up till later?" she says. "I didn't lose track of time, did I?"

I actually completely forgot Hannah was taking me out for fancy cocktails for my birthday.

"Chris and I broke up," I blurt, my eyeballs smarting with tears. "And I got fired."

"Oh, babe, not on your *birthday*," she says, enveloping me in a big hug, while still, incidentally, not letting me inside. "I'm so sorry, he doesn't deserve you, never has. And we already hated Kendra, right? So we just hate them both?"

"I'm not ready to be mad yet," I say, wiping my eyes with my sleeve. "I need some time to wallow in self-pity mode. In nobody-wants-me-and-I'm-going-to-be-broke-soon mode. Speaking of being broke do you think we could talk inside for a sec?"

Hannah glances over her shoulder and grimaces. "It's sort of a tricky moment. We're, um . . . negotiating boundaries. It's a tough state of the union, hardest one this year so far."

State of the union. They literally have names for their arguments. I feel like such a teenager next to them.

She squeezes my hand and says, "I know this is the worst timing, but could it wait till cocktails tonight?"

"Totally." I try to sound upbeat. "It's fine. Could you just let me into the apartment downstairs, then? I only need a place to stay for like a week. No more than a month or two. Probably."

Hannah looks at her feet and sighs, which is not exactly a good sign. "We're kind of working through some new rules around that space, Mo," she says softly. "I'm sorry."

"Oh," I say, stung. "Okay. Can I just sleep on your couch then?"

She gives me a look.

"I'll do your dishes?" I plead.

"If it was up to me, you *know* I'd say yes," she says, her face full of regret. "I'm really sorry. I have to get back to the house meeting, but I'll text you soon, okay? We're still going out tonight, promise."

"Han—" I say, stunned. "Where am I supposed to go? I don't have any other options!"

"Of course you do," she says, giving me a quick kiss on the cheek before she disappears back into the house. "You're like the most resilient person I know."

Ugh. If I *never* hear that word again, it'll be too soon.

And even worse, she's right.

I *do* have another option.

CHAPTER 3

They call Chicago a city of neighborhoods.

But it's more like somebody went and smashed together a bunch of *very* specific small towns. We've got Chinatown and Little Puerto Rico; Ukrainian Village and German Square. There's Boystown. Slag Valley. The Viagra Triangle. One neighborhood is known for having wild parrots everywhere. One actually smells like chocolate.

In theory, Chicago is a place where you can find your people, whether they're promiscuous grandpas or parrot-obsessed birdwatchers.

But now, as a new Uber drives me away from Hannah's—away from the hip restaurants, away from the job I've lost, away from *Chris*—each passing neighborhood reminds me that I don't belong anywhere anymore.

The driver hums along to moody jazz on the radio and takes a right, closing in on my destination as we cross the invisible border of the neighborhood I know best. The neighborhood that's stuck in time. The neighborhood that practically smells like shag carpet and wood paneling.

It doesn't get any more old-school than my parents' block. Their squat seventies-ish bungalow is miles away from Chris's condo in every sense of the word. It's way west, the low-flying planes constantly reminding you exactly how close you are to O'Hare Airport. And no one in their right mind would ever, ever describe it as sleek.

The car comes to a stop in my parents' driveway.

"Thanks a lot," I say to the driver.

I don't move.

"Are . . . you going to get out?" the guy asks, a saxophone wailing weakly from the car's speakers.

Behind each bungalow and two-flat in my parents' neighborhood lurks a network of alleyways, for garages, dumpsters, and a whole community of flies and raccoons and bedbug-riddled armchairs, and I can't help thinking that's what my life has become without me even realizing it. Respectable and orderly on the outside, and just a smelly ol' dumpster-fest out back.

"Do I have to?" I ask.

"Here," he says with a sigh. "Take this bottle of water with you."

A bottle of water. Tears well in my eyes as I remember the last bottle of water I held, the one also filled with lemon juice.

"No, thank you," I say bravely. "I think I should face this one alone."

I step out of the Elantra, hoisting my sad duffel, and trudge up the old, cracked driveway that's slowly devolving its way back to gravel. I stop for a second at the doormat shaped like a can of Old Style, trying to psych myself up to ring the doorbell. It feels like pulling a fire alarm—once I do it, there's no turning back. I take a deep breath and force myself to push the button.

And they . . . do not answer the door.

I know they're home; I can hear someone scrambling around in there.

But no one is coming to greet me.

My stomach clutches, and oh god, do they know? Did Chris call them? They love him, and Mom checks my left hand every single time I see her, and the thought of my own parents being so upset by our breakup that they'd avoid their own daughter *on her birthday* is—well, I just don't think I could take it.

I'm about to ring the bell again, when the door flies open, and there's Dad, wearing nothing but his bathrobe—and a bedazzled pink plastic cowboy hat that says "29 and Lookin' *FINE*." Behind him, I hear Mom yell, "Davey! The hat! You're still wearing the hat!"

I don't think he hears her, though, because he's standing in the doorway staring at me, deer-in-the-headlights style, clutching at the lapels of his robe like it's a string of pearls and he's a '50s housewife.

"It's . . . not the DoorDash," Dad says, sounding strangled.

"If they're going to take so long, I guess I could just *make* some whipped cream," Mom announces as she steps out from the hall that leads to their bedroom. She is also radically underdressed, wearing nothing but very high heels and an apron emblazoned with the phrase, "Who's Your Mama?"

Oh god.

I think the heart attack is coming back.

A FEW MINUTES later, the three of us are sitting at the bright yellow Formica kitchen table avoiding eye contact, but at least everyone's fully dressed. I spin the lazy Susan in the middle of the table like it's a roulette wheel. I don't know why—all I'm doing today is losing.

"It's just . . . *we* like to celebrate your birthday too," Dad says, staring up at the ceiling.

"It was a pretty big deal, you know," Mom adds. "That we succeeded."

Dad picks up. "On account of my low—"

"*Nope*," I say quickly. "We are not talking about this."

And here I thought there was nothing I wanted to talk about *less* than my breakup.

Welp.

"I need to move in for a while," I blurt out. No sense beating around the bush. So to speak.

They share a look that I have zero interest in decoding.

Mom clears her throat. "What happened with—"

"Chris and I are taking a short, very *mutual* breather," I say, hoping that my subtext, DO NOT ASK ME ABOUT THIS, is very, very clear.

"I guess I could empty out your old bedroom?" Dad asks uncertainly.

"Not necessary!" I say as brightly as I can. "I'll just move the boxes off the bed. This is short term. *Very* short term." It's a lie and we all know it.

Dad gives me an awkward thumbs-up.

I'm trying not to take the lack of enthusiasm personally. After all, it's not just them. None of us want me here.

After a moment of silence, Mom says, "Well, what do you want for a birthday dinner?"

I opt for full-on comfort food, and we order a couple pizzas from Raul's, which happened to be my birthday dinner every year until I turned sixteen. The great thing about thin crust tavern-style pizza is you can stuff approximately a million squares into your mouth before you want to die.

Comforting, yes. Also extremely depressing.

Once we've placed the order, I text Hannah and see if she can pick me up at my parents' house for our night out. And also maybe bring a cute outfit I can borrow.

Hannah doesn't text back right away, and I'll admit I'm feeling PRETTY sorry for myself, and rightly so, as a person who just got fired, dumped, and then had to listen to her dad wax nostalgic about his sperm count. But I tell myself she's still state-of-the-unioning, or doing whatever an influencer does during the day. I decide to make the best of things, so I grab some fresh twin sheets from the linen closet and stick my head in my old room.

Ugh.

Dad, *come on.*

It is a literal fire hazard in here. Boxes piled on boxes. Novelty Zippo lighters precariously balanced on top of propane-fueled egg cookers (you know, for camping). The man is addicted to eBay and factory warehouses. When he's not preparing people's taxes in the spring, he's buying bulk overstock sales of the actual dumbest things on earth, and then trying to resell them. That Old Style welcome mat? There are two hundred more in the garage. He always has a scheme. Always some big new thing that's gonna make them rich.

I spend about ten minutes moving boxes of Vienna Beef hot dog air fresheners (no ketchup!) and determine that half a bed is all I deserve anyway. I've just curled up on it pitifully when Mom appears in the doorway.

"I don't understand," she says with a frown. "I thought for sure he was going to propose."

"Well, he did not," I mumble. "He did the opposite of that."

"Maybe he was waiting for you? Did you consider proposing to *him*? Maybe that's worth a try?"

"Pretty sure that ship has sailed," I say miserably.

"Well, what happened? Did you have a fight? What led up to it?"

I decide to leave out the sexy business. "I'd just, um, gotten fired."

"You what?" Her eyebrows go up.

"I . . . also got fired today."

Her lips mash together to form a knife's edge.

"Mom, I'm handling all of this," I say, trying to sound like I mean it.

She sits down on the edge of the bed and sighs deeply, and I can already tell I'm going to hate this so much. I wonder if it would be possible to permanently Freaky Friday myself with one of those propane-fueled egg cookers. Live a simple life. Have a purpose: the cooking of eggs.

I have never been so jealous of a useless gadget.

Mom sighs again, like I might have missed it the first go-around. "It's time to take life seriously, Mo."

"I didn't *try* to get fired and dumped," I argue.

"Maybe not, but be honest with yourself, you have no drive, sweetie—no ambition. Not in your life, not at work. You just take the path of least resistance. Look at Hannah," Mom says. "She's got herself figured out. Found her thing, worked hard at it."

"So I should be an *influencer*?" I snort. "I don't have that kind of charisma."

"You don't have to be anything except yourself. Once you figure that out, everything else will fall into place."

On cue, a Vienna Beef hot dog air freshener falls off the closest box and hits me on the forehead.

I make a noncommittal groan and flop face down into the pillow as she strokes my hair. Then after a beat, she adds, "I just don't want you to forget that you *are* almost thirty."

Forget? I wish.

In a moment of mercy from the universe, my phone pings. It's a text from Hannah. Hannah the Perfect.

> I'm out front. Mo, you cannot stay here.

My best friend in the whole world paces back and forth between the boxes. "This is where you got potty-trained. Where you ate a box of crayons on a dare." She flings her arms around. "The wallpaper is *Finding Nemo*."

"I told you I had no other options."

"Okay, you don't get to blame me for this," she says. "You are a grown-up."

"Grown-ups like fish," I whimper.

She holds her hand out to me. "We're taking a walk."

"What's that gonna do?"

"*Now*," Hannah says. I stand up, but I do it slowly so she knows I don't want to.

It really is nice outside—a mid-August day but not too humid, and unlike my bedroom, it doesn't smell like fake hot dogs. There's a light breeze in the air, and all around us the cicadas are screaming. Same, cicadas. Same.

"I wish I could stay with you," I say glumly.

"I know for a fact that you have some savings," she says.

"Like three months' worth."

"That's plenty. There are tons of studio apartments for rent this time of year. You just need to hit the right neighborhood. Like Buffalo Park. Off the end of the Brown Line."

"*All* the way at the end?" I wail. "Is that even still in the city?"

She stops and gives me a hard look. "I'm sorry, as opposed to your parents' house, which is practically a runway at O'Hare?"

"It is *free*, though," I mutter.

"You have two choices here, Mo," Hannah says sternly. "You can be a hot mess with *Finding Nemo* wallpaper, or you can at least *try* to get your shit together."

I want to explain that I'm a hot mess *without Finding Nemo* wallpaper, too, but I'm too afraid she'd agree with me.

"So what's it going to be?" she asks.

"I'm going to look around for a cheap studio," I recite.

"Good girl," she says, and we start walking again.

"But that still doesn't fix the job problem," I say. "How am I supposed to pay for an apartment? Not to mention all these health problems I've accumulated today."

"You could get marketplace insurance," she suggests.

"Oh, sure. If I want to pay a billion dollars in premiums only to then *also* pay for everything else."

"Okay, so let's put a budget together. What do you think you spend the most money on?" she says.

"I don't know, it just disappears!"

Hannah sighs, and I can tell I've disappointed her with my chaos monkey lifestyle once again.

The truth is that, over the years, I fell into a habit of letting Chris pay for all the essentials, which—I know—does not reflect well on me. I try logic instead.

"Believe me, I *want* to be gainfully employed. But even if I apply for a job today and got an interview tomorrow, it'll take at least a month—"

Hannah stops abruptly. I slam into her. "Oh my god," she says.

"What?" I ask, alarmed.

She turns around with a huge grin on her face. This is not a moment for a huge grin.

"I know you think my predicament is hilarious," I say, "but this is actually my real life."

She points toward the corner across from the grade school, where the neighborhood gardeners have really dropped the ball. A patch of desiccated tulips has fallen over, and impaling them is a plastic yard sign. "We just fixed your job problem."

I squint, reading the sign. This can't be happening.

"Hannah? No. No way. You're obviously kidding, yes?"

But she's not kidding. At all. She puts her hands on my shoulders and looks deep into my eyes. "What does the U stand for in UPGRADE?"

UPGRADE is her assertiveness program on social media, the one that took off and made her a full-time influencer. She helps people upgrade themselves is the whole idea. Simple. Brilliant. And Hannah has always given excellent advice, so it's actually really cool that she gets to use her skills in this way. It's just . . . it also feels weird that the advice she used to give me is now available to hundreds of thousands of fans. I mean, if I ask for her advice now, am I just one of her fans? You can't be a groupie to your own best friend, right? Or can you?

No. I'm going to handle this my way. I shake my head and, only half joking, say, "Don't you dare use your influencer powers on me—"

"Don't be a stubborn baby," she says. "What's the U, Mo?"

"Understand What You Want," I mutter.

"Check! *You* want a job. Now what's the P?"

I sigh. "Pay Attention to Signs."

She pulls the sign out of the lawn and holds it in the air triumphantly. "Here's your sign, kiddo. Happy birthday!"

I read the sign again, each word a nail in the coffin of my soul.

Looking for flexible part-time work with health insurance?
Become a school crossing guard.
Start today.

CHAPTER 4

News flash: I am not good with either kids or traffic. And, as it turns out, kids plus traffic is the sum total of what crossing guards need to be good at.

I've been on the job for two weeks, and every day is a nightmare of screaming, sprinting kids and drivers with a fetish for kid-flattening.

"Heeeeey, buddy," I say, as a kid approaches the corner. I say it the way you might talk to a horse, or a bear—the kinds of animals that can smell fear.

This kid can totally smell my fear.

He's glaring at me and wielding his dinosaur lunch box like he might swing it at my head, but despite this, I squat down to his height, so he can see me as friendly and approachable. I smile like I'm not scared of getting brained by a lunch box. "How about today, let's stop at the curb and wait for me to go out first, okay?"

The kid narrows his eyes at me. I narrow mine back.

"Don't even think about it," I say.

The little turd grins and then sprints at full tilt across the street, flipping off the drivers who, thankfully, for once, are actually paying attention and screech to a halt to avoid steamrolling him.

That's it. I am going to get fired. AGAIN. I have one job here and it is literally to not let anybody die, and it is exceedingly clear to me that sooner or later I am going to fail.

And look, I tried not to take this gig, I really did. I *tried* to come up with my own solution and get a real job. But it turns out word travels fast when you show your (actual) ass in a client meeting. Chicago's a small world when it comes to boutique marketing agencies, and the only thing Kendra loves more than work is work gossip. I figure everybody in the city knew my bra size by EOD.

At some point, I'll need a new job, or even just an extra job, because this one pays peanuts and my savings, as previously indicated, are nil. But my first priority at the moment is insurance, because all these heart attacks aren't going to pay for themselves. I don't even have Chris to hand me paper bags anymore.

So here I am.

Standing on a street corner, wearing a neon traffic vest that very much does not match my fabulous business casual outfit and espadrilles—neither of which are *technically* regulation crossing guard attire, but I just can't bring myself to wear the baby blue polo and knee-length navy shorts that make me look like a deranged mailman. Oh, and I'm holding a stop sign the size of the friggin' *sun*.

And that's not even the worst of it. Kids flipping the bird at speeding SUVs are a minor annoyance compared to my new archnemesis.

AKA: Poodle Dude.

I don't know his name, I just know that he drives a seafoam-green Kia Sportage and has *at least* three standard poodles, because every time he drives past, there's a poodle sticking a white, fluffy head out of each passenger window. He comes through my intersection every day at the same time, and every day he is somehow more pissed off than the last. Best of all—he seems delightfully hell-bent on running me over.

Poodle Dude actually *speeds up* when he sees me and then screams at me for being in his way.

It's definitely personal.

Days like this, I really miss that shitty copier.

"Hey, I mean it, *slow down*!" I shout, chasing after another child with a death wish. Like I needed the job to be any harder, this kid isn't even going the right way—he's hustling *away* from school, like he forgot his lunch or something. By the time I've made it to the middle of the intersection, the kid has already sprinted across the street, toward the construction site on the opposite corner featuring my favorite view: a half-built and possibly abandoned parking garage.

Whew, these suckers are *fast.*

I realize I'm still standing in the middle of the intersection when a car honks at me, the driver yells, "What the hell is your problem?!," and I shuffle back to the curb sheepishly. Meanwhile, the kid ducks under a hole in the chain-link fence surrounding the abandoned construction site. This doesn't strictly seem "safe" or "legal," but there haven't been any actual construction workers here since I started at this job, so I guess it's fine? I mean, what can be in there other than a lot of rusty nails and loose pipes and chain saws and stuff. Totally acceptable shortcut for children.

Anyway, the fence and the construction site are not my realm.

My realm is the street, I think dramatically as I pull out my phone to check the time. *Please let this shift be over soon.*

"You're not supposed to look at your phone," says a kid next to me, looking at her phone.

My face gets hot. "I'm not looking at my phone, I'm checking the time."

"On your phone."

"Well, yeah."

"So you admit you were looking at your phone."

"I . . . that's . . ."

We face off for a second. She's probably twelve and she's weirdly confident and has a lot of pink hair. Her eye contact is . . . intense. Honestly, she terrifies me.

I may be new to dealing with kids, but there's one thing I do know: Don't argue with the tweens. They will destroy you.

After a long, tense moment, I realize that she's actually just waiting for me to walk her across the street. *She* doesn't think we're in a face-off. She couldn't care less, which somehow only makes this even more humiliating. I sigh and step into the crosswalk, stop sign held high, before she and her friends cross.

"Have a good day," I mutter.

"Always do," she says cheerfully.

Must be nice.

I've just turned away from her when I catch a glimpse of the older lady who lives in the house just to the left of the construction fence. She's hard to miss, always sporting a HUGE floppy green hat. That, and she resents me with an intensity that could probably heat my apartment.

My first day on the job, I smiled my biggest "be nice to the olds" smile and tried to crossing-guard her, but as I held my sign up, she stopped dead in the middle of the street. She folded her arms over her chest, and said, "I'm not a child, I know how to do this by myself." She wouldn't finish crossing until I went back and stood on the curb. She even made me turn my back to her so I "wouldn't be tempted."

Another time, she hid behind a tree for a full seven minutes. We locked eyes. "Don't even think about it, ma'am!" I yelled.

"Don't 'ma'am' me, you fascist!"

"Just because I wear a uniform—" I started to argue, but before I got any further, she ran right into traffic, yelling at a car for almost plowing her down.

Needless to say, she is not my biggest fan.

So I'm obviously thrilled she's back.

This time, she ducks between two parked cars, her green hat bobbing above the roofs, like she's in a knockoff *Mission: Impossible* for old ladies. I wave and shout, "Good morning, *ma'am*!" so she knows I'm onto her.

Then, as I'm herding the next wave of children, she speed walks across the middle of the block, nowhere near the crosswalk.

And flips me off in that old Italian way where it's your whole arm.

I flip the bird back at her, going on adrenaline and pure instinct. The kids in the intersection giggle and immediately start flipping each other off. Meanwhile their parents go stone-faced, and whoops—like I said, not great with kids.

I am really doing an excellent job of charming the residents of my new neighborhood.

The first bell rings, which means it's almost time for the grand finale of my morning: Poodle Dude. Worse than judgy parents, mean old ladies, and death-defying children put together. It'd probably be funny if he wasn't out here trying to run me over on the regular.

Every day, I dread the approach of 8:13 a.m. (Poodle Dude is *very* punctual). Getting yelled at and nearly run over is not good for my nerves, which are not good to begin with. My chest feels tight in anticipation, so I try to breathe through it like Hannah taught me. She's the reason I have this job, so what the heck—I might as well lean in and UPGRADE the situation. If that's possible.

And since the G in UPGRADE is for Ground Yourself, I give it a shot.

The breathing doesn't work, of course, but I power through anyway. I'm just wrapping up the four-part breathing, trying to calm myself, when my exhale gets caught in my throat.

Because holy shit. Forget Poodle Dude. My life may be about to change for the better.

But first, let's back up.

So, both my new apartment and my new job are in Buffalo Park—Hannah was right about there being some cheap options up here. But Buffalo Park is in the nosebleeds of Chicago. I might as well be in Wisconsin. And the people who live here are not the quick-walking suits I'm used to. Everyone who crosses the street has either a dog or a kid. And sure, my job is at the junction of a school and a dog park, but still.

Point is, I never thought I'd see someone I *know* in my new neighborhood.

And yet, half a block away, walking toward me and scrolling on his phone, is *Mark Sunari*.

This is a message from the universe. This is hope, in the form of a mustache (they're back again, apparently), a patterned shirt, and cuffed pants.

This is a lifeline.

Mark is VP of Creative at Livewire, another scrappy little marketing agency in the city. We met at a networking event about seven years ago, and he was chill and smart and told me to reach out if I ever wanted to leave Kendra. We've crossed paths here and there, and he always remembers my name.

He hasn't seen me. Yet.

I have to think fast.

I shove my stop sign in the bushes and make my way toward him, remembering at the last minute that I'm wearing a VEST you can see from SPACE. I rip it off, ball it up, and do the only thing I can think of: Shove it down the back of my skirt.

"Oh my god! Mark?" I say, trying to sound casual.

He looks up and does a double take. ". . . Mo Ellery?"

"Yeah!"

He blanches.

Shit. He knows about my little, erm, HR indiscretion.

That's okay—this is part of Hannah's UPGRADE program too. The R: wRite Your Own Story (or Someone Else Will Write It for You). Sure, the R's sort of shoved in there, but the message is solid.

"This is so funny! Do you live around here?" I ask with lots of friendly, nonthreatening eye contact.

"No, but the, um, the guy I'm dating does," he says, and he is literally looking around like someone might save him from me.

Time to turn up the charm. "Nice! I haven't been here long, but I like it. New place, new me! I'm shaking things up!" Then I plaster on a confident smile and lean in, like I'm sharing a juicy secret. "You know, after my short-lived career in accidental Zoom porn."

He laughs at this, a little cautiously, but I can tell he's warming up, all because I broached the subject myself. Man, Hannah is *good*.

I keep up the confessional tone. "It's a very 'lemons into lemonade' situation. It gave me an excuse to move on, find a new challenge. Things were getting a little stale over there, you know? I'd already been thinking, 'I wonder what cool stuff Livewire is up to these days?'"

Boom. Operation Get Hired is officially underway.

"Sure," he says slowly. "But, like, you *did* flash the entire senior leadership team at Midwest Tool Warehouse, right?"

"Look, Mark," I say in my best givin'-it-to-you-straight voice. "I'll be honest. I know I'm pretty spicy property right now, but I respect what you're doing, and I've got a killer portfolio featuring 300 percent increases in web traffic, 200 percent increases in newsletter subscribers, and almost 0 percent nudity."

He actually smiles a little, and I think my spin is starting to work. My mom would be so proud.

"Maybe we could get coffee," I add with a grin. "How's Friday?"

He opens his mouth to reply, but before he can squeeze out the "sounds good" that I so desperately need, a car horn blasts. We both turn to look.

No. Not now.

The seafoam Kia Sportage, poodle ears blowing in the wind.

And it's racing toward my intersection. Meanwhile, I'm halfway up the block with Mark, and if I turn my back on him, he's going to see the vest balled up in my waistband.

But also . . . on the far side of the street, a distracted dad scrolls on a phone, and his kid barrels toward the curb, totally unsupervised.

Come *on*, universe. This feels downright biblical. Do I seriously have to choose between Mark (glorious future) and some random kid (shitty present)?

I watch in horror as the Kia closes in.

And it is not slowing down.

CHAPTER 5

The dad chuckles at something on his phone.

The child pirouettes off the curb.

Shitballs.

"Sorry, Mark, just a sec!" I sprint to the corner and leap into the street, yanking my vest out of my butt and waving it overhead as I reach for the kid.

"Stop!" I yell. "Crossing guard!!!"

Somehow I manage to grab the kid's sleeve and pull him toward me, just as the engine revs and Poodle Dude blows through the stop sign. I can feel a breeze as the sideview mirror barely misses us, and once we're clear and safe on the opposite curb, there's a loud *crunch-crunch* sound from the general vicinity of the Kia.

Brakes screech as the car skids to a stop, and I'm suddenly being hugged by the dad, who has run across the intersection and is now incredibly grateful that his kid narrowly escaped extinction, when we all hear Poodle Dude yell in a gravelly faux-French accent, "Jacques! *Dites-moi!* Tell Papá what hurts!"

It's the first time I've ever heard him talk, and his voice is weirdly raspy—not how I imagined he'd sound, but then again, the guy probably yells at everybody. *Except*, apparently, his dogs, who are now getting some spectacular French baby talk.

"*Mon petit garçon doux!*"

The dad recovers enough to let me go, and we both turn to watch as Poodle Dude leaps out of the car, runs around the front, and flings open the passenger door. The guy throws himself halfway inside.

Where he clasps a limp poodle body to his chest.

He wails.

It's like a scene from *Les Misérables.*

I have a very bad feeling about this.

"JACQUES!" Poodle Dude wheezes. He shoots me a vicious look over his shoulder. "What did the mean lady do to you?"

Mean lady— What?

But before I can process what's happening, two *other* poodles hop from the back seat to the front seat, the limp poodle pops up, good as new, and all three of them are suddenly having a massive sniffing party.

Okay, I think, *terrific. Poodle drama resolved.*

I am wrong.

The guy whips around to face me. I've actually never seen his face, because he's either blocked by poodle heads or hidden by the Kia's tinted windows.

My dude is blond and chiseled-looking and he's wearing workout clothes—the fancy kind that match. He's breathing hard. He wipes his eyes and blinks at me a bunch like he's so mad he doesn't even know where to start. For a second, he grasps at the air around his head, and I realize he's trying to reach the straw sticking up behind him. Why is there a straw? He spins around like a dog chasing its tail, and I see that he's wearing one of those backpacks that hold water so you can be hydrating all the time, and the fact that he can't locate the straw seems to be panicking him.

Should I . . . help?

He finally finds the straw, takes a big gulp, and coughs violently, doubling over and moaning.

Yikes.

"*You*," he says as he recovers. He steps toward me, stumbling a bit. His whole body looks like it's vibrating. "You almost killed my sweet baby garçon."

Dude *really* needs to learn how to enunciate. I squint at his mouth like that'll help me hear better.

"I'm sorry, your what? I can't quite—"

"Dog *murderer*!" he clarifies.

"But your dog is alive," I point out. Alive *and* thriving. The dog is now sitting up in the front seat, licking his own butthole. "Also, I was nowhere near you."

"Exactly," he says, venom in his voice, spittle in the air. "I was trying to avoid that kid, and you *made* me drive straight into that sinkhole."

He slings his arm toward the pothole across from the parking garage-in-progress.

That was probably the *crunch-crunch* I heard—two sets of wheels hitting the hole in quick succession, cracking against the street like an egg.

"Sir, it's just a pothole," I say.

"Sinkhole."

"Pothole."

"Sinkhole."

"Pot—" I can't even finish the word before he interrupts me.

"Whatever! *You* made me swerve, *you* made my sweet boy fly around in the car. I bet he's concussed. Concussed!" He wipes his mouth clumsily. Is he *drooling*? Maybe he's the one who got concussed. Or maybe he's drunk? That would explain a lot.

I move a little closer to see if I can smell his breath.

"I was doing my job," I say, surreptitiously trying to get a whiff. "You were about to hit that kid . . ."

"She's right," the dad pipes up from over on the sidewalk. "I saw the whole thing."

"Oh, *did* you?" taunts Poodle Dude. "You saw the *whole* thing?"

The dad looks at me, confused. ". . . Yes?"

"Was it on your phone?"

The dad grimaces, gives me an apologetic shrug, and then ushers his kid past us toward the school.

Poodle Dude, meanwhile, turns his rage to me and me alone. He huffs, sending a blast of hot breath my way, and though I would not call it *good* breath, it doesn't smell alcoholic. So much for that theory.

Just drunk on rage, I guess.

"The alderman is going to hear about this," he says, mumbling even worse now. His voice sounds weird, like he's a ventriloquist for himself.

"The *alderman*?" I ask, not sure I heard him right. If he was trying to randomly scare me, why not pick the mayor? The governor? Why go for the alderman, who basically makes sure the neighborhood trash gets picked up? I try not to laugh. "Why are you going to tell *him*?"

"He's my friend!" He sticks a thumb into his chest to drive the point home.

Ah.

"That's a good call," I say, as encouragingly as I can. "You should definitely talk to a friend about this." And maybe also a therapist.

But this makes him even more livid, which unfortunately seems to give him a second wind. His mouth curdles into a gruesome grin. "Merle's a *close, personal* friend of mine, and he does not take kindly to illegal roadside activity in his ward by so-called public servants."

"Wait. Illegal?" I squeak. "So-called?"

"I'm taking Jacques straight to the vet. After that, you'll be hearing from my lawyer."

Lawyer? Can he do that? I can't afford to deal with lawyers right now. Do I also have to hire one to, like, do battle with his lawyer? My throat starts to close. I don't know a lot about lawyers, but I do know you can't hire one on crossing guard money.

"I didn't do anything," I squeak.

"And I wouldn't be surprised if the alderman sends the police to your door. He's my *bro*. So watch out, traffic girlie. Alderman Carey knows where you live." Poodle Dude feints at me, and I pull back in time for him to stumble forward harmlessly.

Was he trying to headbutt me? What is going on?

He recovers his balance, shuts the poodles back in the Kia, climbs behind the wheel, and peels off.

My head is spinning, and I'm trying to understand what the hell just happened, how worried I should be, and who I should call for help, when I realize Mark is *still there*.

Standing across the street. Watching me with wide, shocked eyes.

"So, Friday? Coffee?" I holler, trying to pick up where we left off as if none of this happened.

"Oops, I'm getting a call," he says quickly. He speed walks away, forgetting to actually put the phone to his ear.

Operation Get Hired, dead on arrival.

All of a sudden, there's a creaky groaning sound. I look over at the pothole just in time to see a huge chunk of street fall in on itself.

Okay.

Now it's a sinkhole.

CHAPTER 6

My commute home is only two blocks—one block up and one to the right. It's a gorgeous afternoon, sunny and warm. People are out walking dogs, bikers pedal past, there are even some late-summer blooms holding on here and there. But I'm not enjoying one second of it.

I've got the heebie-jeebies the whole way.

The alderman knows where you live, Poodle Dude had said.

But, like, *why*? Why would he know something like that? Is the alderman a perv? Is he watching me? With binoculars? How did this all escalate so fast? *I was only trying to do this job I don't actually want*, I think miserably. I'm suddenly overwhelmed with the desire to be back in Chris's condo, safe and cozy.

Instead, I'm out here on the mean Chicago streets, being threatened by a guy who owns three poodles and a pervy elected official.

"WATCH OUT!" somebody yells, just as a Frisbee hits me in the head.

Streets so mean you have to wear a helmet.

I hand the Frisbee back to a little kid who does *not* apologize, and, head pulsating, I push through the imposing gate to my apartment building.

My new home looms over me. I hate that this is home now. It's a sketchy brick U-shaped monstrosity that crumbles at the corners when the wind blows hard. There are three separate entrances, one for each section of the U, and the courtyard has a distinct prison yard vibe. The studio I rent month to month is a third-floor walk-up in the center of the U, and to get there, I have to pass my landlord's apartment. I'm pretty sure that's why the place was so affordable. Roy, professional landlord, lives on the first floor with a TV blaring the Home Shopping Network 24/7, and every time I walk past, he flings his door open and talks at me.

Every. Single. Time.

Roy is approximately seven hundred years old, exclusively wears blue button-downs with a different food stain on each one, and the top of his head comes up to my boobs, which is convenient for him, since most of the time, that's where he's looking.

Forehead still throbbing, I try to sneak in, but right as I reach his apartment, Roy flings the door open and sidles into the hall, blocking my way. I am extremely not in the mood to hear his usual gossip about other tenants' communicable diseases and medical procedures, but instead he squares off with me, boob to eyeball, and goes, "Someone just came looking for you."

Blood instantly ices in my veins. My voice shakes as I ask, "Who? When?"

"A man. In a hurry. Few minutes ago," he says, very pleased with himself. "I let him up to your apartment."

"You *what*?" I shriek.

"Well, I didn't let him *in* to your place," he says, clarifying. "Just up to the door. Not a friend of yours, I take it?"

I gaze up the stairs.

Holy shit. The alderman. Here. Poodle Dude sent him.

No, Roy, definitely not a friend.

My heart is pounding, heart attack style.

"Is he still up there?" I whisper.

"What do I look like, a snoop?" Roy says defensively and, feelings clearly hurt, slams his door.

Alone in the stairwell, I debate my next move. I'm tempted to run away and maybe start a new life in a new city under a new name, like a DIY witness protection sort of thing. Upside: I've never liked my name. Downside: I will definitely lose my security deposit.

Reluctantly, I creep up the stairs as quietly as I can, which is not very because the stairway is old and creaky as FUCK. It smells like Victorian ghosts, and I have no intention of joining them today.

At the top landing, I peer around the corner, and, seeing no one standing menacingly in front of 3C, I finally exhale. The hallway is short, with no shadowy corners or alcoves to hide in. The alderman must have come by to intimidate me. Damn, these guys work *fast.* Did he leave anything behind? A note, say? Or, I don't know, a horse head?

There's nothing obvious lying around, so I lift the gross old doormat that came with the apartment. Nothing under there but grimy, threadbare carpet. I'm *almost* relieved until I realize he might have picked the lock and could be *inside my apartment waiting for me right now.*

Careful not to make any noise, I press my ear to the door. Are you supposed to be able to hear through wood? I don't hear anything, so I wiggle the doorknob. It's locked. Okay, would he have gone through the trouble of breaking into my apartment and then locking the door behind him? I feel like no?

I unlock the dead bolt slowly and try to subtly ease the door open, just in case there's an ambush waiting for me on the other side—but of course it's humid, so the wood has swelled, and I have no choice but to throw myself against the door repeatedly, wedging my shoulder in just the right spot to get it to unstick.

Extremely *un*subtle.

When the door finally gives way, I stumble into the apartment and instinctively brace myself for another blow to the head. Would that be a thing an alderman would do? I have no idea. When it doesn't happen, I glance around, the tension unbearable as I am forced to scan my grim studio apartment, that yes, fine, gets lots of light and has wood floors, but also has exactly three pieces of furniture: a double bed on the metal frame that comes with the mattress, a faded pink velour armchair I got off Facebook Marketplace, and a small, round side table I brought from my parents' house. It barely looks like anybody lives here—I haven't hung anything up, not a single photo or poster.

This would be a very depressing place to get murdered by a low-level government official.

Or murdered by anybody, I guess.

After a few moments of silence and no head-bashing, I'm thinking about letting my guard down . . .

. . . just as a skull-shattering *CLANK CLANK CLANK* explodes from the corner of the apartment. I whip around and scream.

The fact that I'm screaming scares me even more, and so it's at least twenty more seconds of CLANKing and even louder screaming before I realize the CLANKing is the 1980s beige fridge, just trying to do its job.

"I thought we were *friends*!" I holler, kicking the side of the fridge.

Okay. I am yelling at a kitchen appliance.

I need backup.

"HIIIIIII," I SAY as Hannah's boyfriend Kenji opens the door.

"Oh," he says, instead of hi. "Hannah didn't mention you were coming."

"So weird!" I say, casually squeezing past him into the stairwell. It's not weird at all. I didn't tell Hannah. I knew if I did, she'd put me off until later, and I am in danger *now.*

But *also* now? I smell something *delicious* wafting down from the apartment. I follow my nose up the stairs.

Kenji sighs heavily, and I turn back to him with a shrug. "Sorry, Reuben's cooking is calling me."

HANNAH'S OTHER BOYFRIEND, Reuben, is currently working on his second cookbook (*Getting Even Blacker in the Kitchen*, sequel to his first cookbook, the TikTok hit *Getting Black in the Kitchen*). Kenji's girlfriend Eva is a big-time photographer who focuses on themes of Puerto Rican statehood, but also does the art for the cookbooks, and sometimes helps Hannah with her UPGRADE reels. Kenji is a mosaic muralist, and when he's between commissions, he redecorates their bathrooms into glittering dreamscapes that make you want to poop forever (a compliment). And Hannah, of course, has cornered the white-girl influencer market.

They are my MAGA aunt's worst nightmare (again, compliment).

Hannah and Kenji are together, and so are Hannah and Reuben, as well as Eva and Kenji, and sometimes Eva and Reuben. And Kenji and Reuben are in a casual friends-with-benefits thing, I think? Hard to keep track. Their whole relationship status is literally, "it's complicated."

I offered to be their HR person once, and Eva told me it wasn't funny.

I strongly suspect that Eva doesn't like me.

But now, after my horrible day, this is the only place I want to be. I've got Reuben's cherry cobbler burning the roof of my mouth because I ate it too fast, I'm surrounded by friends (and, okay, one frenemy)—and I actually start tearing up and sniffling.

"I *told* you to wait till it cooled off," Reuben says, washing a bowl at the sink.

"She's not crying because of the cobbler, Reu." Hannah touches my arm. "Mo, did you get fired again?"

I semi-successfully keep the pastry in my mouth and the snot in my nose while I bawl through the highlights: I pissed off somebody dangerous, he has a government connection, and said government connection knows where I live.

"Which is bad enough, but then my landlord let him up to my apartment. He didn't let him *in* but—" I pause, letting them imagine what horrors might have befallen me.

"—God, watch literally any horror movie, *Roy*," Hannah finishes.

I nod, helping myself to another scoop of cobbler. I knew she'd understand.

"So that's why I'm here, guys. I need your help. What if—hear me out—you rotated keeping me company at home?" I glance around the table. Everyone's avoiding my gaze. "Listen, it would only be 24/7 for a few days till I can clear this up. A week, tops. You all work remote, so I figure—"

Eva smacks her fork down, startling us all. "You guys have *got* to do a better job protecting yourselves. You think nothing bad will happen to you, so you just open your DMs up to whoever wants to slide in."

DMs? You *guys*?

"I'm sorry," I say, "what are we talking about?"

"Boundaries, babe." Returning from the sink, Reuben gently squeezes my and Hannah's shoulders. "When you're chronically online, people just kind of—glom on to you. They'll project their shit all over you. Believe me, I've been there. Eva's right, you have to take initiative to protect yourself."

I widen my eyes at Hannah like *Can you believe I'm getting lectured right now?* But she's just staring blankly at her untouched cobbler.

"I have like ten followers on Instagram," I say, my face getting hot. "*You* guys don't even follow me. This isn't a chronically online thing, it's an actual threat to my IRL life!"

They all turn to look at me. Kenji leans across the table to touch my hand. "He threatened to kill you?" he asks.

My confidence wobbles. "Maybe not kill me, *per se*," I say.

Eva groans.

"Okay, fine," I admit, "there is a very small chance I am blowing it out of proportion a very little bit. But the alderman did come up to my *apartment*—" I turn to Hannah for support. "The whole thing was so scary, you have no idea."

My bestie nods. "I do, I do. I get it." She's not facing me, though, she's frowning at Eva, who's glaring back at her, and I'm so overwhelmed with love for my best friend who sticks up for me, no matter what. "And the worst part is," I say, "the poodle was totally fine! Licking its butt like nothing even happened!"

"Oh," Hannah says, turning back to me. "Maybe I don't get it."

"There's a . . . poodle . . . involved?" Kenji asks.

I shake my head sadly. "Three."

A brief silence falls over the table as I wipe my nose on my sleeve. You'd think they could polycule me up a real Kleenex, but *no*. Kenji is anti-single-use products.

"I bet you leave your door unlocked too," Eva mumbles. "It's amazing you made it to thirty in one piece."

"Excuse *me*," I say. "I'm twenty-nine."

"Lock your door, *every* time. Tell the landlord you'll sue him if he lets anyone up to your apartment. Get some pepper spray and stay offline," Eva says, slapping her palm on the table. "There's your advice."

Those two helpings of cherry cobbler are sitting like a boulder in my guts, along with some foreboding rumblings. I really shouldn't eat so fast when I'm stressed-out. This isn't the kind of backup I was hoping for.

I say my goodbyes and Hannah walks me back downstairs. "Your boyfriend's girlfriend drives me nuts," I grumble as I step out onto the porch.

"I know," Hannah says, leaning against the doorframe. "When Eva gets scared, she lashes out. But she does it because she cares. I bet if you walked back in right now, she'd apologize . . ." She glances uncertainly up the stairs.

I seriously doubt that, but I let it go.

Because I've decided what I'm going to do.

I *am* going to protect myself, *Eva*. By beating Poodle Dude at his own game.

I'm going to take some initiative and go straight to the alderman's office.

CHAPTER 7

It's so simple, I can't believe I didn't think of it before. All I need to do is tell the alderman—MY elected official—my side of the story. I'm an upstanding crossing guard! Hero of the corner! He'll see that it wasn't personal, I was just doing my job, no poodles were harmed, and it was all a big misunderstanding.

I can already imagine the whole scene.

He'll lean back in his oversize chair and nod slowly as he chews on a cigar. "Welp, that's my bad," he'll growl. "I shouldn't have come to your apartment. You keep on keeping our streets safe and our kids alive. Just don't let me see you in here again."

It's either that or nobody ever sees me again.

The heady perfume of fear and confidence is making my heart race, so I look up the office address from Hannah's porch, get a rideshare, and race over before I can change my mind.

The driver pulls up to a block with a liquor store with murals all over the windows, a sewing machine repair shop, an empty storefront covered in graffiti, and a "dinner club" with mirrored windows that doesn't look *entirely* welcoming. It's not far from my apartment, and I definitely recognize the block because the Urgent Care I've been going to for the last two weeks is right around the corner.

They don't give out paper bags, but they're nice enough.

Before I get out, I double-check the alderman's office address on my phone. There are no high-rises in the neighborhood, but I was at least picturing, I don't know, *an office building*? Something with an elevator? Or at least a doorman.

What I wasn't picturing was a janky storefront that looks like it used to be an off-brand Taco Bell. The door is absolutely smothered with posters for art shows and improv shows and dog shows and car shows. There's no buzzer. *Anyone* could walk right in. So I do.

Inside, there's a vacant front desk with a bunch of pamphlets strewn all over it, and a plant that is barely holding on to this earthly realm.

And then a giant black mop attacks me. Oh god, I didn't even get a chance to explain myself to the alderman. No oversize chair, no cigar. No grudging mutual respect.

How did they know I was coming? *Touché, Poodle Dude*, I think. *Adios, world.*

It all happens so fast.

"Help!" I manage to squeak from somewhere inside the mop, which also seems to have claws, but I'm thrown back against the door, ripping posters down as I struggle to free myself. Why is *everyone* attacking me?

I'd really hoped to live long enough that flashing my tits on Zoom wasn't going to be the most significant thing in my obituary, but oh well.

"Charlie! *Charlie, down!*" says a voice from somewhere, and just like that, my life is saved.

The mop retreats and now that it's at a reasonable distance, I can see it vaguely resembles a dog. I turn to thank my savior, and the words get stuck in my throat.

"I am *so* sorry," says quite possibly the most gorgeous nerd I've ever seen in real life. She's holding a clipboard and wearing a button that says, "I'm Tasha, she/her, Ask Me Anything!"

And I do, suddenly, want to ask her . . . everything.

Holy crap, why am I blushing? And sweating? Is this an arrhythmia? I'm probably too young for hot flashes. Right?

She gives me a smile and the back of my neck is suddenly on fire.

Is this . . . a crush?

Well, shit. That changes things.

I haven't crushed on a girl since I was in college, and then I was with Chris forever, so it wasn't an issue. And look, I am still with Chris in my heart—plus I am here to take some initiative and resolve an alarming misplaced revenge scheme—so *hey body, why the head-to-toe flop sweat event*?

Thankfully, AMA Tasha doesn't seem to notice. She points sternly at the floor, and the mop-shaped dog lies down obediently. She gives him a little dog cracker.

I get it. I would beg for a little dog cracker from her.

Mo, down!

I distract myself by peeling a poster off my arm. Discount tickets to the *Counter-Productive Lover Improv Show*, it tells me.

Too soon, poster. Too soon.

Tasha scratches the dog's ear. "He's usually better behaved, but he's on new meds, and I think they're making him cranky," she says, shrugging.

"It's fine," I say, pushing my saliva-drenched hair out of my face casually, as if I didn't think I was about to die just a second earlier. "I needed a bath."

Tasha laughs. She has an amazing smile, and a gorgeous mass of curly dark-brown hair with just the slightest hint of auburn, which she's only semi-successfully pulled back. Behind her oversize glasses, she's got huge brown eyes, and she's smiling at me in a way that makes me glad I already have a reason to be wobbly.

Get a grip, I tell myself. *Alderman. Poodle Dude. Remember?*

"So I have a question—" I say.

"Aha! The AMA button works!" She grins. "We just got these. Here, have a seat, we can talk at my desk."

"I'm Mo," I say, following her.

Her desk—a beige metal monstrosity from another era—is just plopped right there in the middle of the open room. It's piled with folders and books and papers and a plastic "inbox" that has an enormous stack of notes in it.

There are a couple fuzzy, gray-walled cubicles stuck together toward the back, and behind those, there appears to be an actual office with a door on the far wall. The ceiling hums with those buzzing fluorescent lights we had in grade school.

"Is this your dog?" I ask, as the dog flops down and puts what I assume is its face on my shoe. I can't see its eyeballs under those mop-strings of hair. "Actually, is this even *a* dog? I'm honestly not sure."

She laughs again.

Is there any chance I could forget about Poodle Dude and the alderman? Just stay here all day and try to make this hot nerd laugh?

"Not my dog, just the resident demon," she says, ruffling the huge mop's head. "A very *fancy* demon who does competitions and everything, doesn't he? Yes he does!" The mop pants and drools and limps around in a circle, trying to catch his own tail. "He's our official mascot."

"That's a thing? Alderman mascots? Do you also have like a

human-size suit of him that runs around at basketball games and block parties?"

"Ha, I wish! That would be incredible!" The dog nuzzles her, and heck yeah, good choice, dog, I want to do that too. I have to force myself to concentrate as she keeps explaining, "He belongs to Alderman Carey's wife, and they both work here so Charlie keeps me company most days. Except for the days he's winning awards for being such a good boy."

He wags enthusiastically at the praise.

"I didn't know dogs could look like that," I admit. "Like sentient mops."

"He's a Puli. Not a super common breed." She lowers her voice conspiratorially, like she doesn't want Charlie to hear us. "He can be a little high maintenance. Total diva."

"Same," I confess.

She smiles again and adjusts the clipboard in her hands. "So, now that you've recovered from being attacked by the slobber monster, what can I help you with?"

"Right. Yes." I suck in a fortifying breath. Here I go. Taking initiative. Protecting myself. "I have reason to believe that Alderman Carey came to my apartment earlier looking for me under the false impression that I was guilty of a crime, and I would like to clear everything up."

Nailed it.

Tasha frowns. There is a very long silence in which I have ample time to regret everything I just said. "So . . . huh. Can you say that—"

"He was at my apartment. The alderman."

She hesitates and then smiles. "Aldermen don't really make house calls."

"Not even for suspected crime stuff?"

"Especially not for that." She smiles again and yeah, I'm still scared and confused, but maybe a little less. "Why don't you give me some more context about your problem?"

I clear my throat. "Well, you see, I'm a crossing guard, and—"

"That's so cool!" she interrupts.

It takes me a second to realize she's talking to me. About crossing guarding. Being cool. "*Is* it?"

But it's like she's been waiting for someone to ask her this question her whole life. She beams at me. "Public service is *incredibly* cool. I mean, people like us, we're the blood and guts of the city. We *are* Chicago. We're the nuts and bolts, the joints and the joists. It's like the city is a matrix of interlocking public service effort and artistry—just this week, for Manhole Cover Monday, I found a totally gorgeous historic manhole cover that no one knew about, and my Instagram notifications are off the charts."

She takes a breath and waits for me to react.

"I . . . I can't say I've heard of Manhole Cover Monday."

Her warm brown eyes widen, and I want to sink into them forever. Is that weird? Yes. But also, I don't care.

"*MO*," she says, and I blush harder, but she doesn't seem to notice. Instead, she pulls out a brochure with a giant manhole on the front. "You've got to join us. Hashtag Manhole Cover Monday. So much great stuff."

Oh, okay. She's not just a normal nerd, she's a HUGE nerd.

And it is doing some seriously butterfly-shaped things to my stomach.

Oh my god, Mo, FOCUS, I think. No way out but through. If I want to get this nightmare over with, I'll have to do something other than flirt. I put the brochure in my pocket, thank her, and get back to business.

"So I was at work earlier today," I say, "and a guy in a Kia full of poodles got really angry at me because he thought I made him drive into a pothole on purpose, but I was just trying to keep him from running over a kid. And *he* said the alderman was going to come after me. He told me the alderman knew where I lived, and then right after that, someone . . . *accessed* . . . my apartment."

She frowns. "Wait. Someone broke into your apartment?"

"Well, that part's a bit hazy," I say. "He didn't come inside, he was more like, creeping around? Outside the door? Stalker-style?"

Am I babbling? I'm babbling. And suddenly I'm doubting everything. Including whether Roy was telling the truth. He does love drama.

"Okay," she says, nodding gently. "It sounds like the guy with the poodles this morning definitely spooked you. But also, he was talking out of his ass. Merle's been here all day with some folks from the Chamber of Commerce, but more importantly, he doesn't go after citizens. He's a good dude."

I guess I'm glad the alderman isn't after me. But that doesn't explain who came to my apartment, or, if there wasn't anyone there, why Roy would lie about it. My confusion must show on my face, because Tasha puts a hand on my shoulder.

"If you're really worried, I can help you file a police report," she offers.

"No," I say quickly. "It's okay. If you're right about the alderman—"

"I am."

"—then Poodle Dude is just being a bully." Projecting his shit on me, like Reuben said. Okay, fine, maybe that *was* good advice.

"I'll keep an eye out for him, steer clear, that sort of thing."

"You're sure?" she asks, and . . . I actually am.

It's a good feeling. The first in a while. *This* is what it feels like to handle something.

"Now that that's settled," she says, leaning so close I can see the freckles dotting her nose, "I can *totally* help you with the pothole situation. Potholes are, in fact, extremely my jam."

I've fully described the pothole and clarified it's actually now more of a sinkhole (it's a hole where the street used to be, that's about all I got), and Tasha's just written down all my info when her desk phone rings. She whispers, "Sorry," as she reaches for the phone and answers it. "Alderman Carey's office, Tasha speaking."

She listens for a moment and then makes a gesture like this is going to take a while. I'd love to stay, but I don't want to make it weird, so I wave and head out. Hopefully there'll be more to discuss about the sinkhole.

Or manhole covers.

Either way, I'd really like to see her again.

Just as friends, obviously.

Obviously.

CHAPTER 8

By the time I get home, I'm ready for Roy. And I've got a few questions of my own.

Taking initiative is *such* a rush. Who's a badass? That's right. It's me.

His door swings open, and instead of being halfway up the next step like I usually am, I'm standing there with my arms crossed, Bad Cop style.

"Oh," he says, looking past me nervously. "Something wrong with the apartment? I can't get anybody out on a weekend, it costs extra."

"It's Wednesday, Roy, and that's not what I want to talk about. That guy. The one you let up to my apartment?"

He screws up his face like he's prepared to deny something. "Um . . ."

"What did he look like? I need you to describe him."

"Oh yeah, yeah, sure," he says. "I can describe him. The stripper."

"The *what*?"

"The stripper."

"Roy," I say, trying to stay calm. "Why did you think the man was a stripper?"

"He was very athletic," Roy says approvingly.

Huh. Poodle Dude is athletic.

"And blond," Roy adds.

Poodle Dude is ALSO BLOND!

Looking more and more like it wasn't the alderman!

"And he was wearing a stripper outfit," Roy continues. "That was the clincher."

"What, like matching workout wear?" I ask, frantically trying to remember exactly what Poodle Dude was wearing last time I saw him. "With logos and stuff?"

"No, no." Roy waves his hand, annoyed. "More like—a sexy doctor."

My heart actually stops.

An athletic, blond, sexy doctor.

"Hey, I don't judge," Roy says, palms up. "Just don't do it on company time. Take it from somebody who knows."

I can't believe it. I was so busy panic-spiraling that I didn't think of the most obvious answer.

Chris was here.

Panic evaporates and is replaced with pure love and light and rainbows and unicorns. Amazing how something I thought was horrific could turn out to be the best possible thing! Goodbye Roy and shitty apartment and angry men with fancy dogs! Hello, beautiful old life!

Roy keeps talking, but I don't register what he's saying, I just leave him in the doorway and float up the stairs, taking them three at a time as I whip out my phone and dial. It's already ringing by the time I get to the top of the landing. I unlock the door, and I've just shouldered my way in when Chris picks up.

Through the phone, his voice is distant. "What's up, Mo?"

Not the most romantic opener, but I'll take what I can get.

"I'm so sorry," I wheeze, trying to catch my breath. Maybe I should have given it a second.

"You're sorry?" He sounds confused. "For the penis thing?"

"No, no. I mean, yes, absolutely," I say, pacing from the fridge to the bed and back again. I'm too happy to stand still. "I'm sorry I missed you today. At my apartment. I heard you came by."

Came by to say you were wrong. To try and win me back. To make this all okay again.

But I don't say any of that. I want to hear him say it.

"Oh, yeah," he says, like he's vaguely distracted by some of the noises on his end of the line. "Yeah, it's cool."

"It's cool?" I ask, stopping.

"Yeah, you got it, right?"

"Got what?"

"Your toothbrush," he says. "The one you left at my place. I slipped it under the door."

That's when I see it.

I wasn't looking for it, so I didn't notice it, but there's my toothbrush, on the floor, pushed up against the wall behind the door. Covered in old floor grime. I'd left that toothbrush at Chris's condo on purpose. It was my toothbrush of hope, my just-in-case-I-end-up-sleeping-over-and-we-get-back-together toothbrush.

But now I understand. When I burst in, bracing for a murderous alderman, I must've kicked the toothbrush, and I was so focused on something big potentially hitting me in the head, I didn't notice the tiny thing that could stab me in the heart.

"Yeah," I say numbly, "I got it."

When I wake up the next morning, my eyelids are puffed up and crusted shut and I feel like death after a quick thirty seconds in the microwave. I roll over and something pokes me in the sternum.

Oh, great, the toothbrush. Just who I wanted to see.

I grope around for my phone and when I find it, I send Hannah a text.

Devastating news. Not being stalked.

Hmm. That sounds weird.

Me: It was Chris returning my toothbrush ugh

Me: Plz don't tell Eva

I wait for the inevitable *you're too good for him, you can do so much better*, to which I will obviously reply *no no he's too good for ME*, and then she'll boost me up again, and I'll argue again, and so on . . . because that's what besties do.

I stare at the screen. Nothing.

Except the notification: Read 7:23 am.

Huh.

The memory of Hannah asking, "Did you get fired again?" echoes in my head. Is she busy or is she deliberately not replying? Is she sick of me asking her for help, just like the rest of the internet?

She's my best friend, she can't be sick of me . . . right?

I glance at the screen again. Still nothing.

But this time, I actually process the read notification.

7:23??

SHITBALLS I'M LATE FOR WORK.

I spring out of bed, throw on some clothes and my vest, shove a bunch of pepperoni in my pocket because my stomach is screaming for breakfast and that's all I've got in the fridge, grab my stop sign, and tear down the stairs. I might not be a natural at this job, but it matters to me that I do it right, that I protect those kiddos, even if they are a bunch of miscreants.

I've almost covered the length of the first block when I think that maybe I should go back to see Tasha after my afternoon shift, check if there's any progress on the sinkhole situation. I need a friend, and if that friend happens to be hot, that's okay. Hot friends happen. We'll go to improv shows together and talk about manhole covers. And I'll stop flirting and sweating so much around her, because we'll just be normal friends, and anyway my heart belongs to another, even if he's making things really hard right now.

I just really, really need a friend.

I could like manholes and their covers, I think, as I become vaguely aware of the *honk-honk* of a car alarm coming from somewhere close by. Then I turn the corner to where my post is and, suddenly, the *only* thing I'm aware of is the alarm.

The alarm, and also the car it's coming from. Which is an SUV.

An SUV that has dived, nose-first, into the sinkhole.

An SUV that is a seafoam-green Kia Sportage.

The back wheels are spinning, several inches off the ground.

Three white standard poodles are gathered by the edge of the sinkhole close to the front of the car, by the driver's-side window. One of them is standing on its hind legs like a person, whimpering. One of them is sneezing uncontrollably. The other one starts barking like crazy and spinning around in circles as I join them.

And then all four of us peer through the window, where Poodle Dude lies slumped over the steering wheel, blood trickling from his nose, his open, glassy eyes staring back.

CHAPTER 9

Wouldya look at that," says a thick Chicago accent next to me. "He's *dead*."

I'm embarrassed to report that my first bewildered thought was that the dogs were talking to me, and that my second thought was: *But aren't they French?*

Let's just chalk it up to the shock of seeing my first-ever dead body.

But then when I turn away from the accident, the brim of an enormous green sun hat smacks me in the face, and it's honestly kind of a relief to see the old *Mission: Impossible* lady.

This is all awful, but at least dogs aren't talking to me.

"Super dead," I agree shakily.

The old lady squints hard into the driver's-side window, lips pursed. She *humphs*, reaches in, and lifts up the dead guy's wrist like she's taking his pulse.

I'm going to barf.

She drops the hand, letting it flop back down lifelessly, and turns to squint at me accusingly. "Did you do this?"

"What?" I squawk. "No!"

But the moment it's out of my mouth, I realize I *did* do this. If I hadn't been late for my shift, I could have made him slow down or directed him away from the sinkhole. He definitely would've screamed at me again, but at least the car wouldn't have crashed. He wouldn't be dead.

Oh god.

This is *totally* my fault.

I'm about to blurt out a confession, but the lady has moved on—she's scoping out the scene, looking underneath the car, peering in the back windows, opening and closing the passenger-side door, which makes the car groan.

"Hey, ma'am?"

She shoots me a dirty look, and I start again.

"Do you think maybe we should wait for—" The rest of that sentence catches in my throat as she *lifts Poodle Dude's head off the steering wheel*, which somehow sets off a DELUGE of what appears to be . . . the totality of his guts? My vision goes wavy, my soul leaves my body, and before I know it, the lady is next to me, snapping her fingers in my face and patting my cheek.

Then she full-out slaps me.

"What the heck!" I yell.

"This is no time to get soft," she says, elbowing me. "They're coming."

I drag my eyes away from Poodle Dude and see what she's elbowing about: The first wave of kids and parents is making their way toward us. Their bright, excited faces and colorful backpacks and cheerful, innocent morning chatter are steadily closing in on this extremely gross dead guy and a lifetime of therapy. "What do I do?" I ask, absolutely panicked.

"I'll call 911," she says. "You cover this up."

"Cover this . . ."

"Cover *him* up. So all those cute little kids aren't traumatized for the rest of their lives." She shoves her green hat in my hands. There are bloody fingerprints smeared across the brim. "There you go."

Oh.

Okay.

Yes.

I can do this. I can keep those kids from owing a mountain of therapy co-pays.

I take a step toward the car and the dogs growl.

I take a step back.

"*Now!*" the lady orders. She waves her phone at me aggressively, and I decide she's scarier than the dogs, so I leap into action, first sticking my hand carefully through the driver's-side window and placing the green sun hat over the dead guy. It doesn't cover all of him, but it's a good start.

The kids are getting closer and as she listens to someone on the other end of the phone, the lady frowns at me and mouths the words *Keep going!* but I have no idea what else there is to do. The windows are tinted, but maybe that's not enough? There needs to be some other distraction, but my brain is just screaming *Save the kids!*, so I do the first thing that flashes into my mind: I hop up on the hood of the Kia and sprawl out like I'm the goofy member of a nineties boy band.

Between me and the tinted windows, these kids are NOT SEEING A DEAD BODY ON MY WATCH.

Unfortunately, I'm so focused on the kids that I've forgotten about the poodles, who now start scratching at the car (not ideal) and one of them is hunching down like he's going to jump up here with me, while at the same time the car begins to groan like it's a centimeter away from dipping perilously farther into the hole. Nope, nope, this isn't good. I lean back hard into the windshield, propping myself on the little pocket where the wipers go. To my everlasting relief, the groaning stops.

The poodles are now going CRAZY, though, barking their poofy heads off at me and their dead papá. Oh god, do dogs eat dead bodies?

I can't let the kids see that.

Clearly the dogs managed to jump *out* of the car windows, what if they jump back *in*?

And time's up, because the first group of kids and parents has reached the opposite corner, where they're all eyeing me curiously.

"Just a little fender bender!" I call, trying to sound chipper. "Don't worry, everyone's still alive!" I look both ways for oncoming traffic, then stretch out my stop sign arm as far as it can go. "No one's coming, go ahead and cross!"

They do not cross.

Instead, they peer past the car at the dogs, and I can't blame them, because the dogs are going absolutely berserk. One is up on its hind legs again, nosing around inside the driver's window, poking at the hat. I try a gentle roundhouse kick to nudge the dog down. Unfortunately, I don't know how to roundhouse kick. Also, I am balanced on a car hood, so I only succeed in straining a groin muscle. I stifle a grunt of pain.

The assembled kids and parents all stare at the seafoam Kia and me, at the dogs and at the old lady who's yelling into her phone, confusion playing across their faces. One parent opens his mouth to ask a question I definitely won't want to answer, so I plaster on a smile and put on my loudest voice.

"Looks clear for crossing!" I say, pointing forcefully toward the street. "It's swimming pool rules today! I'm a traffic lifeguard up here right now! Just go with it!"

Cool. Very normal, Mo.

But it works, or rather, the first bell rings, so they mumble to themselves and walk across the street, and I'm mulling over how I might turn this experience into a bullet point on my résumé, when the old lady yells, "MARLOWE. NO."

It startles me enough that I yelp and almost slide off the hood and straight into the hole. At the last minute, I spin and manage to grip the windshield wiper gap and pull myself back up.

And now I see what the old lady was yelling about.

It's that pink-haired kid again.

She's at the driver's-side window, peeking under the giant hat and taking a picture with her phone as the dogs flank her.

"Whoa," she says. "Dead guy."

"He's just sleeping," I say quickly, awkwardly scooting over so I can climb down onto the relative safety of the street. "And you shouldn't disturb . . . people while they're sleeping."

Marlowe looks up at me dryly, like it's too much effort to fully roll her eyes, but she would if she felt like it. "That is not a sleeping guy. That is a *dead* guy. I've watched a lot of *Law & Order*."

"Marlowe," scolds the old lady again, crossing to join us. "Delete that before I tell your moms."

"You can't tell me what to do, Claudia." The tween crosses her arms defiantly.

The old lady—Claudia, apparently—steps in so the two of them are eye to eye, and she points in the direction of the train station a couple blocks away. It's one of the few in the city on street level, and the early wave of commuters is heading toward the entrance.

"I can see Shoshanna from here," Claudia says. "Do you want me to yell for her? Do you think she'll appreciate being late for her fancy-pants lawyer meetings because her daughter is taking pictures of dead people?"

Marlowe sighs loudly.

"Phone. Delete. Now."

Marlowe groans as she goes through the phone, trashing the pictures. "I wasn't going to *do* anything with them."

"Only a creep says that sort of thing," Claudia declares. "Now get to class."

With one final grumble, Marlowe heads for the school.

Once she's out of earshot, Claudia whispers, "Smart kid. Huge pain in the ass, though."

"So, um, back to the dead body?" I ask, my voice squeaking. "What exactly do we do now?"

"You go help those folks across the street," she says, nodding at a few oncoming stragglers. "I'll hover around the car and shoo off anybody who wants to get too close."

I do exactly what she says, and some people ask about the accident, but most people roll their eyes as if to say, *Of course that happened, it was inevitable, how could that douchebag not hit a sinkhole.*

I absolutely do not mention the corpse inside.

As the latecomers cross, I glance back and see that Claudia has removed the big green hat and is, it seems, taking lots of pictures of the dead guy as the poodles swarm around her, begging for attention.

What's *she* doing?

Just as I'm about to ask her, an ambulance whizzes down the block and I swear to god, I've never been so happy to hear a siren in my life, not even the time I thought my appendix was bursting in Target and I made Chris call 911 and it turned out to be the Italian beef I'd had for lunch.

Still. That was a good sandwich.

The ambulance parks next to the Kia, followed by a cop car and a tow truck. They all block off access to the accident, which makes my job a lot easier. Then it gets even better when the second bell rings, and I am officially off duty.

I shrug out of my vest and join Claudia on the sidewalk, still awash in guilt. The cops are setting up cones around the sinkhole, which feels very too-little-too-late to me, and, since the kids are finally gone, the EMTs pull the guy from the car and plop him on a gurney. They're a little slow to put a sheet over him, and I accidentally catch another glimpse of the body before I catch myself. *The body.* Ugh.

I am trying very hard not to be woozy, and only partly succeeding.

I turn my attention to the poodles, who seem sort of lost. They follow the EMTs from the car to the ambulance, try to hop in, and, after being nudged off, wait patiently after the door shuts and it drives away, no siren necessary. Then they straggle over to us, and for a moment, we all stand there like we're at the most awkward cocktail party ever, until one of the dogs leaps at me. I flinch, preparing myself for an attack—after all, I'm responsible for the death of his person, plus dogs seem to like leaping on me these days. But all he does is headbutt my hip, pushing against my hand, while the other two dogs lie down on the grass, looking pathetic.

He likes me.

Somehow that destroys me even more.

Just then, one of the cops—a youngish white guy with a shaved head and an I-drink-more-High-Life-than-water look—walks up to us with a tiny spiral notebook.

"Did either of you see what happened?" he asks, flipping the notebook open.

We shake our heads.

"Not even you, crossing guard?"

"I got to work late," I say, miserably.

He writes that down. Ugh, why didn't I lie?

"Those your dogs?" he asks.

"These dogs? The dogs that just tried to get into the ambulance?" Claudia says. "No, you dipshit."

I almost choke. "They belong—belonged—to the dead guy. Uh, sir."

He glares at her and writes something in his notebook. "Watch your tone, young lady."

"Me? What did I do?" I say.

He leans into his walkie-talkie. "Get Animal Control up here."

"No!" Claudia blurts.

We both look at her.

"Animal Control will put them in a kill shelter. No way. I'll take care of the dogs," she says.

The cop raises an eyebrow. "And how are you related to the deceased?"

Claudia straightens up to her full height of approximately four feet. Her hair is short and gray and mashed against her head unflatteringly, and she's got the sun hat all folded up behind her back so the cop can't see the body fluids smeared all over it. *RIP, hat,* I think somberly. *Thank you for your service.*

"I'm a friend," she says.

"Uh-huh," the cop says. "So what was his name?"

"Cran Johnston," she says, not skipping a beat.

Cran? That's the best she could come up with? *Cran?*

But the cop checks his notes and nods. Okay then, Cran it is.

Claudia points at the poodles. "Look how fancy they are. They'd hate it in a shelter," she says firmly. "That's like *puppy prison.* But then, you cops love prisons, don't you?"

"Excuse me?" the cop says. They glare at each other again.

"I think what she means," I jump in, "is why use good taxpayer money when you have someone who will take them for free?"

"This is your second warning," he says to me.

What the *hell*?

Luckily, the cop looks like he wants nothing more than to get the heck out of here. He clicks his walkie-talkie again. "Forget it, animal situation contained."

For the first time ever, I see Claudia smile. It doesn't quite reach her eyes, and there's some kind of threat behind it. I would not mess with her, personally. "Great," she says.

Someone calls a string of numbers over Officer High Life's walkie-talkie and Claudia takes the opportunity to look at me meaningfully, which is terrific except that I have no idea what the meaning is.

The cop reaches in his shirt pocket. "Here's my card if you have any more trouble. Don't abuse the privilege."

"Don't worry," Claudia says. She plucks the card from him and, while maintaining eye contact, drops it in the sinkhole. "We won't."

It flutters into the abyss, and he does that thing where he points at his eyes and then at me, like *I'm watching you*. Then he heads back to his car.

"Yeah yeah, we're watching you, too, buddy. Watching you walk away." Claudia gives a loud wolf whistle.

Despite everything, I'm actually starting to like her.

"Here," she says. "Give me your phone. I don't give a flying fuck about calling that guy, but you and me are friends now."

I hand over my phone, marveling at the bonding experience one small fatal accident can be between strangers. The tow truck goes to work pulling the Kia out of the sinkhole as the two of us watch. At my side, the affectionate poodle licks my hand sweetly.

"That was nice of you," I say, petting this poodle who now fully adores me. "To take his dogs. I don't think they'd die with Animal Control, but I'm sure they'd prefer a real home."

"Oh, I'm not taking them," she says as she types her number into the text app and then sends herself a text before handing it back to me.

"But you said—"

"*You* are," she interrupts casually.

I laugh.

Then I stop laughing.

"Wait, what?" I ask.

She watches the cop car screech around the corner. "Fucking cops," she says, shaking her head. "We're on our own, kiddo."

"I *can't* take the dogs," I say, even though I know instinctively that I shouldn't argue with Claudia. "I don't know how to dog."

"Well, I'm sorry but you have to," she says. "They're our only witnesses."

"I'm sorry, witnesses to what?" I ask.

"It's just for a short time, sweetie," she says, patting my hand like a grandmother. "Just until we figure out who murdered Cran Johnston."

CHAPTER 10

"*Murdered?*" I say. "This was a car accident, Claudia. Of the sinkhole variety."

"That's just what they want you to think," she murmurs, bending down and rubbing some grass between her fingers before smelling them.

Ooookay.

The nice thing about living in a city is that you meet all kinds of people.

It just so happens some of those people will be crazy conspiracy theorists.

Don't get me wrong, part of me wishes she's right, because it would let me off the hook. But I'm going to be a grown-up about this and take responsibility for my actions. Even when my actions suck and someone, uh, dies.

"It really wasn't murder," I say quietly. "It was my fault. I was late to my shift. This guy—*Cran*, was it?—drives through every day at a hundred miles an hour. It's the most predictable thing in the world.

And without me here to make him slow down, he drove straight into the sinkhole and hit his head on the steering wheel. Game over. And very much my fault."

Claudia stands. "Then why weren't the dogs hurt?"

"What?"

"The dogs. They're all totally fine."

I look down, where the sweet dog has curled into a ball at my feet. He gazes up at me lovingly. "Huh."

"Exactly."

I shake my head. "No, I'm sure it's because dogs are bouncy or something." But then I think back to yesterday, when Cran hit the pothole, before it was a sinkhole, and was so convinced I'd given one of the dogs a concussion.

That dog wasn't very bouncy yesterday.

Still. No way.

"Okay, then," Claudia continues. "Why didn't the airbag inflate?"

"I don't . . . I'm not a mechanic, Claudia."

"I'll tell you," she says. "It's because the car wasn't going fast. Not fast enough to kill somebody."

"He always drives too fast," I argue, feeling queasy all over again. "That's his whole thing."

"Nope," Claudia says, shaking her head. "Look at the facts. We were the first people to arrive, so we had a pristine crime scene. We know we got there immediately afterward, based on the amount of oil leaking under the car. His positioning indicated that he vomited *during* the incident, not after, which suggests—"

I hold up a hand to stop her while I do my best to not sympathy-barf.

She shoots me a withering look, but gives me a second.

"What about his nose?" I carefully ask when my stomach has more or less settled. "It was bleeding, probably from hitting the steering wheel. How about that, hotshot? You trying to tell me that's not from impact?"

"Fine, but my point is, no cuts or gashes or bruises like you might see in a blunt force trauma. Therefore, *factually*, he was disintegrating internally. You know what causes that?"

I want to know.

I also don't want to know.

"Radium poisoning," Claudia says triumphantly.

And this, right here, is how conspiracy theorists get you. They sound perfectly reasonable, and then they pull the rug right out from under you.

"Now we're in this together." She's suddenly on a roll. "You and me have to figure out who did it, and what their motive was, and it's going to be hard because I can think of about a dozen motives for killing Cran, and that's without even trying—"

"You know what," I interrupt as delicately as I can, because you never want to piss off a conspiracy theorist. "I have to go. I'm sorry. I have a . . . mammogram."

"Oh," she says. "Well, yeah, that's important."

"I'll, ah, see you around," I say, as I back away.

She holds out three leashes with dogs at the end of them.

"Aren't you forgetting something?" she asks sweetly.

For the entire two-block walk home—which takes longer than usual since the three dogs have to smell *every single thing*—I'm in a state of shock. How did I let that woman convince me to take charge of these poodles? I don't know anything about dogs. They definitely aren't allowed in my apartment. I can't afford to get kicked out. And I absolutely do not believe a word Claudia says about them being "important witnesses."

So why did I take the dogs??

It's partly because the sweet one won't let me take two steps without following me and nuzzling. And, well, that's sort of melted my heart. Claudia said it was unusual that he likes me; poodles are "handler sensitive," and since I'm just not really a natural at many things (okay, anything), discovering that I might be a natural "Poodle Handler" has been the best part of a very bad day.

And then there's the fact that it's my fault they're now orphans.

So yeah, I took them.

And now I am going to have to sneak these three enormous dogs through my front gate *past Roy's door.*

Great.

We jog across the courtyard as quickly as possible, and I plaster myself against the bricks next to the door. We're just under Roy's window, so I hope he isn't looking out at this exact moment. After giving it a second, I peek through the front door into the mailroom—everything is quiet.

We slip inside, and while the dogs try to tug my arm off and stick their noses in every dirty, spiderwebby corner of the tiny room, I clamp my stop sign into my armpit and manage to unlock the little metal door of my mailbox.

Ugh.

How do I have an electricity bill already?

I try to shove it in my pocket, which is weirdly already full. I pull out whatever's in there—and I've only *just* processed that it's the breakfast pepperoni I forgot to eat, when the sweet dog vaults over the other two and devours the entire handful with a huge sloppy chomp.

When he finishes chewing, he looks at me, and it is exceedingly clear that it was never me he wanted to nuzzle.

It was the pepperoni.

Welp. Too late to back out now.

I take a deep breath and aim all four of us toward the stairwell, hoping we can run past Roy's door. But the moment we're in, the dogs are everywhere, smelling every inch of the faded brown carpet, and the jingle-jingle of their collars is *really* loud, so when I hear the click of Roy's lock, I panic. I can't outrun this.

I do the only thing I can. I let go of their leashes, point my finger toward the stairs, and whisper, "Fly like the wind."

And stunningly, they sprint right upstairs and out of sight.

By the time Roy has the door fully open, the dogs are gone.

"Oh hey," I say, casually, leaning against the wall.

"Did I hear something weird out here?" he asks suspiciously.

"It was probably me," I say, holding up the mail. "That dang electric company is on my ass."

"I know exactly what you mean," Roy says. "If I had a nickel."

There's a pause.

"Okay, well, see you later," I say.

"Okay," says Roy with a nod. "Good talk."

As I PUSH open the door to 3C, the dogs burst inside and immediately make themselves *way too much* at home. The pepperoni lover heads straight for my tiny kitchen and starts licking the floor. Another one flops down in the middle of the room, sneezing. The third one leaps onto my bed and starts wrestling with my comforter.

"You—" I point at the one on my bed. "Uh, down! No! Stop!" None of these things work. He shakes his head back and forth, growling, and I can hear the comforter start to rip, and the electric bill flashes through my mind, and I *should not* be buying new comforters right now, but then I remember something I heard walking past the dog park the other day—

"Drop it!"

The dog freezes, drops the comforter, and looks at me. Yes. YES. I'm a total dog whisperer.

"Okay," I say. "Now just—stay right there. Don't move." I hold out my palm to him, like I do when my stop sign isn't enough and I need an extra hand signal to get a car to stop.

And suddenly, *the dog pops up on its hind legs and starts walking around on my bed like a person.*

Wait, what? Forget whisperer.

I AM A GODDAMN DOG *WIZARD.*

I put my palm down. The dog goes back on all fours. I hold my palm up again. Dog stands on two legs.

Am I imagining this? Are these *circus* dogs?? Why did Cran have *circus* dogs???

I turn and hold my palm out to the dog lying on the floor. Nothing. It just lets out a huge sigh. Too depressed for tricks, I guess.

Then I turn around and hold my palm out to the dog who was licking the floor, and that's when I notice he's turned his full attention to me. He is, in fact, making very intense eye contact with me. Weirdly intense. He hunches a little bit, and I wonder if this is another trick.

And then, maintaining eye contact, he very slowly starts to hunch even more . . .

"No," I whisper.

. . . as if he's about to . . .

"Nonononono," I plead.

. . . take a crap . . .

"Please no," I say, trying politeness.

. . . right on my floor.

"*Don't* drop it," I say, trying dog-speak.

Desperate, I hold up my STOP sign.

The dog just stares, wide-eyed. There is a delicate plop, and he leaves an actual turd right on the hardwood. He kicks his feet a couple times and sits down next to it proudly.

"You are never getting pepperoni again," I whisper. The other two dogs start barking with abandon, congratulating the pooper, I suppose, as I wave frantically for them to keep it down. Stopping Roy from seeing the dogs is one thing, but keeping him from hearing them is something else entirely.

I quickly dispose of the evidence and throw open the windows, but the odor of stress-poop is still overwhelming in my little studio. I've been a dog owner for five minutes, and already I do not see why anyone would voluntarily choose this life. I must be missing something.

How do I get them to not poop on my floor?

The answer comes so quickly, I can't believe I even had to ask: I'll buy their love.

I hit the internet and place a DoorDash order for a few things: a weird toy you put peanut butter in, "bully sticks," which I'm thrilled to say are actual bull penises, and Himalayan yak chews, which look like string cheese for dogs, and which the internet assures me will keep them occupied for at least a full hour. I realize with a sinking feeling that keeping these dogs flush in other animals' penises is going to be *expensive*. Hopefully this will be a one-penis sort of stay, just until I can figure out what to do with them.

First step, I look up the closest police precinct and dial the number, wishing I'd kept that cop's card after all.

A bored-sounding receptionist answers.

When I tell her I need to talk to somebody about a dead person's stuff, she sounds a little *less* bored and transfers me to the cop on duty.

"Yelloooo, Detective Mierzwiak," says a deep voice on the other end.

I quickly explain that I need to get the three poodles to Cran Johnston's next of kin.

There's a pause, and then he says, "Lady, I'm a cop, not a dogsitter."

And then he hangs up on me.

Old me would've just let it go and dealt with my new identity as dog housekeeper, but new me takes initiative.

So I call again, tell the receptionist that I got cut off, and then when Mierzwiak picks up, I say, very quickly, before he hangs up on me again, "You weren't at the scene of the crash this morning, but *that cop's* card, uh, accidentally got thrown into a sinkhole, and I don't know who else to talk to about this, but the tl;dr is there was a car crash, I took the dead guy's dogs, and that was a mistake."

"You stole the property of a vehicular DOA?"

"What?" I squeak.

"What's your name and address?"

I hear laughing in the background. Are they making fun of me? Or is that menacing "I'm gonna get you" laughter?

My turn to hang up. Would it just be possible to start this day over? Just erase the whole thing—unanswered texts, dead guys, pooping dogs, mean cops, puking corpses? That last image flashes through my mind and I shudder.

I decide on a hot shower to wash off the general morbs, then throw on my comfy threadbare Cubs tank and pajama shorts, and pull out some pepperoni for lunch. The dogs all line up in front of me looking pathetic, so I cave and loop them in on the pepperoni train (after sternly reminding them that they will be cut off if any of them poop inside again). Time for one of my favorite activities: Ignoring the Problem by Watching Some Soothing Haircut Videos on YouTube. Honestly, it works like a dream. I've completely forgotten the dogs and become fully invested in a kicky little bob when I get a text.

Claudia Alonzo: Come to my house in 15.

Claudia.

Shit.

I'd completely forgotten I'd given her my phone. In my defense, it was before she revealed herself to be a total conspiro nutjob, but I make a mental note to not be so loose with my number again.

Now I have to gently let her down.

Me: Mammogram!

Claudia: You don't have a mammogram. Come to my house.

How did she know? Do I have a tell? Ugh. Okay. I'll be less gentle.

Me: I don't go to strangers' houses, and even though we had a traumatic experience together, we are still strangers

Claudia: Fine. Meet you on your corner in 15.

No! No no *absolutely* no.

I decide to ghost this lady, stat. Ghosting isn't exactly the most grown-up option, but sometimes, you do what you have to do.

Unfortunately, she's insistent, sending text after text.

Claudia: I'm serious. You need to be there. You're in this now.

I'm *in this* now? What does that even mean? And more importantly, how do I get *out* of "this"?

I leave that message thread and instinctively go into Hannah's, because she's who I ask about stuff like this, except it reminds me that she still hasn't replied about the toothbrush thing. She can't be mad at me, can she? I mentally flip through everything I said yesterday, can't come up with anything objectionable.

Me: Hey Han

Need to be strategic here. Getting sucked into a phony murder investigation with a crazy old lady leans a little too far into "hot mess" territory. If Hannah's already cranky with me, I don't want to sound too unhinged and needy.

But before I get any further, Claudia sends me another text. I swipe it away. Then there's an attachment. And then another. And another. The more I swipe, the more they keep coming. With a LOT of trepidation, I switch back over to her thread.

Oh fuck.

It's all the pictures she took of the dead guy.

Cran.

Photo after photo of him, slumped over the steering wheel, at different angles and with varying amounts of gruesomeness. The pepperoni in my stomach revolts.

Me: Please stop sending me snuff photos????

Claudia immediately texts back.

Claudia: Then meet me at the corner.

And she sends me another photo.

I take a deep breath. I'm handling it! I have it under control! Hot messes do not take deep breaths! I go back to the Hannah thread.

Me: Quick Q!

How to phrase this? Casual. Non-needy.

Me: Got any UPGRADE tips on how to say no to a job you don't want?

Me: If like the hiring manager is being REAL pushy? Oof!

While I wait for an answer, Claudia sends me two identical close-ups of Cran's bloody nose. HELP.

Claudia: Sorry for the repeat

Right, that's definitely the problem here.

And then, to my relief, Hannah finally responds.

Hannah: OMG a new job! Mo! Congrats!

Wait.

No. I was clearly too casual. *Too* not-needy. Faking being normal is SO HARD.

Me: Hahaha thanks but like what if I REALLY don't want this job

Hannah: You can totally keep looking

for your dream job while you're pulling in a paycheck at not-dream job! Right now money is the thing, right? Go go go! You got this!!

Something still feels off. Is Hannah faking normal too? She's not usually *this* cheerful.

But then I wonder if she has a point. Would Claudia pay me? I wonder.

My phone pings with a close-up of Cran's vacant eyes. Jesus.

Nope. There's no money in this, only suffering.

Hannah: What's the job??

Oh. Oops. Of course she would ask. She's a good friend.

Time to pivot.

Me: Tell ya later - oh hey btw guess who flirted with a hot government official yesterday?

Hannah: !!!

Hannah: NATURE IS HEALING

Me: Ha ha, yep!

Thankfully, Hannah has always been easily distracted by romance. She's a pushover when it comes to that stuff.

With her derailed, I grimly face my destiny in Claudia's text thread.

Me: Fine. I'll be there.

Claudia: 10 minutes.

Me: What happened to 15??

Claudia: Tick-tock.

I groan and reluctantly ditch my comfy outfit to put on a pair of jean shorts, socks, and shoes. And then I have another thought. If Claudia's going to be so pushy, then *she* can take the dogs.

"Come on, fellas," I say, and the dogs scramble to their feet. "You're going to stay with Aunt Claudia."

CHAPTER 11

I don't usually take the back stairs. They're a little too "condemned building" for my taste, but: desperate times.

I lock the back door behind me, and then the guys and I slowly make our way down the creaky wooden stairs, descending past 2C (who recently wreaked havoc on the building's pipes with his colonoscopy prep, a fact I wish I did not know, thanks, Roy), and then past 1C (where Roy's own dangerous-looking hammock chair collects mold). The four of us creep through the back gate into the alley, and while I wouldn't exactly call the dogs chill, I'm glad we're at least all moving in the same direction.

As soon as we turn the corner onto the sidewalk, though, they start straining at their leashes and wheeze-panting and yanking me almost out of my shoes. I can see Claudia up there on my corner wearing a thankfully unfamiliar (and clean) lemon-yellow bucket hat.

But as we close in, it becomes clear that the dogs are fangirling about the person she's with: a surprisingly hot guy closer to my age, with a nice set of exposed forearms and impressive pecs that are currently fighting for their life against his T-shirt. For a moment, this whole Claudia thing has a silver lining. Me, a down-on-her-luck crossing guard and him, a stupid-hot city lumberjack! What a classic meet-cute! My recently dumped brain can't help but imagine us telling the story of how we met: Brought together by conspiracy and tragedy! Adorable! Sad! Sexy!

I'll admit, two crushes in two days makes me feel like a massive traitor, but until Chris wakes up from this nightmare and realizes he made a terrible mistake, maybe a crush here and there is okay?

The dogs drag me over, the guy takes his index finger and points down, and holy shit, all three dogs sit obediently in a line in front of him.

Extra hot.

Apparently I'm not the only dog wizard in town. He squats down and pets them, while they nuzzle him affectionately.

"How did you *do* that?" I ask as he appears to inspect them.

"Did anyone follow you?" Claudia asks, trying her best to interrupt my fantasy where this guy falls for me right here on this street corner, and I have to tell him that I already have an imaginary government girlfriend and an actual boyfriend, at least as soon as that boyfriend comes to his senses.

Ooooh, maybe all three of them will fight over me. Could happen.

"I wasn't checking," I say.

"Amateur," she mumbles.

"Look, Claudia," I say, as diplomatically as possible. "I'm a crossing guard because I need insurance. Like, health care. I'm just trying to live my life. Please don't put me in charge of a so-called murder investigation."

"In charge?" she scoffs. "Not on your life. You're lackey material."

"Well, thank you, I think," I say.

The guy stands up from where he's been playing with the dogs, brushes his hands off on the thighs of his, *phew*, really nice-fitting jeans, and in addition to that and the forearms, he's got these bright green-blue eyes, and—

He thrusts half a pepperoni in my face. "Did you feed these dogs *pepperoni*? Are you *kidding* me?"

Hmm. Maybe we could do, like, an enemies-to-lovers sort of thing.

"The dog food hasn't been delivered yet," I say, flirting. Fine, I'm a bit rusty.

"*Pepperoni* is *dangerous* for dogs," he says passionately. He points at them dramatically. "Claudia, on top of everything else, we now also have an *attempted* murder on our hands."

Okay, he's working the enemies angle pretty hard.

Claudia puts a hand on his shoulder. "Easy there, Benny, I made her take the dogs, remember?"

"Right. About that," I say. "I would like to return them."

"Oh, that's not an option," Claudia says.

"*Maybe it should be*," Benny says, stepping up to me.

"*Yeah*," I say, giving it right back.

"Okay, kids," Claudia says with a sigh. "Let's walk."

So Claudia, who previously wouldn't let me or my stop sign anywhere near her—who would in fact *hide behind a tree* to evade me—makes me walk out into the street and pretend to cross her and Benny, who takes the leashes for the dogs. She tells us we're going to go all the way around the intersection, until we've walked in a full circle.

"Just to be clear, I'm not a crossing guard at the moment. I don't have my vest or my stop sign," I say. "And school isn't in session."

"Well," she says, "you wouldn't come to my house, so here I am, doing this on your turf. If you have complaints, then next time, make different choices."

I sigh as I step into the intersection. Next to me, she makes Benny hold her arm while she fake-hobbles at an unbearably slow pace, and next to him, the dogs form a unified front.

After a few steps in silence, Claudia whispers, "Benny, this is Mo," and—wait. How does she know my name? I don't remember telling her my name.

Benny, she says, continuing with the introductions, is Buffalo Park's most sought-after dog trainer. "Tons of experience," the old woman adds. "Used to work for Cran, as a matter of fact. The poodles love Benny."

Unlike you, Pepperoni Pockets. It's like she's rubbing it in my face. *You'll only ever be able to bribe someone to love you.*

"Great," I say to Benny. "Then you take the dogs."

"No can do," Benny says.

"Maybe Mo would feel closer to them if you told her their names," Claudia prompts.

Benny points at the pepperoni lover. "That's GCH CH Bellevie Qu'ils Mangent de la Brioche CGC."

I blink. "That's a name?"

"He goes by Jean Valjean for short."

"Oh, does he?"

Finally, Benny looks chagrined. "Well, Jean for short."

"Right."

Next, he points at the sneezer. "GCH CH Bellevie Liberté Égalité Fraternité CGC." He pauses. "AKA, Louis XIV."

As if on cue, Louis sneezes.

"Sure, why not," I say.

"And finally," Benny continues, "GCH CH Bellevie Après Moi Le Deluge CGC. But you can call him Jacques Cousteau."

"Wow, enchanté, obviously," I say. "And why, again, do *I* have to keep them? Why aren't we giving them back to someone, *any*one else?"

"If Cran was murdered, the dogs will know who did it," Benny says, looking around cautiously, like someone might be listening to us. Out here. In the middle of the wide-open street. "They were always with him, they would have sensed something dangerous."

"You just said 'if' he was murdered," I point out.

But Benny doesn't take the bait. "I didn't see the accident, but I trust Claudia's gut on this. And I knew Cran. He loved his car. And his poodles. He wasn't a drive-into-a-sinkhole, Thelma-and-Louise-but-with-dogs kind of guy."

Sure, I think. *More like a drive-into-a-crossing-guard guy.*

"Poodles are really smart," Benny says. "We just need to get them in front of the murderer and they'll tell us."

"Poodle detectives, why didn't I think of that!" I try to keep a straight face. "So how's this going to work? Are we doing a dog lineup? Are they going to look through a one-way mirror at all our suspects?"

"Of course not." Benny rolls his eyes. "They'll tell us by sniffing, or whining, or pawing at the guilty person, something like that."

"So by doing generic dog things, got it."

Claudia holds up a hand. "Mo, I've known Benny for a long time. There's no one I trust more. You're new to the neighborhood, so to help you on the case—"

"Look, I love neighborhood gossip as much as the next guy, but I'm not 'on the case'—"

"—you'll need a little background. Cran Johnston and his brother are the ones building that hideous parking monstrosity." Claudia waves her hand at the construction site across the street, the one all the kids like to sneak through. "I've been digging into their business dealings. *Very* shady."

She starts talking about rezoning things and I do my own personal rezoning. Zoning *out,* that is. Ooh, sick burn, Claudia.

But seriously, does Benny work out all the time, or are those forearms a good-genes thing?

Also, for a lovesick person, why am I so horny all the time now? It's really confusing.

Oops. They're both looking at me.

"Oh no," I say, vaguely.

"*Exactly*," Claudia says.

"So the Johnston brothers have been pressuring Claudia to sell her house," Benny explains. "They want to put up fancy condos attached to the garage."

"That's my place." Claudia points to the little bungalow next to the construction site. "But I won't budge. I bought that house when I got my first job and so help me, I'm gonna die in it. No communal living for me, I'm not a *hippie*."

She spits, which seems unnecessarily harsh on hippies.

"It wouldn't be the worst thing for you to downsize," Benny mumbles, and I can instantly sense this is not the first time they've had this conversation.

"Plus," Claudia says, pretending she didn't hear, "all this construction has opened up that sinkhole, which proves my point. And Cran was not well-liked. He's pissed off some very important people."

"Like who?" I ask.

"Like *me*, for one," she says indignantly. "Benny too."

"He fired me a couple weeks ago," says Benny with a shrug. "Guess he thought the dogs didn't need me anymore."

"So *you two* killed him?"

"That is not what I'm saying," Claudia huffs. "I'm explaining that he was very murderable! Why are you deliberately misunderstanding me?"

"Because *nobody* murdered him, Claudia!" I say.

"Then where did the radium poisoning come from?" she asks, like she's got me.

I throw my hands in the air—enough is enough. "You guys are nuts. Cran was an angry dick who drove too fast, and when I saw him yesterday, he was swerving and stumbling, slurring his words, and making drunk guy faces. *Clearly* he liked to start his day off with a one-man party and it should be no surprise to any of us that he ended up in a sinkhole. Okay? Can we all just let this go?"

We've made a full circle and reached our final corner, thank goodness, but Claudia looks at Benny, whose eyes widen.

"Mo," Benny says. "Cran didn't drink alcohol. Ever."

I roll my eyes. "How could you possibly know that?"

"*I* know it," Claudia says. "Every time Cran saw me with my afternoon Chardonnay and ice, he said that he 'wouldn't touch it with someone else's lips,' and I needed his homemade sauerkraut to detox my liver."

She smiles, giddy, and this feels like very bad news for me.

"So what does that mean?" I ask reluctantly.

"It means *you* just gave us our first clue."

Shitballs.

I came here to end this.

And somehow, I'm making it worse.

CHAPTER 12

Thanks to the so-called clue I accidentally pointed out, Claudia is more convinced than ever that Cran was, in fact, murdered. So she takes the next logical step and tells me I have to go to his funeral.

deep sigh

According to her, the murderer will almost certainly be there, and it'll be a perfect place for the dogs to have their John Grisham moment. She instructs me to attend as a mourner and wait for the dogs to tell me who the bad guy is.

When I suggest that the two of *them* do it, Claudia just snorts and reminds me that since they both have bad blood with Cran, it would look suspicious. It has to be me. A nobody.

She actually says that part out loud.

"I don't think that's a good idea," Benny argues. "There will be family at the funeral. People who are actually grieving."

"For Cran?" Claudia snorts. "That'll be the day."

"*And* it'll be too chaotic for the dogs," Benny adds.

"Ooh yeah, I agree with Benny," I say, and he gives me a long look. Yes! It's already happening! He and I are moving past enemy territory! I consider seductively touching his arm to cement the transition, but then he jerks a thumb at me.

"Plus, she's not exactly a smooth operator, she might actually make things worse."

Okay, rain check the seduction.

Claudia shakes her head. "She's what we've got to work with." And at that, the meeting is officially adjourned.

Two days later, I am putting on a black dress and killer heels so I can take three huge dogs to a stranger's funeral.

I know what Benny said. He's probably right about the funeral being a little chaotic for the dogs. And about me being too chaotic for this funeral.

But I have an ulterior motive, and it's not uncovering a murder.

It's about returning the three small horses I'm currently hiding in my studio apartment to their loving family of origin. And doing that very quickly, before any more cops can accuse me of stealing them. Plus, there's the financial aspect of this situation: These dogs are colonizing my life. The snacks alone are going to bankrupt me.

So here I am, getting ready to go to a funeral.

Claudia mentioned that Cran's business partner is his brother. And honestly, who *should* be taking care of these dogs? Their dog uncle, obviously. So I'm going to bring the dogs, like Claudia wants me to, and then when the brother takes custody, it won't be my fault. It'll just be the way it is.

Sorry, Claud.

My phone buzzes.

I'm downstairs, says the text.

Right, so actually, I have two ulterior motives.

"I DON'T GET it," Chris says as he makes a left turn. "You knew this guy?"

"Yeah," I say with a deep, sad sigh. "Through my new job. I mean, I haven't known him for long, obviously. But he made a real . . . impact."

It wasn't easy to convince Chris to spend the afternoon at a funeral with me, but when I told him that tragedy had struck and I needed his support, he finally gave in. And it's working out exactly the way I'd hoped. First of all, the dogs fit perfectly in the back of Chris's coupe. But even more than that, what brings people together? Grief!

It'll play out like this: When Chris sees me in mourning, he'll think about death, and how short our time on earth is, and how he wants to spend that time with me, and then he'll realize he's still in love with me. He'll beg me to come back, and after some stoic resistance, I'll throw myself into his arms and we'll never be apart again.

Yeah, I have a grand, romantic plan. I also *very much* want to get in his pants. That breakup sex flipped a switch inside me, and I can't stop thinking about it, or Chris. Or sex in general. Heck, the Hancock Building set me off the other day. There's also something about the fact that I don't have any realistic options at the moment that makes me want it even more.

So right now, just being in the car with Chris is making my whole body buzz. Like one of those old electric mosquito catchers that accidentally also fries moths.

It can't be just me feeling like this. Right?

"So you have a new job?" he asks, and I search for any inkling of flirtation in his tone. Nothing. That's fine, we have all afternoon.

I gaze out of my window wistfully. "Yeah."

"What is it?"

"I'm a . . . traffic management consultant for a government agency." Nailed it. "They were desperate to have me."

He sort of grunts.

I wipe away a fake tear.

"Don't tell me you're allergic to dogs now," he says.

"I'm not," I say.

"Then what's wrong with your eyes?"

I'm clearly moving too fast in the grief-brings-people-together department.

I play it cool for the rest of the ride to the funeral home, and once we get there, everything starts off just the way I imagined: We walk up together, me leaning on Chris because the stairs are steep and my heels are high, all three dogs following behind us like a fluffy, white Cerberus. We look amazing.

I open the door and all five of us step/trot inside, but before we can go any farther, a gangly, anxious, and *very* pale man with a mustache and a practiced look of regret cuts us off.

"I'm sorry, ma'am, you can't bring those dogs in here," he says.

"Why not?" I ask indignantly.

"It's a funeral home, ma'am."

"And these dogs are the deceased's next of kin," I say in a rich-person voice. "They have suffered a great loss."

"Ma'am, please." The man leans in. "We can't run the risk that they might cause a commotion or chew on . . . something."

The bull penis flashes through my head, but I can't retreat now. Not when my salvation is in the next room with that corpse.

Instead, I gasp. "Are you suggesting," I press my hand to my chest for full effect, "that these impeccably trained *angels*—"

As I look to Chris for backup, his face goes puke green and he freezes in terror, leaving me hanging.

And here's where the plan starts to unravel.

Mostly because I underestimate, again, how much Chris hates conflict.

"I'm not suggesting anything," the man says quickly. "We have a strict no animal policy."

I feel bad for him, but this really doesn't work for me.

Right behind the man, there are several rooms, one of which has a large picture of Cran on a tripod by the entrance. And beyond that, in Cran's designated room, I can see people in suits milling around. It's so close I can taste it. I *have* to get in there. And it has to be with the dogs.

Time to try another tactic. I cover my face with one hand and clutch the leashes to my chest with the other, as though I'm just barely holding myself together. "Dear, sweet, deceased Cran begged me—*begged me*—to promise that if anything happened to him, his beloved babies would have one final moment to say goodbye. And now you're taking that away from him?"

A few heads are poking out of the funeral room to see what's going on, and the man looks like he'd rather be in the coffin than deal with me.

Chris suddenly caves under the pressure.

"I'll wait in the car," he blurts, panicked. He spins around and in two steps he's back out the door, leaving me all alone.

I'm about to be furious, but actually, if I play this moment just right, it could be the break I need.

Because I am now a grieving woman *abandoned*.

I try the tear-wiping/wistful-look-into-the-distance thing again. And this time it works.

Mr. Eternal Rest watches Chris go with a frown and then looks at me with some tenderness.

"All *three* of them need to say goodbye?" the man whispers.

I nod, sniffling delicately.

The man looks from me to the dogs to the room and back. I open my mouth to wail again, and he pats my shoulder to stop me. "All right, all right," he says. "Just keep them on a short leash and make it quick."

I grab his hand with my free one and hold it tightly. "Bless you," I say. "You are an angel."

Mr. Eternal Rest straightens up, sucks in his cheeks, and then nods. "But if they misbehave, you're all leaving."

I nod in return. Back to business.

We're in.

We make our way across the muted rose carpet into Cran's room. Nobody's sitting down, but there are about eight rows of somber, dark-green chairs set up, all of them facing the open casket, which is at the front, surrounded by flowers. The room swims for a second as I think about Cran lying up there, peaceful, versus the last time I saw him, gruesomely slumped over my sinkhole.

Jean Valjean must sense how unsettling this is, because he steps closer to me, suddenly acting like an actual support dog, and it's sort of sweet. I reach down to pet him, except then I realize that he's not leaning into *me*, he's sticking his nose into the huge red purse of the tiny older woman standing in front of me, chowing down on something inside. For chrissakes. Fool me once, right?

"Jean!" I snap and tug him back toward me.

Except *that* pulls on the woman's big red bag, which is almost as big as she is, and the bag pulls on her, and she stumbles into us, catching us in the act. I freeze with a guilty grin, as she cranes her neck to squint up at me.

But instead of being mad, she takes one look at me and the dogs and bursts into giggles.

Not what I was expecting.

She claps a hand over her mouth, trying to stop herself, and then whispers through the laughter. "I am *so* sorry, I always have the most inappropriate reactions at funerals. Always gets me in trouble. Something about all the emotions flying around?"

"Oh yeah, this place is lousy with emotions," I say, distracted by pushing Jean's butt down so that he's sitting politely like his two brothers.

She leans in conspiratorially. "I think that one found my purse dog."

"Your . . ."

She glances around quickly and then pulls a half-eaten brat out of her purse.

Oh my god, I think, both horrified at what Jean has done and also making a note for later. Purse dog. *Genius.* This woman is my hero.

She giggles again. "He's already eaten half of it, can he just have the rest?"

"You know what, go for it," I say, and she laughs even harder as Jean scarfs up the rest of the hot dog.

"I'm Leslie," she says, wiping a tear from her eye.

"Mo," I say. "Nice to meet you."

"So you've taken the dogs? You seem like a wonderful girl."

Finally someone who really sees me. "Thank you," I say modestly.

"I thought they might go to Benny." She wrinkles her nose like his name smells bad. This lady is the best.

"Ugh, right?" I say. "You know Benny too?" I wrinkle my nose to show I agree.

"I have known him," she says carefully.

I don't *think* she means in the biblical sense—she's easily three decades older than me—but that would explain his complete disinterest in me.

In any case, this conversation got really awkward really fast. Time to redirect. "Have you seen Mr. Johnston's brother?" I ask quickly.

"Leslie!" someone bellows across the room.

"I'm sorry, dear," she says with a slight eye roll. "My husband calls."

"It was nice to meet you," I say as she disappears back into the crowd.

That's fine. We have our own appointment with destiny.

It's time for The Great Poodle Handoff.

Now, the question of the hour: Who at this funeral looks like the brother of Cran Johnston? Would he be another blond, snarling gym rat? Or the opposite?

I wind my way through the small clusters of mourners, which would be a lot simpler if I didn't have an entourage of dogs with me. They keep getting their leashes wrapped around the chairs, sniffing the carpet and feet and chair legs and going in all different directions. Each time they get tangled on something, I have to bend over to free a leash and manage to catch a snippet of conversation.

Thing is, *none* of the chatting is about Cran. A couple people in suits are exchanging business cards; someone in a silk shirt is asking about commercial rentals in the neighborhood; another trio is arguing over something to do with insurance. I've almost made a full circuit around the room when I realize everyone here is *networking*.

Benny was wrong—it doesn't seem like anyone is here to grieve. Yeesh, that's depressing. Cran was a dick, but maybe even dicks deserve a little respect at their own funerals?

We're nearly to the front when the dogs suddenly stop weaving around the chairs and instead drag me straight ahead, toward the casket. Sweat explodes from my armpits as I think about Mr. Eternal Rest and his warning. These guys are really pulling hard, and I have a vision of knocking the entire casket over, which would just be the cherry on top of this terrific week. I glance around for a quick exit, fantasizing about leaving the dogs here. Funeral home dogs! That's cool, right? Part of the package?

On the other hand, if Cran's brother *is* here, he'll probably come talk to a stranger with his brother's dogs standing over the casket. Right?

Against my better judgment, I take a quick peek at Cran, just lying there on a smooth bed of satin. He's obviously all cleaned up, and he doesn't look like a person who had a car accident, but then again, fixing that is somebody's whole job. And they did a good one too. He looks not quite serene, but quietly satisfied, like he just yelled at a cashier for not making his smoothie fast enough.

The dogs settle in around the casket like it's just a cozy Saturday for them, so okay, sure, I'll just hang out here with the corpse until the brother sees me. This is fine. I'm fine with corpses.

I stretch my calves a bit and wiggle my toes in these cramped heels. Nobody is looking my way. No one bears even a passing resemblance to Cran. This could just as easily be a casual business function that happens to be taking place in a room with a dead body.

Maybe I should check in on Chris. I turn back to poor dead Cran with my back to the room for privacy, pull out my phone, and start typing.

Me: Hey bb it's really sad in here, we're sharing memories, prob good you didn't come in

Nope. I delete the last bit.

Me: Hey bb it's really sad in here, we're sharing memories, thinking about you

That's not it either.

Me: What do you say we get outta here and go to pound town?

Hands down I am the horniest person at this funeral. Obviously not sending that one.

At this point, I'm so focused on crafting the perfect message that the funeral crowd behind me fades into the background. I rest my elbows on the casket and lean over Cran's body, thinking, *What are some classy synonyms for pound town?* when Louis suddenly leaps to his feet and barks, startling me into dropping my phone.

I go for the save and bobble it like I'm some kind of sports guy, but it falls anyway, and as I reach down to pick it up, I discover that they put Cran in an *unnecessarily* slippery suit and all I can do is watch in horror as my phone slides away from me.

Disappearing deep into the coffin with the dead guy.

CHAPTER 13

Okay, no big deal.

I desecrated the body.

I'll just *un*desecrate it real fast before anybody notices.

I'm about to stealthily retrieve my phone when Louis barks again, a man steps into my periphery, and I panic, doing the first thing I can think of, a thing that makes perfect sense in the moment: I throw myself over Cran, grieving mobster-widow style, and fake a sob.

It makes a lot *less* sense in the moment afterward, but it's too late. I've committed to this, now I have to see it through.

"Are you okay?" the man asks tentatively.

My face is pressed into a dead man.

I am definitely not okay.

"It was just so sudden," I mumble into Cran's chest, subtly trying to feel around for the phone without this guy catching on. "Er . . . could you find me a tissue?"

The guy hesitates and then says, "I'll be right back."

While he steps away, I quickly get more aggressive in my search—when my hand hits something hard, I instinctively pull it out, even though I almost immediately realize it's the wrong size and shape (a matchbook—did it fall out of his coat pocket?), but I don't stop to put it back, I thrust my hand farther in until I feel the familiar edge of my phone. I yank it up just in the nick of time.

I will be sterilizing this hunk of metal the second I get back home.

Also showering for an hour.

And no more playing in coffins.

"Here you go," the guy says, returning.

"Thanks a ton," I say, sniffling into the tissue. "I'm Mo."

"Hi, Mo," he says with a nod.

Unlike the rest of the room, this guy actually seems a little sad. He's easily got a foot and a half on me, and his overgrown dark hair makes him look even sadder. In one hand, he's holding half a turkey sandwich from the refreshments table, and I prepare to forcibly hold Jean back from eating it, but for once, he doesn't seem interested.

Instead, the massive poodle is leaning against the back of my legs. I silently pray that Leslie's purse dog didn't make him sick—one thing this funeral clearly doesn't need is dog barf everywhere to really drive home the futility of life.

The guy reaches out for a handshake. "I'm Tond."

"Nice to meet you, Todd," I say.

"*Tond*," he corrects me, like everyone has heard of that very common name. "How did you know Cran?"

Since I deployed the crying-in-the-coffin strategy to cover my grope for the phone, I'm sort of stuck with that vibe. "How did I know him?" I echo, running my finger along the edge of the casket and thinking fast. "I was his girlfriend."

He frowns. "You don't look like a model."

"Um, *wow*."

He frowns harder, studying me too close. "No, I mean—Cran said you were a model and I just thought models were . . . taller."

"Right, no, I was his other girlfriend. His *secret* girlfriend. That he was *ashamed* of." Nope, too far. I try to laugh casually. "And how did you know him?"

"He was my brother," Tond says.

"YES!" I say, before I catch myself and quickly follow up by leaning in and touching his cheek tenderly as though I'm overcome. "Yes, I can see the resemblance, how remarkable."

They look nothing alike.

I may have overplayed my hand.

"*So* great to finally meet you, *Tond*. And sorry about your brother." I shake my head sadly. "Who was also my secret boyfriend."

"I . . . didn't know about you," Tond says awkwardly.

"It was new," I say, and then quickly add, "but meaningful."

"Meaningful?" Tond says, his voice bitter. "That's a first."

Interesting. Some bad blood between siblings?

"You know how it is." I sigh, trying to get misty-eyed as I rack my brains for the remnants of high school Latin. What was that thing about love conquering all? "Semper fi, as they say."

"Are you in the marines?" he asks, taking a dainty bite of sandwich.

Oh nuts. Nope, that's a bumper sticker I saw last week.

I need to get this back on track. "So, *any*way, the last thing Cran said to me was that if anything happened to him, he wanted you to have the poodles. I'm sure they'll bring you a lot of comfort," I say, holding out the leashes.

Tond is now straight-up bewildered. And not as grateful as I would have thought. "He wanted me to have his poodles?"

"They've been very sweet and no trouble at all," I lie. I force the leashes into his non-sandwich hand.

"Oh, that's okay," Tond says uncomfortably, like they're dirty underwear or something. "You're the meaningful secret girlfriend, you can take them." He stuffs the leashes back in *my* hand.

"I insist—" I say, trying to hot potato the leashes back to him.

"It's fine—" he says, pushing them back at me.

We both let go and the leashes drop down to the plush red carpet between us.

Stalemate it is.

I could run. If I run, Tond will have to take the dogs.

Unless, of course, the dogs think we're playing a game and they chase me out of the funeral home and back into the car, in which case I've just made it all worse.

No, I need to stand firm. I need to DWHWD (Do What Hannah Would Do), which is to say: This is a moment for UPGRADE. I need the A for Act Confident. Because whether I walk or run or crawl out of here, I am *not* doing it with these dogs.

I can't wait to tell Han about this application of UPGRADE.

Or some of it, anyway. The part that doesn't make me sound like a maniac. Does any part of this funeral tableau not make me sound like a maniac?

Eh. I can retcon it later.

"Tond, I'm gonna level with you. These dogs need a stable home. The kind of home you can provide. They shouldn't be with me. Look at me. I'm a secret girlfriend that Cran wouldn't tell his own *brother* about. The cops want to *arrest me* for having these dogs."

That last part definitely might be true.

And I finally have his attention. "The cops are involved?" he whispers.

Bingo. Time to think fast. And think *good*.

"Oh yeah. The cops? Involved? *Majorly.* There's this big-time cop who just got transferred into town, right after a breakup, just him and his, um, houseplant, and he has a real chip on his shoulder about all of it. Oh, and his partner? Phew, his partner just wants to see some action." Tond looks positively green at all this, and that means . . . he doesn't recognize that I'm ripping off the plot of *Hot Fuzz*, the last cop movie I saw.

Unfortunately, I have just exhausted my memory of that movie because I fell asleep on Chris's couch while we were watching it.

Ugh, Chris's couch.

Ugh, Chris is waiting outside, gotta move things along.

"*Anyway*, this lady Claudia was the one who called them because she just loooooves the cops, so she made sure they were looking into everything, and I mean *everything*, Tond, including me and my possession of these dogs, so now the uh, big-time cop-slash-detective is *fully* up my butt about this case, and plus on top of all that, you know, poodles are sensitive, they really struggle with strangers." I only stop because I have completely run out of breath.

Tond blinks. Like about a hundred times. "I just . . . need a minute," he says, pale under the dark mop of bangs.

"No problemo," I say as he glances toward the refreshments table. Probably needs a glass of water. Or whiskey. I know how jarring it can be to suddenly become a dog parent.

I, meanwhile, am ecstatic. I am killing this UPGRADE! Hannah would be so proud! I Acted Confident. I Didn't Doubt! I'm already at E for Execute! Let's doooo this!!!

I pick up the leashes, deposit them in Tond's hand, manually fold his fingers around them, and give him a quick wink. "I'll just run to the ladies' room so you guys can get reacquainted."

In the bathroom, I do a little victory dance in front of the full-length mirror, feeling light for the first time in days. Then I pull out my phone to text Claudia. She won't be happy but at least this way I don't have to tell her to her face.

Me: Well I tried but dogs didn't sniff out a murderer

Me: So I gave the dogs to Cran's brother who was moved to tears by my generous gesture

I pause for a second, finger hovering over the send arrow. But I really need to be firm here. Crystal clear with no room for argument.

Me: You and Benny do what you want but I really can't be involved anymore

I put my phone on silent and tuck it in my bag. I'll deal with the repercussions later. Right now—time to get out of here.

But there, standing in the hallway, is Mr. Eternal Rest, frowning severely and holding the leashes of all three dogs.

I think I audibly whimper, but I'm in kind of a fugue state so it's hard to say.

He holds the leashes out to me gingerly, like he's holding the tail of a dead rat. "Mr. Johnston told me to wait here for you. He said you'd be leaving with these creatures."

"No!" I say, then compose myself. "I'm sorry, you're mistaken, those are Mr. Johnston's dogs now." I try to skirt past him, but he's quicker than he looks. He blocks the way so I have no choice.

After I finally take the leashes, he looks at his hands with revulsion. "I'm going to go wash up, and when I return, all *four* of you had better be gone from my establishment."

I nod meekly. "My apologies for disturbing everyone."

He nods, then disappears to the men's bathroom, at which point I race back into the funeral room.

Thankfully, Tond is tall, and I spot the back of his head across the room, sticking up from the crowd. I push my way through, elbowing cranky real estate agents and landscapers and contractors to get through as fast as possible. I'm almost to Tond when Jean tugs at his leash, trying to crawl through a pair of legs to get to something. I can just make out the giant red bag and a tiny pair of feet beneath it, which means he's in the mood for another of Leslie's purse dogs, and who can blame him—but this is no time for a nosh.

"Jean!" I whisper sharply, and he turns to look at me, irritated. "Later."

He seems to accept this, but unfortunately, the brief detour took us off course, and a woman with an impressive set of biceps steps between Tond's back and me, yammering on her cell phone and not looking where she's going. She wedges me against the wall with her solid and immovable shoulders.

Probably CrossFit, dang it.

Behind me, I see Mr. Eternal Rest peek into the room as he speaks into a walkie-talkie. I hide behind CrossFit, in the clear for now.

As I look for an opening to squeeze past the buff broker, I hear Tond deep in conversation with somebody I can't see.

". . . she said Claudia's got the cops sniffing around. You told me this was the end of it and that nobody would find out—"

My blood suddenly runs cold. The other guy says something, but I can't hear him over the buzz of the room.

Tond interrupts. "No way, I didn't sign up for *this*. I'm out."

And *that's* when Mr. Eternal Rest spots me, gestures toward a security guard, and in a first for me, I'm pretty sure I'm about to get kicked out of a fucking funeral.

As the security guy barrels his way toward me, I finally hear the guy Tond is talking to, loud and clear this time.

"Cran was your ticket in, don't go soft on me now. Just take care of her."

Take care of?

Her?

Oh my god.

Was Claudia right?

It *was* murder? And these are the guys who did it? His own brother?

And "*her*" is next?

Who is "*her*"?

ME?

I need a paper bag, I need a paper bag so bad.

Calm down, I tell myself, except then I think of the dogs. How Louis, who hasn't made a single sound except to sneeze, barked when Tond walked up. How Jean, who will eat *anything*, ignored a perfectly good turkey sandwich, just because it was in Tond's hand.

Oh my god. Claudia and Benny were right.

The dogs told me who the murderer was.

And Tond freaked out *the moment* I brought up the police.

I'm definitely breathing too fast. And I still have not one single solitary paper bag to hyperventilate into. But I do have the next best thing. I have Chris.

Vision's getting sparkly. No time to think.

Get to Chris. Fast.

The security guard is trying to push past the buff broker now, but she's still on her phone and yelling at him to get his hands off her, so she's inadvertently acting as *my* security guard.

Thank you, CrossFit, I say silently as I squeeze myself and the three dogs back the way we came. I catch a glimpse of Mr. Eternal Rest making his way through the crowd to cut us off, and I realize even worse than getting kicked out of a funeral would be *getting detained* at a funeral (can they do that?) and I do not want to get detained while spying on murderers. I elbow my way harder, the four of us *just* managing to spill out into the lobby before Mr. Eternal Rest can clamp a hand down on my arm.

"Hey!" he calls from his spot next to the poster of Cran's face.

"Great funeral, thanks for hosting!" I call back to him as I run toward the exit.

I throw the door open and almost bowl over Leslie, who's inconveniently about to make her tottering way down the front steps.

Jean, meanwhile, is thrilled to get one last shot at a second course.

"*Not now, Jean*," I say, crushing his hopes again.

"Oh, I don't mind," Leslie says as I fly past her. "I'm out of purse dogs, but I do have—"

"Can't talk right now . . . thank you . . . have to . . ." I hot-step it sideways down the terrible steep stairs and straggle-run across the parking lot in my heels and black dress, the dogs loving this spontaneous jog, while I wave frantically at Chris. The windows are up and he's drumming passionately on the steering wheel while clearly singing at the top of his lungs, which I would find cute if we weren't in mortal danger.

"Chris! *Chris!*" I yell, but he doesn't hear me until I slam my body into the passenger door and tug at the handle. "Unlock the door! There's murderers!"

He jumps and blushes and turns down the volume. The doors click open, I get the dogs in the back seat, then leap into the front.

"*Go*," I yell. "PUNCH IT!"

"What?" Chris blinks at me, distinctly *not* punching it.

"Murderers!" I say again, gasping for breath. "We have to get out of here, stat! Oh god, I need my inhaler. Where's my inhaler?" I root through my bag. "You don't have any lunch bags in here, do you?"

Chris starts the car, but he doesn't put it into gear. Instead he turns to me disapprovingly. "Once again, you don't have asthma."

"THAT'S what you want to respond to?" I shriek. "Not the murder part? Seriously, you need to *drive*."

He finally pulls out of the lot.

"Okay, fine," he says calmly. "What's the murder part?"

"Cran's brother murdered him! And I'm next!"

"So this guy you know from work," Chris says, "his brother *murdered* him? This was part of the funeral service?"

"*No!* I overheard him talking."

I turn in my seat, straining to look past the dogs and through the back window. It doesn't seem like anybody's following us. But good lord, in the time we've been sitting here, tiny old Leslie has tottered down the stairs, gotten into her massive Escalade, and squealed out of the parking lot.

You know, like *we* should be doing.

"Are you sure?" Chris says gently. "Maybe you misheard."

"No way," I say, feeling the heat rise up in my face. "You always do this! You always second-guess me!"

"To be fair, you overreact a lot—"

"I'm not overreacting this time! They're murderers! And you're pissing me off!" I groan with frustration, as he reaches over and pushes my hair back from my face. But he doesn't stop there. He runs his fingers through my hair and back to my neck.

I look up. He's got a smoldery look in his eyes that I haven't seen in forever.

Wait, what? Is this happening? Did my plan actually work? And also, why'd it have to work *right* after I identified some murderers?

"But the . . . murderers," I manage to whimper as Chris slowly sucks on one of my fingers.

"I know a great secluded parking lot," he says, his gaze lingering on my cleavage. "They'll never catch you there."

CHAPTER 14

I decide to put the whole murder thing on hold for just a minute.

Maybe twenty minutes.

Tops.

We pull into the parking lot of a former abandoned elementary school that's now an abandoned cop academy and park behind the dumpster. It feels sexy and dangerous—maybe not as dangerous as murder, but I'm not thinking about that now.

I'm thinking about Chris and the hand he's sliding up my leg.

With surprisingly little effort, he swings me up and over so I'm straddling him in the driver's seat. The car is clearly not made for this, but as long as my ankle doesn't get stuck between the door and the seat, I can work with it.

I can *also* work with what Chris has currently going on in his pants.

While I grind on his lap, Chris goes back to sucking my finger, and it occurs to me that maybe I should mention that the finger in his mouth was recently digging around in the coffin of a dead man.

Which reminds me that I should give Claudia another quick update about the whole situation, so that she can start thinking of a plan to protect me, and I can really relax into all of this instead of worrying.

And honestly, I think I'll just skip telling Chris—he's having a great time, no reason to distract him.

I push his head into my boobs with one hand while I use the other one to slip my phone out of my bag and hold it behind the headrest where Chris can't see. I keep grinding as Chris motorboats me—or am I motorboating him? Philosophically speaking, which of us is the motorboated and which is motorboating?

Putting that aside for later, I compose a quick text. The dogs are definitely confused, but thankfully they're just sitting on the back seat, watching as I multitask.

Me: You were right, it was nursery

Nursery? Dammit, autocorrect.

Me: I mean, murder, it was murder

Me: I'm in danger

Just then, in one swift motion, Chris decides to go for the gold and yanks my dress over my head, sending the phone flying into the back seat. Before I can protest, I feel his lips on my stomach.

Ah fuck it.

I spin and trust fall backward so my head's on the passenger seat, pressing against the door, and I'm arching my back over the center console, which gives Chris the perfect angle.

His tongue is now sliding along my hip bones. Then he's tugging at my black silk underwear *with his teeth*. Holy hell.

Why did it take us breaking up for sex to be exciting and fun?

This is a very important question that I should probably answer for myself at some point, but now is NOT THE TIME.

Now is the time to prop a foot up on the steering wheel so that he can get the underwear all the way off me and then hoist my legs over his shoulders so I'm in a kind of tits-up wheelbarrow situation, giving him an all-access pass as he starts slowly kissing up my thighs.

That's when my phone starts buzzing.

I'm going to ignore it, I really am, because this is like *life-changing* sex, but the phone just keeps buzzing, so I twist my head, and spot it through the gap between the two front seats.

I think I can get it.

Or at least see who's calling.

I arch my back a little more, and then inch my arm through the gap, doing everything I can not to have any impact on Chris's really excellent work. Unfortunately, the dogs are starting to get restless, and they seem to think we're playing a game now, so as I grope around for the phone, they keep nudging my hand out of the way.

UGH, why is it so hard to just *live*?

By now, the windows are steamed up, and the slow, careful teasing Chris started out with builds in speed and pressure, so that my whole body is shaking, and not just from the strain of holding this impressively acrobatic position. It's like the dogs sense it all the way from the back seat because they start howling in unison, and I'm thinking yeah, actually, good idea, so I howl too.

This is exactly what I needed!

And who cares about murder anyway!

I'm here, in the car, safe with Chris!

Chris, who makes me feel so good!

Chris, who is about to make me explode!

Chris, who I love!

"*I love you!*" I gasp.

And that's when he *stops*.

He gophers his head up from between my legs.

"*Why are you stopping?!*" I cry.

Chris frowns. "Did you just say you *love* me?"

"For god's sake, *don't stop now*!"

He slides my legs off his shoulders and looks away as he hands me my dress. I don't even know what to do with it for a moment—it's like my rational mind has been completely scrambled.

"You should probably get dressed," he says, avoiding eye contact.

"But . . . I thought you wanted . . ." I awkwardly reposition my legs so they're facing forward again and hold the dress up in front of me like a bath towel.

I thought you wanted me.

He shrugs his shirt back on and sighs. "I don't get it, Mo. Aren't we past all that?" he says. "I thought your text was just about some fun breakup sex."

"Past all *what*?" I say indignantly, pulling my head through the neck of my dress. Then I freeze. "Wait, what text?"

He shoves his phone at me.

Mo: What do you say we get outta here and go to pound town?

Oh.

Balls.

I hand the phone back and muster up as much dignity as I possibly can for this next bit. "Right," I say. "I can explain that. I must have accidentally sent it when I dropped my phone in the coffin."

He goes a pale green color again. Really, for a doctor, he's awfully squeamish.

"But, Chris, listen," I continue. "Wasn't that fun? Funeral hijinks and steamy, albeit *unfinished* car sex? You can't deny that we make a great team."

Chris sighs, puts the car in gear, and without looking at me, says, "I've actually just started seeing somebody. Casual. But still."

It feels like I just got punched in the stomach.

And then I'm shrugging my dress back on as he drives out of the parking lot, kicking off the most awkward forty-five-minute car ride known to man.

He couldn't have waited to say that as he was dropping me off?

Because now I have to ask who it is, and of course he won't tell me, he'll just say, "you don't know her," which is how I'll know I *do* know her, and it's probably another doctor, and then I'll have to ugly cry as I think of all the ways she's cooler or smarter or hotter than me, and just imagining it is all so humiliating I can't even work up the nerve to actually ask the question out loud.

I've almost psyched myself up to say something mature and selfless by the time we pull up in front of my building, but as he puts the car in park, he clears his throat. "I think we should take a break."

"What?" I blurt incredulously. "How could we be any *more* on a break, Chris?"

The absolute coward looks away. "I mean, I think we shouldn't talk for a while."

I bite my lip until I know my voice won't crack, and then I give him a very inappropriate two thumbs-up. "If that's what you want," I say. "Thanks for the ride."

The dogs and I slink out of the car and walk-of-shame ourselves right into the building without even pretending to hide, because frankly, I can't bring myself to care about Roy seeing us. It would still be the fourth-worst thing that's happened today.

But the god of breakups throws me a bone; there's a note taped to Roy's door. "On Vacation! Call Sheila (my mom) if you need something."

Upstairs, I throw my bag on the table, let the dogs loose, and realize my dress is on backward, because of course it is. I take the stupid dress off and put on my Cubs tank. It's no-pants night, baby. Too early to go straight to bed, though. I grab a beer and a pint of ice cream and throw myself pathetically into the ratty pink velour chair. That's when I notice the matchbook that's slid out of my bag and onto the floor.

Right. The matchbook that was in Cran's corpse's suit pocket, from that time I shoved my hand in his coffin.

I flop out of the chair, crawl over, and study it half-heartedly. It's from the bar down the street from me, Dickie's Tavern. Dickie's is one of those bleak neighborhood bars that puts red wine in the refrigerator and has no lights except a lit-up Old Style sign in the window.

Why would Cran go there if he doesn't drink? Sure, they nominally have pizza, but he wouldn't go there for that—believe me, I've ordered that pizza and the Yelp reviews are right. Plus, didn't Claudia say Cran was a health nut?

CLAUDIA.

SHIT.

I totally forgot that I need to talk to her! I check my phone, and it was her calling while we were in the car—she called twice, but didn't leave a message either time. And she didn't reply to my texts.

I try calling back. She doesn't pick up.

Then I text again.

Me: I'm sorry we keep missing each other, but I really need to talk. Murder plot real. Johnston brother in on it, but there's a mastermind, identity unknown. Any leads??

Then, because I need her to know how serious this is, I text again.

Me: Please, this is urgent. Need to know who other guy is

By now I've finished my beer and yes, I'm a little tipsy, but I can feel myself getting worked up about this, and I have to find a way to not completely freak myself out.

Why won't Claudia respond? Is she ignoring me because I tried to offload the dogs to Tond and quit the investigation?

Petty, yes. But on-brand? Also yes.

After about three minutes of stewing about being ignored, I decide to just go over to her house and beg for forgiveness. I mean, I know where she lives. And it's so close. That's not weird, right?

Well, it's definitely not weirder than anything Claudia does.

Maybe I'll take her a beer.

As a house gift.

It's closing in on 9 p.m. when I get there, gift beer in hand. We probably only have a few more weeks of summery weather, and even though the sun has set, the sky is still a light, glowy pink.

Claudia's bungalow, on the other hand, is totally dark.

I knock lightly on the door, loud enough that she'd hear if she was still up, but not loud enough to wake her.

No answer.

Is this situation urgent enough to wake Claudia up by ringing the doorbell?

Claudia's voice rings in my head. *I dunno, Mo, is* murder *urgent?*

Then Chris's voice: *You took what you heard out of context and blew it way out of proportion. This was so obviously an accident.*

Ugh. Dick.

My finger hovers over the bell, which is one of those video doorbell camera thingies. Of course Claudia's got cutting-edge security. This is peak crime-prevention stuff. She's probably got a friggin' *panic room* in there.

I lean into the doorbell, because I might as well cover all my bases.

"Claudia," I whisper. "It's me, Mo."

Yes, obviously it's me, this thing is a camera.

I keep going.

"I'm sorry, okay? *Please* don't give me the silent treatment right now. I heard Tond say he wants to 'take care of' me . . . Which really does sound kinda murdery? I'm not *scared* scared, but Chris thinks I'm overreacting, which I have—okay, fine—*occasionally* been known to do. Right, you don't know Chris—he's my boyfriend. Ex. Long story, not my fault. He is GREAT in the sack, though, which still makes me kind of want to trust him and honestly, I'm just really confused right now, lots going on, you know? Could use an assist."

Phew, this went off the rails fast. *Bro, you* really *need therapy* pops into my head, and I make a mental note to eventually deal with that.

"Anyway," I continue whispering into the doorbell, "I'm sorry I didn't believe you at first. Call me when you watch this?" I pause for a second. "Okay, um, bye."

I hustle home, drinking the gift beer as I go, which unfortunately just makes me feel more paranoid. After pacing around my apartment and polishing off my third beer of the night, I break down and pick up my phone.

"Yellooooo, this is—"

"Hi, Detective Mierzwiak, it's Mo. Ellery. We talked before? I think we got off on the wrong foot."

"Ahhh yes, Chicago's most notorious dog thief."

"I am not—look, I tried to give the dogs to their uncle and he's making me keep them and anyway, that's not what I'm calling about. I think someone is trying to murder me. I overheard them talking about it at a funeral."

"No kidding. A funeral? I'll get my best guy on the case."

A thousand-pound weight is lifted from my shoulders. "Really? Thank you so—"

"No, not really! And stop calling me or you're gonna be in some real trouble."

He hangs up.

So that went well.

CHAPTER 15

I wake up the next morning to one new text.

Claudia: It's murder

Great, thanks, Claud. Super helpful.

I can't tell if she's being passive-aggressive about me doubting her or if she'd just had a little too much of her Chardonnay and ice last night, but right now I can only think about how unfair it would be if I got murdered or arrested before I've had any caffeine.

I roll over and discover a searing pain in my left arm. And that's not all: My mouth is dry, my heart is racing, and my whole body somehow feels both hot and cold at the same time. And my throat is definitely closing up. I put my hand on my chest as my breath starts to come fast, and part of me just wants to stay in bed and wait to see if this massive heart attack passes or kills me.

But then a velvety wet nose nudges my hand. Another one sniffs at my face. I weigh my options. I could get up and be a grown-up about this, or I could die and run the risk of being breakfast for three circus poodles.

I grit my teeth. "Ugh, fine."

JESSIE, THE WEEKEND receptionist at Lincoln Urgent Care, audibly groans when I sidle up to the counter. "Hope you brought your punch card, Mo," she says. "What'll it be today? Tetanus? Skin infection? Ebola?"

"Very funny," I say. "We both know Ebola never made it to Chicago. I'm having a heart attack."

"Then go to the ER."

She's right, of course, but the idea of going to the ER is somehow *scarier* than a heart attack. "Can't you just squeeze me in? My left arm really hurts," I say, rubbing it and wincing to show her I'm not lying.

"You're not having a heart attack."

"I could be," I say, picturing my parents getting the call that I died in the lobby of an Urgent Care. *That tracks,* they'll say. *Bet she didn't even try to get to the ER—if only she'd had some ambition.* "This is medical malpractice."

Jessie groans, pressing fingers into the bridge of her nose. "No, Mo, it's *triage.* And I'm really busy today. With people who are actually sick."

I look around the waiting room. There's no one else here.

Jessie sighs and types something into her computer. "Just, you know, make an appointment online like everyone else."

Two can play this game.

I head out to the sidewalk, pull out my phone, and make an appointment for fifteen minutes from now. Busy, my ass. Once I get the confirmation, I shoot Jessie a cute look through the window just as Hannah texts me about hanging out. I leave her on read—it's just not a good time for me to sound like I have my shit together, what with my current heart attack—and then I go back to my thread with Claudia.

> **Me:** If you're mad at me for doubting, I will make it up to you. But until then, could use a little help? Figure out who the mastermind is so I don't get killed, etc??

I've just hit send when a voice startles me. "Well, if it isn't my favorite crossing guard."

If it's possible to nearly jump out of your own body, that's what I do. But it turns out the voice isn't coming from a potential murderer.

It's coming from the hottest, nerdiest government employee I have ever met. And sure, the alderman's office is like two doors down, but also, this is a Sunday. What's she doing here?

"Workaholic, much?" I joke, trying to pretend she didn't just give me the jump scare of my life.

Tasha is wearing a short-sleeve button-down and, I'm sorry, a *bow tie*? Somehow she just got ten times cuter, which honestly seems illegal. I, meanwhile, am still braless in my ancient Cubs tank, sporting a puffy face and bedhead.

She doesn't seem to notice any of this though. Instead, she breaks into a huge grin and gives me a hug while I whisper to my deodorant, *Hold the line.*

Tasha, meanwhile, smells kinda sweet, kinda spicy, and totally delicious. This is all very bad timing because it's making my heart race mid–heart attack.

"Don't get too close," I say, pulling away from her, and then accidentally blurting out the least sexy thing imaginable. "I might be contagious."

"Oh," she says, concern flashing across her face. "Flu? Covid?"

Too late to backtrack. No way out but through.

"No, uh," I say. "Heart attack."

She laughs.

"I'm serious!" I say, smiling despite myself. "My left arm hurts!"

"Can I?" she asks, pointing at my shoulder.

"Yeah—O-o-okay," I stammer.

She starts gently massaging my shoulder, and it feels amazing. "I bet I can guess why."

Maybe this is about to be sexy after all.

"You've been walking a big dog," she says.

The laugh dies in my throat, and the wave of paranoia that started yesterday at the funeral crashes over me.

How would she know that?

Has she been watching me?

Seriously, why *is* she working on a Sunday?

"What?" I ask, glancing up and down the street. Was I followed?

"A dog," she says cheerfully.

I step out of the massage. "Why would you say that?"

"Sometimes I take Charlie out when the dog walker isn't available, and that dog yanks so hard, my shoulder hurts for days." She cocks her head. "You okay?"

I cringe. "Sorry, it's been a weird week." Everything she said was, in fact, totally normal, because *she's* a totally normal person who does not get herself embroiled in murderous conspiracies. "I am, indeed, doing some dogsitting, and it's a good theory. But the pain is," I throw some air quotes, "'radiating down my arm' and WebMD says—"

"Dr. Google is a slippery slope, Mo," says Tasha. "Trust me, I've been there. Better just to resist the urge."

"Well . . ."

She peers at me through those dark-rimmed glasses, sees that I'm unconvinced, and smiles. "You *have* had a stressful week. How about this: I've got to get back to the office—elections are around the corner, projects are really stacking up, and I want to get ahead of the week. But after I'm done, let's grab a drink? Unwind a little?"

"Oh," I say, and my entire vocabulary abandons me. "Oh."

"Is that a yes?"

"That sounds—" My voice cracks. Oh god, I am an eleven-year-old boy. In so many ways. "That sounds definitely. Very great."

Good lord.

"Cool," she says. "How about Dickie's?"

Dickie's Tavern. The matchbook!

"My fave," I say, rubbing my stomach like a cartoon. Seriously, I need flirting lessons or something. Do they have those at the park district?

Tasha takes off, and I watch her walk away until I realize it'll be weird if she turns around and catches me ogling, so I go back inside, waving my phone triumphantly at Jessie. "Checking in for my appointment, right on time."

She sighs. "Have a seat."

ONE $25 CO-PAY later, and I am officially heart-attack-free. Tasha was right: strained muscle with a side order of spasms. I tell the doc that Advil's not going to cut it this time, but when he suggests the alternative would be several very expensive rounds of some kind of off-brand Botox injections at a real hospital, I decide that Advil will be fine.

On the walk home, I obsess over tonight. Is this going to be a date, or are we just new friends unwinding over a beer? A couple of days ago, I would have been fully committed to the friend camp, but now that Chris is seeing somebody else, why can't I?

Maybe this whole life explosion won't turn out so terribly after all?

I'm rolling this revelation around in my head as I get home, check the mail, and then head into the stairwell. Roy's door opens and for a second, I'm surprised that he's already home—until I see that it's not him.

It's sort of like an alternate universe version of him.

Essentially Roy, but with faded orangish hair from a bad dye job.

"Sheila, I presume?" I ask the wizened old lady standing in front of me.

"Hello, dear," she coos. "You must be No."

"*Mo*," I correct her.

She frowns and pats the pockets of her flowered apron in distress, like she's trying to remember where she put something. "I was so sure Roy's note said that your name was No."

"It's okay," I say reassuringly. She's so cute and grandmotherly, I already want to hug her and make her proud of me. "You call me whatever you want."

She beams up at me, her eyes twinkling. "You're such a dear. Just a moment, I have some fresh cookies."

With that, she disappears into the apartment, presumably to get me some fresh cookies. Why can't this lady be my landlord?

She returns a minute later with a bunch of cookies on a massive cooling rack. "Take as many as you like," she says cheerily.

"Oh, Sheila, you shouldn't have," I say, as I grab two cookies and take a big bite of one. It's amazing—oatmeal and warm chocolate, and the slight hint of spices I can't place. "Wowzers."

She winks at me. "That's my mother's recipe."

"Mmmm," I groan. "It's just incredible. Thank you. My weekend started off so badly, but between hot civil servants and delicious cookies, things are looking up."

"Was it because of the dogs?"

I promptly choke, cookie crumbs suddenly clawing at the inside of my throat.

"What?" I manage to croak.

"Your bad weekend. But never mind that! Sounds like that cookie went right down your Sunday pipe," she says, nothing but sweetness. "Let me get you something."

She disappears again as I keep coughing.

Sheila knows about the dogs?

When she reappears, the oven mitts are gone, and she holds a shot glass of what looks like whiskey.

"Go on," she says encouragingly.

I shoot it, and it is, in fact, whiskey. Cheap, brutal, and very definitely whiskey.

"There you go," she says, patting my back as the coughing subsides, instantly replaced by the burn of the alcohol. "I thought you might need it."

"For the cookie?"

"Oh, no, dear. For the blackmail." She winks again.

"I'm sorry," I say weakly. "I think I've lost track of what's happening."

"Oh, that's because I haven't told you yet." She takes the shot glass back and dries it out with the edge of her apron.

Note to self: no more shots with Sheila.

Then she smiles at me again. "I know you have dogs up there. Now see, my Roy can be a little naive, like most men, but I wasn't born yesterday. I know about the dogs *and* I know you aren't allowed to have dogs as per your lease." She puts on a pair of readers and pulls my literal lease out of her apron pocket, perusing it with her lips pursed.

"I . . . I . . ."

"Don't try to deny it. *Buuuut* . . ." She draws the word out, as she flaps the lease in front of my face. "I don't *have* to tell Roy about them."

"You don't?"

"Thing is, he's got me on a pretty strict allowance, and I could use some going-out money. Mama needs some horizontal refreshment."

I squint at her. "I'm sorry, some—"

She rolls her eyes. "Nookie. Whoopie. Oh, what is it you kids say—hot beef injection?"

A small squeak escapes my throat.

"So I'll need forty-five a week to keep your little secret. You can Venmo me."

"Forty-five . . . *dollars*?"

She just smiles pleasantly.

I'm suddenly grateful for that whiskey. Between horny ol' Sheila and the bull penises, these dogs are going to bankrupt me.

I have no choice but to agree to her terms. It's already clear: You don't haggle with Sheila.

And as I trudge upstairs, eating the other cookie, which somehow doesn't taste nearly as delicious as the first cookie, I make a resolution.

The poodles have got to go. ASAP.

CHAPTER 16

Six hours later, I still haven't solved the poodle problem.

Mostly because it takes me the entire time between Sheila's blackmail and now to figure out what to wear to meet Tasha. After trying on everything I own, I've settled on some jeans that make me look like I actually have a butt and a tank top from one of my favorite bands, Boss Fight. It's casual, a little punk, but it also looks like an actual outfit.

Just for the heck of it, I spritz some saltwater tousling spray on my hair, something Hannah gave me after the company sponsored one of her posts. It's supposed to give my limp hair a little body, but all it does is make it look slightly sticky.

Gross.

I check the time, and since I still have fifteen minutes, I hop in the shower and quickly wash out the tousling spray.

Apparently, though, I don't shut the bathroom door all the way.

Just as I'm about to reach down to turn off the water, Jacques Cousteau lives up to his namesake and leaps into the shower with me, which makes me scream bloody murder *Psycho*-style and pull down the shower curtain bar on both of us, bonking myself hard just under my eye. Very cool to be almost blinded today, on top of everything else.

Jacques prances around, apparently loving all this.

"I will call Animal Control!" I yell, sliding around the slick tub and banging my knees as I try to stand. "You wouldn't last an hour in that hellhole!"

He absolutely doesn't care and leaps back out of the tub to pounce on the puddles that are now all over the bathroom floor. The other two dogs watch from the doorway, looking amused.

I finally untangle myself from the curtain, shut the water off, and get out, first drying myself and then tossing the towel down to mop up the water. I'm simultaneously swabbing the floor and cursing out Tond for sticking me with the dogs, when suddenly I realize I *still* haven't heard from Claudia about all my funeral revelations. Makes sense that she'd be the grudge-holding type.

Tomorrow, I'll grovel like I've never groveled before. She'll give in and help me figure out who's the mastermind of Operation Kill Cran and Possibly Mo.

Who's the crime boss/Moriarty/Funeral Deep Throat.

Who's got Tond wrapped around their little finger.

The woman's a born meddler; she won't be able to help herself.

When the floor's mostly dry, I check the clock—five minutes until I'm supposed to meet Tasha. Crap.

After a few quick swipes of deodorant, I throw my clothes back on, grab my shoulder bag, and go.

I jog down the stairs and past Sheila/Roy's apartment, almost tripping over a package on my way out of the front door. I apologize silently to whoever it's for, kick it into the corner of the mailroom, and tear down the path toward the gate. I'm already halfway down the sidewalk when I hear the gate clang shut after me.

The whole way there, I try to walk fast enough that I won't be too late, but not so fast that I show up sweaty. Tasha already got that version of me once today. I need to show her I've got range.

As I turn onto Lincoln, Dickie's Tavern appears in front of me, humming softly from the neon glow of the Old Style sign.

I suddenly feel a little queasy, and not just at the thought of two-star pizza. Here I am teetering on the edge of all things unknown.

I mean, I might be murdered at any second.

AND I'm not sure if this is a date.

Which is worse? I don't know. But somehow, I'm going to tackle both at the same time. *This will be fine*, I tell myself. *I know how to multitask.*

THEY KEEP THE lights low in Dickie's, which I assume is so nobody can see the layer of grease and dust on everything. The wood is dark, too, and so is the red vinyl of the booths lining the walls. The dim light unfortunately does *not* hide the fact that the place smells like the ghost of a thousand sad-guy cigarettes. A quick glance around tells me that Tasha's not here yet. Might as well do a little recon to pass the time.

To start: The Cran/Dickie's connection just doesn't square. Every scummy inch of the bar reinforces my original theory that it's not the sort of place Cran would hang out. Not without disinfectant wipes and, like, kale. So why did he have the Dickie's matchbook in his pocket at the funeral? Did he just pop in to grab some matches one day? I'm sure he wasn't a smoker, so why would he even need them to begin with? Was he a scented candle guy?

My sense of the man just gets fuzzier and fuzzier.

I linger in the doorway for a half second, scanning the room and clocking three middle-aged sports guys at the bar and a couple at a far booth, their heads so close together I can't tell what they look like. The bartender, an older woman with tons of tattoos, leans against the wall behind her, checking her phone.

"Everything okay?"

I spin around, embarrassed to be caught mid-recon, and there's Tasha, looking a little tired but happy to see me. "Sorry I'm late," she says with an apologetic grimace. "I just can't get out from under my workload these days."

Lucky workload, I think.

"No sweat," I say and wave toward the booths. "Any preference?"

"How about that one?" Tasha's hand grazes my lower back, and my brain instantly puts a pin in the sleuthing and screams *DATE DATE IT'S LOOKING LIKE A DATE* as she gently steers me to the empty booth. She's not in work mode anymore, and she's let her hair down and—even sexier—unknotted her bow tie, which hangs loose around her neck. I'm on an actual date with the after-hours James Bond of civic engagement.

High five to myself.

I let her slide into the booth and then ask her what she wants. "First round's on me."

"There's going to be more than one round?" she asks with a grin.

"I have *a lot* of unwinding to do," I say with a matching grin. "I'm guessing you do, too, workaholic?"

"Guilty as charged." She holds up a hand. "What can I say, I'm a beast for public service. If I'm not in bed, I'm probably at work."

"Sounds like you need to spend more time in bed," I suggest, raising an eyebrow.

"Get me that drink and you can tell me your pitch."

HOLY CORPORATE-STYLE FLIRTING, BATMAN.

I float over to the bar with her order, and as I wait for the bartender to pour a couple pints of Green Line, I scope out the wall above the cash register. It's crammed with a bunch of haphazardly taped-up photos from one of those rebooted Polaroid cameras, and I search for Cran's trademark sneer, but come up empty—just a lot of poorly framed shots of strangers toasting or making Malört face.

I sneak a look at the three sports guys, who are glued to a TV screen playing a Cubs game. One of them has a hand resting in a bowl of nuts, like he's getting a manicure and needs to soften his cuticles first.

Mental note: Don't eat the nuts here.

Follow-up note: Those guys are probably not part of any potential crime syndicate.

A quick glance at the couple in the booth tells me they are full-on making out, so also probably not involved in much crime-ing.

How does recon work if people don't just walk up and admit stuff to you? I'm starting to get the distinct impression that I suck at this. *Soldier on*, I think solemnly.

As the bartender works, I try a little casual chitchat.

"So, you get a lot of suits in here?"

She stops midpour and shoots me a baffled look, like I've asked her about local Serbian politics.

Maybe that's just not the right question.

"Cool matchbooks." I point to the little bowl of them. "How many do you think you go through in a month?"

She squints and I think this is *also* not the way to go.

One more try. "How do you decide who gets to go up on the wall?"

Finally, she answers. "You have to be somebody I like."

Then she gives me a look that clearly says I will not be going up on the wall.

That's enough recon for now.

"Two Guinnesses," she says, plopping the pint glasses down in front of me.

I check behind me. Nobody new has entered the bar. "I don't think these are for me."

"Sure they are," she says, already looking at her phone again. "That's what you ordered."

Apparently I suck at recon *and* getting beers.

When I slide into the booth a second later, Tasha's smothering a laugh so hard she's tearing up. "I heard the whole thing," she manages to say. "Your small talk could use some work, but you definitely did not order those drinks."

"Should I—"

"No!" she says, still laughing. "This is perfect." She takes a big swig from her pint and sets it down with a smile and a thick foam mustache. I can see every freckle sprinkled across her face. She grins at me, and my stomach flips over, so actually . . . ? I'll come back and do recon another night, because this is way better. I just hope I don't fuck this up.

As soon as the thought crosses my mind, I realize I'm *definitely* going to fuck it up. Then I can't stop thinking about all the ways I'm going to fuck it up. There are, literally, an endless number of things I could do wrong.

I take a very long pull on my beer, which helps, but only a little.

"Are you *allowed* to have a beer right after a heart attack?" Tasha asks as one side of her mouth quirks up.

"It's part of my treatment plan," I say. "The doctor said I actually had a beer deficiency."

"Well, we can fix that here."

"I'm looking forward to it," I say, and we clink our pint glasses together. This beer is going down faster than usual because I'm so nervous. After another long drink and a moment of terrifying silence, I add, "You were right, by the way. It was just a pulled muscle."

"I'm so glad," she says. "*Much* better than a heart attack."

I lean in to her. "So, government hotshot, what's it like knowing things?"

She waves a hand dismissively. "You know things."

"You get what I mean," I say. "Secret nerdy government things. The seedy underbelly of Chicago."

"Are you talking about Manhole Mondays again?" Tasha asks with a wicked smile. "Because I've noticed you have a real thing for manholes. I saw you checking out those three." She waves toward the sports guys.

"Not really my type," I start, but I'm suddenly unsure about the subtext of this conversation. "I mean, I have in the past. But I also have an appreciation for . . ."

Don't say it. Don't say it.

But the beer's got me now.

". . . ladyholes."

We blink at each other for a second and I turn a Crayola shade of red as she bursts out laughing.

I have no idea which way this is going until she finally catches her breath, and in between gasps for air, she says, "Well, thank goodness, that answers *that* question."

CHAPTER 17

Several beers later, the baseball game is over and the old guys have left. The other couple is long gone. A few new people have arrived, and they drink in small clusters at scattered tables, but it's still pretty quiet.

Approximately half the drinks we've gotten have not been what we ordered—it's like we stumbled into a game of Bartender Russian Roulette.

But, most importantly, I have not fucked it up.

It's Tasha's turn to grab drinks, and she comes back with a couple of shots. This time she slides in next to me and places a shot glass in front of each of us. Her leg is against my leg and I think I really like it there.

"Okay, this time, I made sure we got what we ordered," she says.

"No way," I say to the shot. "This is such a bad idea." The floor is tilting, and I don't actually remember how many beers we've had.

"Yes way," Tasha says. "Because this little baby is called, wait for it . . . a sinkhole!"

We both double over laughing.

"Okay, okay," I say. "You're right. We have to."

We hold up the shots to toast. The liquid looks gold and a little sparkly. We're both mesmerized . . . or maybe that's just me.

I stare into the depths of the shot glass.

"What do you *want*?" Tasha asks suddenly, her eyes soft, her words slurring just the slightest, cutest bit.

Wow.

First date, huh? My lips are tingling and my good sense has evaporated, so here goes.

"I want to not feel sad and heartbroken anymore," I say, and boy, just saying it sort of helps? I keep going. "I want to have more than like five bucks in my bank account. And this next one isn't a *want*, per se, but I probably *need* to learn how to cook something other than hot dogs and cereal? And I want my parents to stop worrying about me and also to know that I'm just different from them, and yeah . . . I guess I want to know who I want to be in the first place. And I want to stay alive and unmurdered and I want to kiss you."

"Thank you for that long and very complicated answer," Tasha says sincerely. "I appreciate you telling me all that. But actually, I wasn't asking you. I was asking *the shot*."

"OH MY GOD," I say, promptly dying of drunk humiliation.

She smiles, gently swirling her shot glass as she holds it up to one eye and closes the other. "I don't know, doesn't it look like a portal to another dimension or something? Like it would speak if you asked it the right question?"

"I think it wants to swallow us whole," I say, dropping my head on the table. "Which right now, I'd be okay with."

Tasha finds my hand and puts it on my shot glass. "Here's to the sinkhole that brought us together," she says.

I pull my head up off the table, we clink glasses, and then shoot it, and it is *revolting.* We're both instantly gagging and making weird faces. "What was that?" I ask, trying to scrape the lingering taste off my tongue with my teeth.

"Malört and tequila!" she says with a giggle.

"You are a menace," I say.

"I'd like to kiss you too," she says, and time stops.

"So gimme a kiss, you menace," I say, grabbing the ends of her bow tie and pulling her toward me.

And suddenly *we* are the couple making out in the booth. She tastes like beer and Malört and tequila and she is a very, *very* good kisser.

When we come up for air, it's clear that neither of us wants to be done, but there's not much more we can legally do in this booth.

"What do you think about maybe getting out of here?" she asks, our foreheads still touching.

Chris flits through my mind, and I tell him to get lost.

"I like that idea," I say. "But not my place. There's an infestation. Poodles."

She nods sagely.

"I have to close my tab," I say and stumble up to the bar. The bartender turns around to close me out and I wait for my card, my eyes drifting over the pictures again.

And that's when I see somebody I do recognize after all.

Who is *that?*

My drunk brain tilts, trying to match the face to a name.

I've almost got it when Tasha comes up behind me and buries her nose in my hair. Her lips find my neck and her hand grazes my wrist and I am going to need an underwear quick-change, or an industrial-strength hair dryer, if we don't get them off me soon.

I sign my name, and I've already forgotten the photo as she takes me by the hand and we get out of there.

If this is a mistake, I can't wait to make it.

It turns out Tasha lives a short walk in the opposite direction from my apartment, so we get back to her place pretty easily, if inefficiently. We have to stop every few steps while she drunkenly—but adorably—tells me something about zoning or tree-trimming or license plate stickers.

She lives in a one-bedroom, and her building is classy-old, as opposed to should-be-marked-for-demolition-old, like mine. Her place is on the first floor, and as she lets us in, I'm extra glad we didn't go to my place, because this apartment is cool and fashionable, like her, and everything actually goes together in a quirky, accidentally-on-purpose perfect kind of way.

As soon as she's turned the lock behind us, I spin her around and push her up against the door, our hands all over each other. I kiss her again and then tug her hair so I can get at her neck. My lips are numb from kissing and from that bad-idea shot, and I start to worry that maybe my sex personality is "big slobbery dog," and then I wonder if Chris thought that, and *what the hell*, get out of my head, CHRIS.

Then Tasha slips past me, glancing over her shoulder and reeling me in. I pretend I'm a fish she just caught, and I try for sexy fish as opposed to realistic fish, but to be honest, it's unclear exactly how successful I am.

In the bedroom, everything slows down. We're kneeling on the bed and she pulls off my tank top, throwing it on the floor somewhere, and I am instantly SO glad I showered that sticky stuff out of my hair and ALSO that I went with my one set of good underwear even though I had no idea if this was a date, because *IT WAS INDEED A DATE*, yells my brain, which seems to just want to speak in all caps right now.

LET'S DO THIS, yells my brain. *AND BY "THIS" I MEAN TASHA.*

I'm wearing a lacy black bra that she quickly gets rid of, and she holds me by my hips, running her tongue from my waist up and up and up, between my tits and then along my neck, then biting softly as she fiddles with one of my nipples, and never has *anyone* enjoyed doing their civic duty as much as I am right now.

She's still kissing my neck as I fumble to unbutton *her* shirt—her bra clasps in the front, and as I unhook it, it's like opening my favorite book.

Oh, hell yeah.

A book with boobs in it.

Then we topple over and we're on the bed, and our pants are coming off, and it's hot and dirty, and I'm kissing the tight muscles of her abdomen and along her side where her skin is so impossibly smooth, and she's making these fantastic noises, and I work my way down and down and down her body, and OH MY GOD I HAVEN'T HAD SEX WITH A WOMAN SINCE COLLEGE.

All at once, I am very sober.

I can't fuck this up.

But also, I've been cohabitating with a dick (yep, I mean that both ways) for the last ten years, what the hell do I think I'm doing here? Literally, WHAT AM I DOING HERE?

Okay, think, think, think. Maybe it's like riding a bike. Come on, muscle memory. Come on . . . any memory.

The alphabet.

Do the alphabet!

Sure it's Girl Sex 101, a total bush league trick, so to speak, but you gotta start somewhere. In this case, with "A."

And slowly, it all comes back to me.

And then, after a little trial and error, it comes to her.

If you know what I mean.

CHAPTER 18

Between us, we had approximately three and a half orgasms before we collapsed in a satisfied heap. I wasn't planning on staying over, but before I know it, Tasha's alarm is going off, and it's officially Monday morning.

Somehow, I feel totally not hungover. I'm not even cursing Malört, which is a first.

"It's the sex," she says, nibbling my thigh. "All those good chemicals compensate for the booze."

"Don't tell me you're a scientist too," I say. "Is there *nothing* you can't do?"

"I can't be late for work, unfortunately."

I roll over and boop her on the nose. "Then let's get decent. Or try to, anyway."

The downside of feeling fine is that I'm exactly clearheaded enough to remember all that really personal stuff I said last night when I thought we were having a heart-to-heart over Malört and tequila. Does Tasha remember? Is this like when I told Chris I loved him and he made us break up a second time? I feel the creeping dread of anxiety all over again. I don't want to ruin this.

But also, what is *this*? A one-night thing? Or a thing-thing? And what do I want it to be? Are we supposed to talk about it, or not talk about it? I'm spiraling, I can tell I'm spiraling, and all I want to do is hide under the cool paisley duvet and go back to sleep.

Get it together, Mo!

I manage to calm myself, and I even turn my head and smile at her to show off how calm and not anxious I am.

"Oh my god," she says, pointing at my face in alarm.

I shoot up, patting my face. "What is it? Zit? Spider bite? Necrotizing fasciitis?"

"I'm so sorry, did I . . . do that to you?" she asks hesitantly.

"You did a lot of really awesome things to me," I say, not sure where this is going.

"No, your eye," she says, frowning.

I check myself out in the classy art deco mirror on the wall and discover I'm sporting a shiner on my right eye, not huge, but noticeable enough.

"Nope," I say. "Not you. It was Jacques Cousteau."

She blinks in confusion. "The French oceanographer?"

"Ah, right. No, a *poodle.* Named Jacques Cousteau. He jumped into my shower, uninvited, and perpetrated a catastrophic incident."

"Oh. Of course. That makes much more sense," she says, snorting. She kisses the bruise gently and grabs my ass. I squeal. "Showers are dangerous. Probably shouldn't do it without backup."

"You're probably right," I agree, and she leads me toward the shower.

Two more extremely efficient mind-blowing orgasms later, we are freshly showered but still on time. This woman is a marvel.

We share a quick kiss on her stoop, and then an awkward moment where I wonder if I should say something to sum up the last twelve hours.

"Well," I say. "It's been a hoot."

Oh good.

She laughs; I blush.

"I'll text you later, k?" she says.

"Yes!" I say. "Do that."

And with that, I head home to walk the dogs and grab my stop sign and try not to overthink this whole thing.

THANKS TO TASHA's alarm, I report to my corner in plenty of time, even after a leisurely morning stroll with the poodles. At some point over the weekend, the sinkhole got even bigger, and the metal plate the city dropped on top like a haphazardly applied Band-Aid is really just doing lip service. I should probably call someone about that.

Just not right *now*, because I'm very busy playing back last night, moment by sexy moment.

Sure, some of it's a little foggy on account of the number of beers involved. But I still remember *plenty*.

Including the embarrassing confessional moment.

Don't think about the embarrassing moment, Mo.

Think about the *sexy* ones.

Right.

Back on track.

And then a pink-haired tween rudely appears out of nowhere. "Whoa, what happened to you?"

"Marlowe!" I shout. "You can't sneak up on people like that."

"I'm standing directly in front of you," she says. "This is not me sneaking. You'll know when I'm sneaking up on you. Or you won't, is the point. So, anyway. What'd you do this weekend? Join Roller Derby?"

"I . . . I am not telling you that," I stammer, because right when Marlowe interrupted me, I'd been imagining Tasha doing something extremely excellent and X-rated to me, and wait—is *Roller Derby* a euphemism that the kids use these days? Suddenly I'm breaking out in a nervous sweat that this literal child can read my mind.

"Looks like somebody punched you with a tiny fist," she says.

"OH. *The black eye.* Right." I try to wipe the guilty look off my face. "No. Yeah. That was a dog thing." I remember Sheila and my rapidly vanishing bank account, and it's really taking the fun out of thinking. "I have to get rid of those dogs."

"You should make an adoption video," Marlowe says.

"A what?"

"You know. A cool video you can post that shows off how awesome and adoptable they are. Adoption agencies love when you do that. Animals with great reels always get adopted faster."

I hold her back from crossing as a fire truck whizzes up the street and parks in front of the construction site, followed by some kind of utility vehicle. Gas company, looks like.

Marlowe jogs into the street without waiting for me.

"Hey, hello, remember me? Crossing guard?" I run into the street, stop sign first, even though no one's coming.

"I'm trying to see what's going on over there." She cranes her neck, but the fire truck is blocking everything.

"Probably some routine construction-related thing," I say. "If there was a fire, I'm sure it would have its lights on or something."

"But they stopped construction there a month ago. For safety stuff."

"Oh, right," I say.

"You really should pay attention to your surroundings," she says. "As a crossing guard."

"I am paying attention, and I'm telling you there's no fire."

Just then we hear some sirens, and an ambulance wedges itself next to the curb in front of the fire truck.

Marlowe gives me a look. "I'm going to go check it out," she says.

"Marlowe, it's just normal stuff. They probably always send an ambulance, just in case." I put on my best grown-up voice. "And don't you have to go to school?"

"I've got ages before the first bell," she says dismissively, jogging diagonally across the street before I can stop her.

Get your head in the game, Mo. Guard this crossing. Save those kids.

Still, that was a really good idea about making a video. And I know just who can help me. I take a quick glance around, and it's still pretty quiet, so I hop on my phone, just for a sec.

Me: Hey hey!

Hannah: Heeeey

Me: What's up

Hannah: Woof they are handing out stalkers like candy these days

Me: Ha ha what tho

Hannah: You know

Hannah: You had that stalker

Me: ?

Hannah: Government guy? Who was creeping on your apartment?

Me: Him! Right! Wow that was so 3 days ago

Me: Anyway that turned out to be Chris

Me: Speaking of Chris- I HAD SEX WITH SOMEBODY NOT CHRIS

Hannah: Oh wow

Me: Also, can I borrow Eva's green screen and some other equipment? I'll be fast, she won't even notice

Hannah: I guess so

Hannah: Also, can we talk soon

Me: How about I call you after my shift? I'm not supposed to be on the phone right now

Hannah: K

I slide my phone back into my pocket and walk a few kids across the street, my mind bouncing back and forth. I'm thinking about good things for once—replaying sexy times with Tasha, imagining doing it again, and fantasizing about how I'm going to make a totally fantastic adoption video that will solve my poodle problem for good—when I notice Marlowe walking back toward me, slowly this time.

I step into the crosswalk to escort her when I see the look on her face. She's pale, her eyes wide and watery. I stop, right in the middle of the street, suddenly terrified of what she's going to tell me.

"It's not the construction site," Marlowe says, her voice so quiet I can barely hear her. "It's Claudia. Claudia's dead."

CHAPTER 19

Well, she got what she said she wanted.

She didn't have to downsize and give up her perfect little bungalow.

Claudia died in her house.

I want to throw up. I can't believe I've been so self-involved, so worried about my own ass that I didn't see the truth right in front of my face.

When the unknown mastermind/Funeral Deep Throat said "take care of her," HER didn't mean ME.

"HER" meant CLAUDIA.

Oh god.

And Claudia's text: It's murder

That wasn't a passive-aggressive snark attack at me for taking so long to figure it out. She was telling me that *she* was going to be murdered.

Hot tears spring to my eyes. None of this makes sense. Why wasn't she more *specific* with her cry for help? If only she'd texted "it's murder NOW, for ME" I would have run straight to her house. Maybe I could have saved her.

Holy shit. I could have saved her.

I've gone from a zero-murder life to having two back-to-back murders weighing on my conscience. First Cran, and now—

"Claudia? When? How?" I can barely get the words out.

"There was a gas leak sometime this weekend," Marlowe says, wiping her nose with her whole arm. "That's what the firefighters said."

A gas leak. If Claudia was suffocating on gas, she probably *couldn't* have been more specific in her text. It probably took all her energy just to get those two words out.

Impossibly, I feel even worse knowing that.

"They said the whole house could've blown up if she'd even switched a *light* on, but she must've been asleep, so she asphyxiated instead," Marlowe says.

"The firefighters *said* this to you?" I say, horrified.

She shakes her head angrily. "I'm really good at lipreading."

Suddenly she tackles me with a hug and starts sobbing.

Sometimes I forget, but Marlowe's just a *kid*. And this kid deserved to have her Claudia around for a lot longer. I pet her streaky pink hair. This is bigger than me and my guilt. There are consequences to murder. You can't kill a niceish old lady, make a scary tween cry, and get away with it. Not on my watch.

"Do you want me to walk you to class?" I say. "I'm going to call out for the rest of the day anyway."

"Why?"

"I, uh, have some errands to run," I say, looking very innocent.

She lasers in on me. "I'm coming with you."

Shit.

"What? No. I'm going to, uh, make those dog videos we talked about."

"No you aren't. You think this was murder. You're going to investigate."

Okay, *can* she read my mind? How does she know that?

Marlowe fiddles with her phone for a second. "Claudia wants me to help you solve the case," Marlowe says. "Avenge her death, et cetera."

Okay I'm sorry, *what?*

"See?" Marlowe thrusts the phone in my face. Sure enough, it's a text from Claudia, from Sunday night. Marlowe frowns. "I'm just not totally sure what the second half means yet."

Claudia: Hells no apple the cat invite affluent odor

Oh good lord.

"Okay, so this is all incredibly awful and traumatic, but Marlowe . . ." I put a hand on her shoulder, "that is definitely the gas leak speaking."

She narrows her eyes at me, no doubt coming up with some devastating insult. "And," I continue quickly, "even if it *wasn't*, you can't investigate with me. I draw the line at a kid sidekick. School. Now."

The first bell rings, right on cue.

She folds her arms over her chest and juts her chin out. "You need me."

"I do not."

Actually, I definitely do.

She holds her phone out again. "Too late, things are already in motion."

There's a sound file on-screen. Marlowe presses play. A woman's voice says: "Hey, Sue, it's Shoshanna Golden. Marlowe woke up with a fever today, so we're keeping her home—"

Marlowe presses stop. "Gonna deploy one of my deepfakes," she says.

"One of—? How do you—?"

"—send it while making it look like it's coming from *her* phone?"

Oh for sure, that was *exactly* what I was going to ask.

"Easy. I set up a partition." She boop-boops on the phone then holds it back up to me. Now there's a profile photo of a middle-aged woman with short gray hair and blue eyes behind funky thick-rimmed glasses. Under the photo it says "Shoshanna's phone." She dials a number, waits for the voicemail line, taps the screen, and lets the recording play out.

Okay, color me impressed.

I sigh and silently apologize to Claudia, the universe, and Marlowe's hopefully not litigious lawyer mom.

"Fine. And only because I do, actually, need your help," I admit.

I'm acting on pure feral instinct here, but if Claudia was butt-texting Marlowe and murder-texting me, she clearly had access to her phone. Maybe ours weren't the only messages she sent. And maybe we can figure out who else she was in contact with.

And then there's the doorbell camera. That's probably on her phone, too, right? Claudia must've had an app or something that showed her the footage. So if someone came to the door, or near the door, or pulled up in a car around the time she was killed, well, that's a clue, isn't it?

"Her phone," I say. "We need to figure out how to get into Claudia's house and find her phone."

"Way ahead of you," Marlowe says, typing away at her *own* phone. "And I know just who can help us."

At this point, I'm fully expecting this kid to be best buds with a cat burglar, or maybe a mob boss, but instead she shows me a YouTube video. It's titled IMPERSONATE TO INFILTRATE and it features an old guy with a little mustache and a big bulbous nose trying on different hats and saying: "Nobody pays attention to your face, all they see is *hat*. Trust me, it works," in a Chicago accent that gives Claudia's a run for its money.

"Rodney O'Malley, PI. Best in the biz," Marlowe says.

"What biz is that, exactly?" I ask.

She rolls her eyes so hard I'm worried they're going to pop. "Um, private investigator?"

PI, right.

I scroll his account, and there are like a thousand videos with titles like TAILING SUSPECTS 101, WHOSE CLUES?, RED HERRINGS = INDIGESTION, and YOU CAN PICK YOUR FRIENDS, YOU CAN PICK YOUR NOSE, YOU CAN PICK THAT LOCK: A SIX-WEEK COURSE. Each one has over a million views.

"I did his lockpicking course. You got a door? I can get in it." She tries on this guy's Chicago accent, and I snort.

"That's great that you're becoming a tween criminal," I say, handing the phone back. "But I'm not letting you pick Claudia's locks."

"We don't have to," she says. "See? The door's wide open."

Sure enough, they must be airing out Claudia's house because the doors and windows are flung wide.

There are also several firefighters, a couple cops and EMTs, and a whole passel of gas company workers milling around outside and chatting like it's an emergency barbecue.

Marlowe sees my concern and pats my arm. "We just have to get you the right hat."

CHAPTER 20

As I crouch by the corner of the construction fence, trying to avoid the rampant dog pee, I wonder what Hannah would think of Rodney O'Malley. After all, isn't "wear a hat" just a version of "act confident"? I'll run it by her later, if this works out and it's not a massively embarrassing failure. Which it could—

"NOW!" Marlowe whispers in my ear as she shoves me through the hole and onto the construction site.

She gives me so much momentum, it's a miracle that I manage to stay on my feet, especially when I hit the patch of gravel and have to wave my arms around to keep my balance. Thank goodness the mesh on the chain link keeps me hidden in here—that graceful move would have blown my cover immediately.

Like most of the kids, Marlowe is well-acquainted with the empty lot, and she told me what to expect. At first glance, there's not much except dirt and gravel, some concrete chunks, a few stray metal rods, and a giant ladder hooked over the edge of what looks to be a bottomless pit. No thank you, bottomless pit.

And then, across the lot, I see what she sent me in here for.

A lone hard hat, abandoned over by a mound of dirt.

I grab it, and with the hard hat plus my crossing guard vest, I do actually get a burst of confidence. I slip back through the fence onto the sidewalk, where I stand up casually, like I was always there, just doing some kind of typical . . . gas business. Marlowe's across the street now—having made sure the coast was clear for me to go in and get the hat, she's now keeping an eye on the outside of the house, so she can alert me if there are any developments while I am—fingers crossed—inside.

We nod at each other.

Then I take a deep breath and try to manifest Big Gas Company Energy.

I adjust the hard hat with a jaunty tap, fix my eyes on the house, and business-walk my way toward the front door.

And holy hell, it works—I breeze right past the literal gas company truck, the fire truck, and the police car, and no one even looks at me.

This Rodney guy knows what he's talking about—I should probably check out the rest of his videos, or at least scrub through a couple of them.

I give Marlowe our agreed-upon sign—a knock on the hard hat—as I slip inside the house.

Apparently, what I'm looking for is an elaborate charging station—a sculpture? a statue?—in Claudia's bedroom upstairs. Marlowe says I can't miss it. Turns out Claudia was some kind of artist? I feel a pit in my stomach at the fact that I didn't know this, and now I'll never get to ask her about it.

I slip through the front room of the bungalow, and yeah, wow, the gas smell is *strong*. Better make this quick.

No one seems to be around, so I take the creaky stairs two at a time, down the burnt umber carpeted hallway with its wood paneling and into the bedroom with the rose comforter. Okay. There's a bedside table with a lamp and a digital clock. A long low dresser with a mirror. A closet, a floor lamp, and a human-size sculpture of . . .

Is that Link from *The Legend of Zelda*?

All grown up and ready to party?

Shirtless with rippling abs?

This is Claudia's sculpture?

Wow. Way to go, Claud.

I lift the bottom of my shirt to cover my nose and mouth. I must already be feeling a bit dizzy and out of it because I swear this Link looks very familiar. I can't place it, but I know that face and bod, and not from my days of playing the game, because canon Link is a scrawny kid.

So where's the phone?

I check Link's hands; one is resting on his hip and the other looks like it's blowing a kiss. No phone. It's not on his trademark hat or his beefy shoulders, so I walk all the way around and—wow—she's *really* lovingly crafted his ass, but there's no phone in there either. I'm starting to doubt myself, when I suddenly see it: a seam running along the edge of his abs. I press on his six-pack and the abs pop open and BOOM.

Claudia's phone.

Fully charged, baby.

I grab it, tuck it in my pocket, and run down the stairs.

Where I slam right into a giant fireman cosplaying as a friggin' mountain.

He frowns. "What the hell are you doing?"

Uh-oh.

"I—"

"How many times do we have to tell you guys it's not safe until we find the source of the leak? You'd really think the *gas* company would know that."

Right. Gas company. That's me!

"Sorry, sorry, I—got here late, didn't get the memo. Leaving now!"

I try to skirt around him but he steps in front of me again. My heart is pounding so hard it has got to be visible through my shirt.

"Hey, tell your guys it's not the oven or the furnace or the meter connections. Gotta be the line under the house." He shakes his head. "Good thing you turned the gas off for the street. Could've been way, way worse."

"Right," I say. "Roger that."

He looks at me weird but steps aside so I can leave.

The line under the house? What does that mean? It's not something I've ever thought before—but *man* I wish I understood utilities better.

I get outside and glance next door at the construction site. Marlowe mentioned safety issues there. Was it *gas*-related safety issues? It really seems like there's some connection here—the construction site, Claudia not selling her house, her death by gas, Cran's death and evil Tond and the Funeral Deep Throat.

My head is spinning, and not just from sucking in gas.

As I dizzily make my way back to the street, I spot a few gas company guys leaning on the truck. One of them is smoking a cigarette, which seems ill-advised under the circumstances.

Ugh, I suck at recon. But what else can I do? *Confidence, Mo. Think of the hat. Do it for Claudia.*

"Hey!" I shout, sauntering over. Their vests are slightly different from mine, but they also look like they don't give a shit. I thrust a thumb back at the house. "Big fella in there told me the leak is coming from the line under the house."

One of them snorts. "Yeah, no shit."

I lift my hard hat and wipe the sweat from my brow dramatically. "Good thing no one was working on that parking garage when this happened, huh? Could've been way, way worse. Remind me why that is?"

The three of them look at me for the first time. There is an extremely awkward pause.

"What's up," I say.

"I'm new," I say.

"Welp," I say.

The smoker takes a long drag.

"They stopped construction because of the gas line." He shrugs. "But they didn't cover up the hole so maybe something fell in there, nicked the pipe. Or maybe a rat chewed on it. Bam. Lady died two, tree hours later."

"Right," the second guy snorts. "A rat fell into the hole, bounced all the way under the house, chewed a hole in the pipe, and then the wind blew the gas right into the old lady's window. This jagoff's a friggin' Einstein."

"Yeah or it was your wife, cuz she's tired of chewing on *your* pipe, heyo!" the third guy says, high-fiving the second.

"What did I tell you?" the smoker shouts, flicking his cigarette. "What did I fuggin' say?"

"Great, yep, awesome, thanks, guys," I say and slip away while they yell and poke index fingers into each other's chests.

It wasn't a rat. Or a rock. Or, uh, that guy's wife. Somehow, *someone* messed with Claudia's gas pipes and killed her on purpose.

No, not someone.

Tond.

And whoever his funeral buddy was.

Which I'm about to find out.

I subtly hold the phone up, and from down the block, Marlowe gives me an approving nod.

In short order, Marlowe convinces me we need to look at the doorbell footage on a big screen at her school's media center.

"We need to see all the details," she calls, already halfway to the school. "High-def!" I toss the hard hat over the fence where it belongs and stuff my vest in my back pocket, jogging to catch up, already deeply regretting every decision that has led me to this moment.

The front desk receptionist clearly adores Marlowe and checks us in with alarmingly few questions. A few minutes later, we're in the media center.

"Mrs. Warren." Marlowe breaks into a huge grin and waves the phone at the media specialist behind the counter. "How's big Tony?"

"Oh, he's doing much better, kiddo, aren't you sweet for asking."

Marlowe leans on the counter, lets Mrs. Warren ruffle her pink hair. "Mrs. W, would you be able to patch this phone into the big screen? I'm testing out some new AI enhancement software on door cams for the 'ship."

"Of course," Mrs. Warren says, beaming. She turns to me. "Marlowe is such a smart cookie. This whole independent study tech internship you gave her is exactly the challenge she needs."

It would have been *really* super if Marlowe had given me a tiny heads-up. "Yes," I say. "The internship . . ."

Marlowe jumps in and saves me. "This is Mo. She's new at eWolram."

"Haven't I seen you before?" The librarian studies me.

"Doubt it," I say quickly. "I'm usually at . . . corporate headquarters."

"Just showing her my latest project," Marlowe explains.

"Wonderful!" Mrs. Warren says, beaming. "I'll grab the cables!"

As she ducks into an office I turn to Marlowe, who shrugs. "Yeah,

yeah, I made up a fake company and gave myself an internship so I could have a little wiggle room during the day."

"It's your own name backward."

"Nobody's noticed yet."

I have no idea how Marlowe has convinced this whole school that she's nothing but a cute and harmless genius, but in this moment, I'm just grateful.

Returning with the cables, Mrs. Warren patches Claudia's phone into the big screen at the front of the room and leaves us to it while she reshelves books. I squat in one of the tiny grade school chairs, preparing myself to watch a snuff video prologue.

Marlowe punches in Claudia's password—it's 5465 (L-I-N-K, obviously)—and we start scrolling through approximately a million doorbell videos with unhelpful file names that don't resemble dates or times.

It's mostly just being triggered by birds, squirrels, and the mailman, wearing a pair of short shorts.

"Helloooo, is that package for me," mutters Mrs. Warren from over in nonfiction. She's not wrong, and any other time, I'd be all in, but right now all I feel is a terrible sense of anticipation.

"Hold on," I say, as another video starts. "Stop here. That's me."

"*Claudia*," the demented ultra-close-up of me hisses. "*It's me, Mo. I'm sorry, okay? Please—*"

Suddenly I have this vague recollection that video-me is about to go into NSFW territory talking about Chris, and I leap up so fast, I knock the tiny chair backward and grab the phone from Marlowe, who protests.

"We can just fast-forward, nothing to see here . . ." I mute the video to be extra safe, and then speed through my message. The video shuts off as I walk away.

I hit the next video. It's still night as the vague outline of a—cat, maybe?—casually strolls across Claudia's front steps. The camera doesn't have *great* night vision.

In the video after that, it's daytime again. Squirrels chase each other.

More squirrels.

More.

"Hang on," Marlowe says. "What's this?"

The time stamp for the next video says 4:46 this morning. The two of us watch the enormous screen as a guy walking a bunch of big shapes—dogs!—comes up to the front door. It's super dark, but the closer he gets, the more I can make out his features.

"Who is that?" I say, squinting. "I think I know him."

"It's Benny," Marlowe whispers. "He walks dogs in the neighborhood."

There's something in his hand. He ducks down out of frame, and there's a little creak which I use my powers of deduction to, uh, deduce is him opening the mail slot in the door. He's down there for a little while, and then he pops up, looks left, looks right, rattles the doorknob, and then shoves his shoulder against the door, hard.

End of video.

"Wait," I say. "I want to see that again."

Marlowe hits play.

Well, I'll be damned. *Benny* was the model for the sexy Link sculpture in Claudia's bedroom.

And that's not all.

He was the person I drunkenly recognized in the photo at Dickie's and then promptly forgot about. My stomach turns.

This makes him the one, oh, let's call it a LINK, to Claudia *and* Cran, and thus to Tond.

And to a possible break-in to Claudia's house around the time of the gas leak.

I feel sick.

CHAPTER 21

We shakily thank Mrs. Warren for her help and then leave through the playground exit, somehow keeping our shit together until we reach the jungle gym, where I have to grab a monkey bar to steady myself.

"Benny killed Claudia," I say out loud to see how it sounds.

"But *why*?" an anguished Marlowe demands, kicking a stray dodgeball hard. It bounces off the gate and then rolls to a stop.

She's right. We need a motive. What do we *really* know about Benny?

"Benny's a dog walker," I say slowly. "He was recently fired—*by dead Cran*—as the poodles' handler. So I bet he needs money."

I just so happen to know that motive *very* well.

Marlowe begins kicking other assorted playground equipment as she mumbles bitterly, "But Claudia trusted him."

"Yeah, exactly. She *trusted* him. So he was the best person to convince her to sell her house," I say, warming up to this idea. "And maybe if he succeeded, Tond would pay him big bucks. But Claudia was stubborn, and when Benny lost his job, he was desperate, so he had to use more drastic measures."

I replay the conversation in my head when Claudia made us walk around in a circle. Benny had definitely muttered something about how it wouldn't be so terrible for Claudia to downsize. And it was clear this wasn't their first argument about it.

And wait.

Oh my god. I can't believe I didn't think of this.

Benny made a case against me going to the funeral.

Why? Not because it would be bad for the *poodles*. Not even because I'd quote-unquote *make everything worse.*

Because it would be bad for *Benny*. He wanted me to stay out of his business.

Cran fired Benny.

And then *at* the funeral, Leslie wrinkled her nose when I mentioned him. Not because she knew him biblically. She knew he was bad news.

Because Benny is Funeral Deep Throat.

Except—wouldn't I have recognized him in the crowd?

Well, hang on. I didn't recognize his photo at Dickie's, or his cheekbones (and ass) on the statue. He's got one of those faces, handsome but forgettable.

Holy cow—did I just crack this case??

I'm about to hyperventilate, but in a good way. We have the perp, we have the motive, *and* we have actual proof.

"We need to send that doorbell video . . ." I force myself to say the words casually. ". . . to the cops. Can you do that?"

Marlowe nods and then kicks a plastic dinosaur—but not as hard as she could've. I figure giving her something to do will help.

I have a brief spasm of guilt at making a tween protect me from the cops.

But if the rest of the cops are anything like Mierzwiak, they're going to need some convincing to take this seriously. Ideally by someone who's not me.

And Marlowe's not the only one who feels helpless right now. *I* need something to do too. I take a deep breath to clear my head.

"Okay," I say. "The video puts Benny at the scene of the crime, so next step, maybe the cops'll bring him in for questioning. And I've got, not to brag, a pretty airtight theory here, but we still need proof. Something concrete. Otherwise the video is just, what's it called—"

"Circumstantial evidence," says Marlowe.

Something's been nagging at me about the video. I feel like I'm missing something. Something important. I run through the video in my head. Benny comes to the door. Ducks down. Opens the mail slot. Pops back up—

Bingo. I snap my fingers. This is a toothbrush situation.

"What?" Marlowe says.

"Benny put something in the mail slot. Maybe it's still there."

"Still? No way." Marlowe frowns. "That place was crawling with cops and firefighters and gas company people. They would've found it."

"I don't think so." I start running, Marlowe close at my heels. We jog through the playground gate and around the side of the school, back toward Claudia's house across the street. The gas van and cop car are gone, and only the fire truck is there. The front door is still wide open, confirming my suspicion. "They've had the door open this whole time. They weren't *searching* the house, they were *airing it out*—they probably just threw the door open and left it that way. Whatever the thing is could still be wedged *behind* the door."

Marlowe jumps from foot to foot excitedly. "They're gonna seal up the house," she says. "We don't have much time."

My phone buzzes in my pants pocket, and it's a number I don't recognize. I'm thinking (hoping?) it's Tasha, so I answer it, still peering around the corner.

"Hello there," I say, in a smoldery but quiet voice.

"Hi, is this . . . Mo Ellery?" Ah crap, it's a dude. At least it isn't Mierzwiak.

Marlowe makes a hand gesture like she's going to run across the street and distract the firefighters. I try to stop her but she's too quick.

Shitballs.

I realize I've said this out loud into the phone, when the voice clears his throat awkwardly.

"Anyway," he says, "this is Eddie from LookShopNow—"

"Oh, no thanks, I've already got one," I say.

"Wait!" he says as I'm about to hang up. He chuckles nervously. "No, you don't understand. You applied for our marketing writer position? We'd love to schedule an interview."

Oh . . .

Right. I sent out tons of applications weeks ago, right after Kendra canned me. Most places didn't even respond. I should jump on this. Like Benny, I need money. I don't want to end up vulnerable to bribery, especially with how rampant bribery seems to be in this neighborhood.

I can do this. I'll schedule an interview real quick. Just put on my corporate-whisperer voice and pull out my calendar, and—

Across the street at the front of the fire truck, Marlowe gives me the all-clear signal.

"You still there?" Eddie says.

"Um . . ."

Marlowe takes a few steps in front of the firefighters—the mountainous man and a small but clearly very strong woman—so they're facing away from Claudia's house, and starts crying convincingly.

The woman crouches in front of her, and the man is rubbing the back of his neck and looking very uncomfortable.

Marlowe has put her trust in me. She expects me not to leave her hanging. She needs me. And so does the ghost of Claudia.

Nuts.

"Can I call you back?" I say. "I'm kind of in the middle of something."

"Oh," Eddie says. "Sure, I'll be around from—"

Three-weeks-ago me wouldn't believe it, but I *hang up on him.* Something small and feeble inside me, oh let's call it my grown-up brain, squeaks *nooooooo* but I quickly squash it and make an appointment to regret this decision later.

Instead, I run across the street and slip behind the truck. My heart is pounding as I count down from three for courage and then run into Claudia's house, no hard hat needed. I close the door slightly and look behind it.

Yes.

There's a thick brown envelope, with a solid layer of packing tape keeping it closed. Centered on the envelope is a label with Claudia's name. And under her name are scrawled the words: *This is just for starters—T.J.*

HOLY CRAP.

THIS IS DEFINITELY A CLUE.

And I know who *T.J.* is because Mo Ellery wasn't born yesterday.

It's Tond Johnston.

God, isn't it nice when the pieces of the puzzle just snap cleanly into place?

Benny and Tond. In cahoots. Tond ready to do whatever it takes to get his dirty real estate dealings done, Benny desperate for Tond's money, willing to deliver secret packages while pretending to be an innocent hot neighborhood dog walker. It practically writes itself.

Mystery solved, bitches.

I give myself a mental high five and glance around to see if there are any scissors I can use on this tape, when my phone buzzes again. *Oh my GOD, Eddie, give it up already*—but when I check the screen, it's Marlowe.

"Marlowe?" I ask.

"Code red!"

"What? I don't know what that means, Marlowe!"

"They're coming inside!"

I don't say anything else, just shove the phone in my pocket, grab the envelope, and do the only thing I can think of—I race through the kitchen, out the back door, into the yard, and past Claudia's back gate into the alley.

I hide behind a neighbor's garbage bin to catch my breath, and my phone buzzes again.

"*What now,*" I wheeze.

"Code, um—" she starts.

"Forget the code, dude, just tell me what's happening!"

"Okay, Code I Might Be in Trouble."

"Yeah, that's good," I say. "See? Now I understand what you're trying to tell me. It's a little long, but it's very clear."

"*Mo,*" she whispers. "For real, I might be in trouble—"

"What do you mean?"

"Hey—" She breaks off, and I hear the grunts of a struggle. Her voice gets distant. "*Let go of me!*"

"Marlowe?"

The phone goes silent.

CHAPTER 22

"*Marlowe?*" I yell into the phone and press it hard against my ear, straining to pick up anything.

"No," I hear her say. "You can't make me."

"Sure I can, kiddo," says a voice on the other side of the phone.

Shit.

She's actually in trouble. Who is it? Can't be Tond or Benny; it kinda sounded like a woman's voice. Please don't tell me there's another player in this that I haven't thought of yet! Figuring out this murder was exhausting enough!

I spin in place for a second, clocking my options. Back the way I came, the firefighter is pulling Claudia's back door shut, so I can't run through the house. The shortest way to the sidewalk where Marlowe's standing is down the alley for half a block, *around* the construction site, and then right onto Claudia's street. I sprint down the alley and all I can think is that I am not in good enough shape to save this poor child in time.

"Marlowe!" I yell into the phone. "Punch her in the tits!"

"Who's that?" says the voice.

"HEY!" Marlowe says. "You can't take my PHONE!"

I'm fully panicking now, imagining this mystery lady wrestling Marlowe into an unmarked van, and *this is exactly why you don't get a kid sidekick*!!

"Hello?" says a new voice.

"I KNOW MMR, YOU MONSTER!" I yell into the phone. Dammit—I'm almost past the construction site, but I know I'm too late. "I KNOW MMR!!!!!"

"You know . . . measles mumps rubella?" asks the voice.

"I am a martial artist!" I yell, clocking that I may have messed up the acronym.

"Um, hi, this is Shoshanna Golden? Marlowe's mom?" the woman says into the phone. I stop dead in my tracks. Crap, wasn't she a *lawyer*? "I don't know what you're talking about, but I was just alerted to the fact that my *child* deepfaked my voice for a school absence. If you've been aiding and abetting her truancy, you're in huge trouble."

Oh my god. I slow down and peer around the corner, my heart still pulling some kind of Blue Man Group shit in my chest. Sure enough, there's Marlowe sulking on the sidewalk, and the woman in the photo from her "partition"—the middle-aged woman with the hip glasses and short hair—is pacing back and forth, calmly eviscerating me over the phone.

Marlowe conveniently left out that detail.

I try to catch my breath.

"Certainly not," I say in my grown-up voice, while hiding out of sight. I pull out my vest—I'm supposed to be *protecting* kids. And yeah, Marlowe will hate me for throwing her under the bus like this, but believing that something bad was happening to her was the scariest thirty seconds of my entire life, and honestly she really should be in school. "I'm the Walters crossing guard, and I noticed she was playing hooky." None of this is *technically* untrue. "I'm so glad you are there to take her back to school, where she belongs."

Shoshanna Golden is silent for a moment, and I can hear her lawyerly brain trying to figure out if I'm telling the truth. "Why do you have her phone number?" she asks.

"I have all the kids' contact info," I say (ACT CONFIDENT). "Just in case of emergency."

"Marlowe," she says. "You are in big trouble. It's one thing to deepfake an absence, it's another to treat this crossing guard like your own personal truant officer."

We say an awkward goodbye, and I hang up to hear Marlowe's yell echo through the neighborhood. "MO!!!!!!!!!!"

Yeah, I know. But I'm an asshole because I care.

I am also a coward, because I hide around the corner, pressed up against the construction fence until I'm sure they're inside the school. From my spot, I can hear as the fire truck drives away, too, and the block is finally quiet.

"Oookay, that is just about enough sleuthing for today," I mutter, taking into account that I'm sticky with sweat and the mystery envelope is getting soggy under my armpit. I'm a little nervous to look inside; it's probably got naked blackmail photos of Claudia or something. I should definitely weed out the most embarrassing ones before I turn it over to the police, but I am not looking forward to it.

I push myself off the fence and am finally about to head back home, but stop before I get very far, because—what the HELL—now there's someone *else* in front of Claudia's house, pacing on the sidewalk, raking a hand through his floppy dark hair, and talking feverishly into his phone. He runs up to the door and rattles the locked doorknob, then tries to peek into the mail slot, then kicks the door, all with the casualness of someone who is currently being electrocuted.

Well well well, if it isn't the big fish himself: Tond.

Based on how freaked out he seems, he *knows* something went wrong.

And it's not hard to figure out what it was: If *I* had someone killed, I definitely wouldn't want a clue full of nudies sitting around with my name on it. This murder bro came back for the envelope I am currently clutching in my armpit.

Totally fine. Totally not scary at all.

He yells something into the phone, shoves it into his pocket, and starts taking huge strides in the opposite direction.

Okay, I know I just clocked out my imaginary detective time card for the day, but this is probably an opportunity, right? Tailing him is the obvious next step.

Didn't Rodney O'Malley have a tailing video?

I fumble with my phone and pull up his YouTube Channel, but Tond is already slipping away, so I hustle after him while also scrubbing through the video titled TAILING SUSPECTS 101: IS THAT YOUR TAIL OR ARE YOU JUST HAPPY TO SEE ME.

I catch a few useful things like "keep your distance" and "don't panic" and "pretend you're supposed to be there," along with a long rambling story about the time Rodney tailed a perp through the city sewers and ended up in the hospital with *E. coli*, which is personal nightmare material. The rest of it feels pretty generic, as far as advice goes, so I pocket my phone and a minute later, I'm tailing a murderer down the block while wearing a neon vest so bright it could be seen in the deep sea.

I keep my distance, partly because I can't walk as fast as Tond—this man is definitely stress-walking. He turns the corner at the end of the block and so do I, but then he whips around, and *oh shit he's looking at me.*

PRETEND YOU'RE SUPPOSED TO BE HERE flashes through my brain, so my lightning-fast reflexes hurl me onto my knees in a random lawn, where I suddenly become a crossing guard who also happens to be pulling up weeds. My hair hangs like a veil, shielding my face, and I *think* I've managed to shove the brown envelope under my vest in time. I silently pray to every known deity that no one is watching me from the front windows as I yank up a hunk of what is probably perfectly good grass.

Tond starts walking toward me, and I double down my lawn duties, holding up and studying what is very clearly just a leaf. "UNBELIEVABLE," I say loudly and pull out my phone to . . . what?

I decide on a fake phone call.

"Yeah, get me Smitty," I say. "Yep, it's exactly what we thought. No, of course they don't have a permit, what do you think?"

Tond stops dead (ha) in his tracks. He spins on his heels and hustles back down the street.

I'm going to pass out. That was TOO CLOSE. I'm just not built, constitutionally, for this kind of stress.

In my periphery, I see him go up a walkway and let himself into the one weird, modernist box-shaped house that sticks out like a sore thumb among the old brick bungalows lining this block.

Figures that this would be the Johnston Bros lair.

I need to get into that house.

I stand up, my whole body shaking, and promptly plop back down on the grass. I need to get into the house . . . but maybe not *right now*, when there's a murderer in there, and I've got his blackmail shoved in my bra.

I limp back home to safety, take the dogs out (through the *front* door this time, a luxury I might as well take advantage of while Sheila's here), and then dig around my kitchen for the scissors I "borrowed" from Chris.

It takes me a minute to find them, especially because Jean thinks I'm going to give him another treat (which of course I do, just to get him off my back). Then I finally get too impatient and grab a knife instead. I slice open the packing tape and pull the envelope open.

My guess was wrong. It's not geriatric nudie photos.

It's *money.*

The envelope is absolutely bursting with hundred-dollar bills.

I flip the envelope over again and reread the message scribbled on the paper.

This is just for starters . . .

CHAPTER 23

I'm not sure how long I've been sitting in my pink chair. I'm not sure how many times I've counted the money.

But I know that every time it comes out to $11,500. (Except for that one time I missed a bill and it was $11,400.)

And it is in stacks all over my floor.

No wonder Tond wanted it back. I, too, would want to recover $11.5K in cash stuffed into an envelope with my literal initials on it. Especially if it happened to be lying on the floor of a dead woman's house.

The dogs sniffed at the cash, and then daintily settled themselves down, and now I'm wondering if this sort of thing is normal for them. Because it is not normal for me. On the contrary, I am *freaking out.*

WHY does this neighborhood run on murder and bribery??

I'm just about to count it again when my buzzer goes off and I jump about a mile in the air. It's fine, I tell myself. Just a package delivery or something.

Not that I'm about to buzz anyone in while I have all this cash lying around like a friggin' drug kingpin.

I ignore the buzzer and sit still in my chair. They'll just go away. They'll leave the package outside the door and go away.

I believe this for about two minutes, until someone bangs *on my actual apartment door.* A thousand warnings flash through my head, the loudest of which is HIDE THE MONEY! So I rocket out of the chair, scoop an armful of hundred-dollar bills off the floor, and run to the bathroom, dumping it all in the tub. It takes me a few trips, and all the while someone is banging down my door. *Goddamnit, Sheila, if you let this person in and I get arrested or murdered here, I am going to haunt this place so bad you and Roy never rent it again.*

Once I've got all the money in the tub, I swing by the kitchen counter, grab the knife I'd used to open the envelope, and then head to the door. I look out of the peephole, clutching the knife in my sweaty fist. The person at my door is younger than I'm expecting.

Marlowe.

A very mad Marlowe. I put down the knife.

"Open up, Mo," her voice comes from the other side of the door. "I know you're in there. I've tracked your phone."

I open the door and try to position myself in the doorway to keep her from coming in, but she breezes past me. She takes a look around at the boxes and the piles of clothes and shoots me a look of disgust.

"I just moved in," I say meekly.

"Whatever." She shrugs and plops down in my pink chair. "I can't believe you lied to my mom."

"You lied to your mom first," I say, shutting the door and slumping back against it. "But for real, Marlowe. If I told your mom the truth, I guarantee we would not be working together anymore. And I can't afford to get sued, okay?" I take a deep breath. "Also, I thought something really scary was happening to you. Two people have been *murdered*. You can't blame me for being relieved it was just your mom."

Her expression softens. "I guess. Anyway, they couldn't hold me for long. Fake internship for the win."

"School isn't *jail*, you know," I say.

She ignores that and continues. "I'm here because I thought you might want to know: I sent the video to the cops during recess. And I got to thinking— If Benny really is getting a kickback, I figured I might find evidence in his apartment. So after math class, I staked the place out."

Is it possible that I am *her* sidekick? No, I refuse to accept that. I am the grown-up! I am the grown-up!

"*Marlowe.*" Also this kid is going to give me a stress migraine. "First of all, you should not have gone on a *stakeout* alone. You absolutely can't do that again."

She raises an eyebrow. "And second?"

I sigh. "Second, what did you find out?"

Marlowe grins and makes me wait for a moment—this kid is such a little dirtbag. Finally, after she's milked the moment as much as she can, she says, "Well, I didn't get a chance to pick the locks and look around because the cops beat me there. They took Benny in for questioning."

This is amazing. I can't believe it. We did it. The cops might just take this whole thing more seriously.

"Now he'll get all jammed up," Marlowe adds viciously. "Just like he deserves."

I pause. "I'm sorry? What now?"

"You get brought in for questioning in the city, you get jammed up. Rolled. *Burged.*"

"Still not sure what you mean."

The twelve-year-old sighs like an old film noir detective. "You know how it is. Just like Rodney O'Malley says." She makes ominous fist-in-palm motions.

"I'm not sure *every*thing Rodney O'Malley says is true."

"And you know so much about the Chicago penal system?" Marlowe says impatiently. "That's what I thought. So what'd you find in the house? I can tell you found something or you wouldn't be so weird and shifty."

I heave a defeated sigh and walk to the bathroom, where I wave Marlowe over and open the door. From the doorway, we take in the scene.

$11,500 in cash, *mostly* in the tub. Also in the tub are three dogs, piled on top of each other and contentedly wallowing in the money.

"Whoa," she says. "That's a lot of bribe."

"Yeah," I say.

She picks a bill up off the floor and studies it. "You think I could keep this hundo? Claudia would have wanted me to have it."

"No," I say firmly, plucking it out of her hand, spinning her around, and pushing her toward my front door. "Claudia would have wanted you to be *safe*, which is why we are not keeping *any* of this money."

"Not nearby, anyway. This is screaming for an offshore account."

"*Marlowe.* We're turning it in to the police."

"Kidding, obviously. About the offshore account, anyway—but you can't hand over the cash." She paces back and forth in front of the front door. "Bro. What we have here is *leverage*. Rodney O'Malley talks about this in his video USE WHAT YOU GOT."

"Please tell me this is PG."

Marlowe ignores me. "The money implicates Tond. Now we need to shake him down for the straight dope by dangling all this cabbage in front of his greedy little peepers."

I bite a hangnail nervously. "Do you think you're watching too many of those videos?"

"Tell me I'm wrong."

She's not wrong, of course. Marlowe is always right. The money clearly ties Benny to Tond, and if I'm going to go to the cops with this, I need evidence. But "we" are not doing anything. I can't forget how scared I was when I thought I'd put her in danger. I won't risk that again. So I play dumb and hope I look convincing.

"I don't know what to do, Marlowe. I've never seen this much money in one place in my life," I say. "But I do know that right now it's safe in the tub, and more importantly, I need to take these poodles for a walk before they leave me another aromatic present on my floor."

The dogs clearly know what I'm talking about—they're out of the tub and swarming us within seconds. I silently thank them for their unholy pooping habits and, apparently, telepathy. "See?" I say. "They've got needs."

She reluctantly concedes, shooting me a salty glance as she leaves and heads down the stairs.

"And stop tracking my phone!" I call down to her from my doorway.

"I can't hear you," her voice floats up the stairwell. "I'm already too far away."

This kid is either going to be president or a master criminal, and it's unclear which one at this point.

Though I suppose *both* isn't off the table, either.

I shut the door behind her as the excited dogs bring me their leashes and I reach down to peel a hundred-dollar bill off Jean's butt.

I need to hide the tub money where Tond will never find it. And then I need to go back to that house, threaten Tond with what I know, and get him to confess to the murders of Cran and Claudia. Oh, and I also need to record that confession. And then get out of his house alive.

Noooo problem.

"Come on, guys," I say. "Let's go shake down a murderer."

WHERE WOULD TOND not expect the missing money to be? The one place it *should have been*—Claudia's house! The four of us head over and try her front door, but of course it's locked now. All the windows are shut, and when we circle the block into the alley, and through the yard to try the back door, we find it locked too. I think about watching the lockpicking video, but I obviously don't have time for a six-week course, and there is no way I'm involving Marlowe.

I didn't really notice before, but Claudia's got a real mullet situation here with her yard—the front is perfectly manicured, but aside from a cleared path to the alley, the back is a dense tangle of brush that she's let go wild. The dogs, of course, are loving it.

I let them run around and dig while I investigate the garage. No luck—the whole thing is locked up tight, even the little window.

Damn. I'd counted on hiding the envelope *somewhere* at Claudia's, but this is sort of a bust.

I decide to take one more pass of the house and yard when Lou suddenly does a dive roll in the tall grass, releasing a huge puff of pollen and sneezing accordingly. As I try to pull him out of the yellow cloud that he is clearly allergic to, I spot a cellar bulkhead door butting up against the house.

Very *Wizard of Oz*, Claud.

It looks like it's rusted shut, but I give it a hopeful yank, and it opens with ease. *Yes.*

The steps look sturdy enough and not excessively spidery, so I make my way down into the basement. There's not much light from the small windows, so I hit the flashlight on my phone, hold it up, and instantly scream as a murderous Benny stares me down.

Okay, it's not *quite* Benny.

It's sort of a messed-up Benny?

It takes my brain *way* too long to realize this is just a statue. It's probably Claudia's rough draft of the Link statue upstairs—where she was clearly working out the . . . anatomical kinks. I'm standing in her workshop, while messed-up Benny looms in front of me, his chest cracked open, and his legs disappearing into one single stalk of clay.

"Smart, Claudia," I whisper as my heart slows down. "A creepy basement scarecrow to keep prowlers away."

I take a look around. There's a couple empty shelves, a worktable, and a sign from the gas company saying they've shut off the gas (*man*, I would love to have seen their reaction to this horror statue) but it's obvious where I should hide the money. Claudia made a hidey-hole in this prototype Link's abs too. Boom.

The envelope is almost too big to fit, but I jam it in there, and with the 11.5K securely stashed in Benny's chest cavity, I close those chiseled abs, and let myself back out of the basement.

"Part one accomplished, boys," I say as I lead the dogs back to the alley. "Time for our next stop."

We retrace my steps from earlier that day, and as we get closer to the house Tond disappeared into, the dogs start straining against their leashes. They go from impatient to insistent, and it takes everything I've got to keep them from running to the front door.

Do they know their uncle is in there?

The blinds are drawn and the lights are on, and I see a shadow moving inside. I quickly duck down into the geometrically sculpted shrubbery in a way that would be extremely suspicious to anyone watching from across the street. The dogs reluctantly follow me into the bushes, their collars jangling loudly and Louis sneezing, neither of which are ideal for skulking, but hey, we do our best.

After a moment, the shadow passes, and I coax the dogs along through the shrubbery to the side of the house, hoping for a window I can see into. Branches scratch my arms and legs, but it's all worth it because a little farther down the side of the house, there's a window that looks like I *might* be able to see in it if I stand on my tiptoes.

We inch our way down, and the window's starting to look a little too high for me, which makes me wonder—do these circus dogs do pyramids, and would they maybe let me be the top of the pyramid, just for a little bit?

I'm right under the window, about to figure out my next move, when there's a loud explosion inside. It sounds, unmistakably, like a gunshot.

Something dark red splatters all over the window.

CHAPTER 24

What the actual hell? *Who is there left to murder, Tond??*

I hyperventilate in the middle of the shrubbery for a hot second and then try really hard to get my shit together. I can*not* stay here. I'm way out of my league, way too unarmed, and this is way too many murders for one neighborhood.

My brain screams *Abort! Abort!*

But then there's a second bang from inside the house, and I flinch, instinctively reaching up to cover my ears. Which means I accidentally drop the leashes, giving the cursed dogs their much-desired freedom. They make a break for it.

"NO!" I whisper-scream, my soul leaving my body. I dive through the bushes to catch the leashes as they snake away from me and disappear into the night.

Shitshitshit.

I pick myself up and chase the dogs back into the front yard, just in time to watch them bolt up the front stairs where Jacques proceeds *to stand on his hind legs, press on the door handle, open the door, and trot inside.* The other two follow happily. I make a sort of gurgle sound and run after them.

Okay, this is the exact opposite of *Abort! Abort!* But what am I supposed to do? I can't leave the dogs there with a murderer. I've got to think on my feet. I've got to stay calm and take control of the situation. I've got to channel both Hannah and Rodney O'Malley. As much as I want to run, I can't retreat when I'm this close.

The door is wide open, and I step inside the entryway, cautiously checking both ways for somebody waving a gun around. All I see is Jacques's tail to the left, disappearing through the archway into the living room, where Jean and Lou are jumping on and off the sofas in a frenzy. The house is quiet, except for the sound of jingling collars and dog breath.

And also someone crying.

It's coming from farther into the house.

Shitshitshitshit.

I inch through the archway, hoping I won't have to do anything heroic, because I really had not thought past this moment, and also I am not a heroic type of person.

But I'm sure as hell not getting this far and then leaving here without the confession I came for.

I duck next to the couch and reach for Jacques, who's the closest to me. He gleefully dodges my outstretched hand and trots off across the living room and through the doorway to the kitchen.

Where Tond is.

Get back here, Jacques! I scream in my head. *There's a killer in there! With a gun!*

The killer's voice wobbles out of the kitchen as he sings . . . the "Ave Maria"? From somewhere in there, Jacques begins to howl along.

How is this my life.

"Tond! Let the dog go!" I call out from behind the couch cushion that I am currently holding in front of me as a shield. "Put down the gun and let the dog go, and I'll give you back your money!"

Hey, wow, not bad, actually. I sound pretty legit.

There's a pause while he sniffles. "Who's there?"

I clear my throat and try again.

"Tond! Who did you shoot? Is someone hurt?"

"Everybody Hurts!" he announces, before launching into a new song.

Really thought a murderer would be a little less, I don't know, ADHD about it? "Tond! Who did you just kill?"

"I think—I think I killed the calendar," he wails.

My heartbeat is pounding frantically in my throat and my face and my eyes as I creep closer to the kitchen—until finally I see the carnage.

Tond is sitting on the floor near the kitchen table—surrounded by jars of pickles and other unidentifiable vegetables in jars. Across from him is the red splatter, and at the base of the wall below it lies a shattered jar that once held . . . beets?

Okay then, Tond murdered some beets.

A second shattered jar—what looks like pickled okra—apparently hit the wall a few feet away, against a calendar. Turns out the difference between gunshots and pickle jars shattering is not as big as I would have guessed.

Tond looks up and spots me.

"You?" he asks, wiping his nose pathetically.

I step into the kitchen and wave.

He frowns. "The secret girlfriend?"

Oh right.

"Hello again," I say, caution sensors blaring in my head. "So you didn't shoot . . . a person?"

He points sheepishly at the calendar on the wall, which I can now see is a kind of pinup calendar but of Cran and his three dogs. The August photo has him lying on the grass, the three dogs sitting behind him in a line. One dog—Jacques, obviously—has his paw resting on Cran's shoulder. There's something inappropriately sexy about the whole thing.

"I threw the last jar of pickled beets, Cran's special recipe." He starts to cry again. "He'll never make any more."

There's an awkward pause and then he picks up the bottle next to him and takes a big swig of . . .

"I'm sorry, is that *cooking sherry*?"

"Secret girlfriend, you are very observant." He takes another swig. "Cran didn't drink, so this is all he has, okay? It's disgusting, but I deserve to be punished."

Oh. This is *Cran*'s house. No wonder Jacques knew how to open the door—wait, nope. A dog opening a door is not reasonable, no matter how you cut it.

Tond wipes his eyes, then pinches a pickle out of a jar and chomps on it, staring directly at me. It feels aggressive, but I'm not sure why.

"I guess you could say I like to dance with death," he says, accidentally spitting pickle bits in my general vicinity.

Now that I'm face-to-face with the neighborhood murderer, who seems to be both drunk and sad, I'll admit he seems more pathetic than scary. I also can't say I understand the pickle situation, but maybe that's how murderers operate, by undermining your confidence with weird stuff.

Not this time, buddy.

Weird doesn't even faze me anymore.

"Time to turn yourself in," I say. "I know exactly what you did."

"You do?" He blinks at me. "How?"

It's go time. The big moment. Is. Happening. Okay, Mo. Muster all your grown-up confidence here. And also . . . see if you can find your recording app with the phone still in your pocket.

Oof, really shoulda had that ready to go.

Time to stall.

I make my way across the kitchen tile, trying not to step on any glass shards, as I shove my hand in my pocket and hope I get the PIN right without looking. "Where to even begin?" I say. "It's a classic case. I mean just *look* at you."

He whimpers a little.

Hmm, can I pull my phone out just a *little* bit without him noticing? I turn away like I'm examining the beet-splattered calendar and peek at my screen. Shit. Messed up my PIN. I unlock the phone and spin back around. "You *murdered* your brother!"

Tond gasps and chokes a little bit on a pickle. He starts coughing and wheezing. Do I need to do the Heimlich? I don't know the Heimlich.

He holds up a finger. "I'm okay," he croaks. "I'm okay."

"You are the opposite of okay!" I say, discreetly thumbing through my apps. Do I HAVE a recording app, even? "You wanted Cran's house and his life! He was cramping your style. He had to be *eliminated*."

YES! Found it.

Ugh, what? I need to put in my *email*? Jesus.

I keep stalling. "Because you wanted Johnston Bros Real Estate to be Johnston BRO Real Estate, didn't you? Didn't you? *BRO?*"

Okay, I've finally got the app going, and I hit record just in time. God, I'm good. I'm looming over him now in what is hopefully an intimidating way, so close I can smell the nose-tingling aroma of pickled beets and sherry.

Tond pauses midchew, eyes welling up with tears. “You guys had something really special, I can see that now.” He nods. “You deserve to know the truth.”

Oh shit.

Here we go.

CHAPTER 25

Cran died of botulism!"

Tond is crying again. Blubbering really. Snot *everywhere.*

I'm staring at my phone, making sure it's getting all this, when his words belatedly sink in. "Wait, say that again?"

"And I'm such a *fuckup*, I can't even kill myself as good as Cran," Tond says, rubbing his nose with a paper towel until it turns red. "Always second best, that's Tond Johnston!"

"No, back up. Cran *what*?"

"Died. Of. Botulism. That's what the coroner's report said. Not the car accident—*botulism*!"

"You can't honestly think I'm going to buy that," I say, abandoning subtlety and shoving my phone in his face. "Admit it to my phone! Admit you killed him!"

He lowers my phone and puts a jar of sauerkraut in my other hand.

"I'm not hungry for cabbage!" I yell. "I'm hungry for the truth!"

"No, listen, Cran made his own pickles because he said they were healthier! I kept telling him to be careful." He stares forlornly at the sauerkraut. "I don't know how to run a *business*! I don't even know how to balance a checkbook."

"You guys still use check—"

"My only choice"—he grabs the jar back and holds up a pinch of sauerkraut like it's chewing tobacco—"is to botulism myself too." He swallows the sauerkraut and washes it down with cooking sherry, then hiccups. "That one almost came back up," he says, patting his chest.

How did this get so off the rails?

Okay, *think*, Mo. Cran was definitely murdered. Tond said so at the funeral.

"I know you murdered your brother," I say, pointing at him. "Because I heard you *admit* it at his funeral!"

Tond puts on a thinking face and then shakes his head. "Not possible, because I didn't murder him."

UGH, this guy is good. Time for a new tactic.

Benny.

"*And* I know all about you and Benny," I say. "So don't even think about denying that."

"Wait, who's Benny?"

This guy's got to be the world's most annoying murderer. "What did I literally just say?"

"Sorry, sorry," Tond says, rolling his eyes. "Got it. You know all *about* me and Benny."

"You and Benny, you're murderers in cahoots. You told him you wanted out after the Cran murder, but he wouldn't let you out, would he? No way. He needed your money. So he told you that first you had to 'take care of her' and I thought HER was ME but HER was Claudia!"

Tond suddenly turns a greeny pale. Gotcha, turd.

"I can explain," Tond says slowly, side-eyeing my phone. "That conversation was about, um, a transaction of a very *legal* amount of money to Claud— To Ms. Alonzo. For transactional purposes. A legal real estate transaction that was 100 percent not *illegal*. I can't tell you *who* I was talking to, for very official, professional reasons. But it wasn't this Benny person. And there are no cahoots."

"Oh sure, maybe it started that way. But then Benny got Claudia to trust him and the two of you left her that envelope of bribe money. Oh yes, I know all about that. In fact, I have the money—"

"Wait, you do?" Tond says. "Oh thank *goodness*, that is honestly a huge load off."

"Don't interrupt me when I'm making you confess, that's so rude!"

He puts his hands in prayer position in front of his face and bows a little at me to continue. I can't help but see he's in much better spirits now.

I've lost a little momentum. Gotta get it back.

Gotta bring the hammer down TOUT FUCKING SUITE.

"But Claudia couldn't be bought, could she? No, she wouldn't sell her house for your big fancy parking garage. So you had Benny kill Claudia. Just like you killed. Your. Brother."

Check and mate.

He scrambles to his feet, and I realize I've only got my fists, so I hold them up like an old-timey boxer and hope I look intimidating.

But he just starts hyperventilating. He leans against the counter to support himself. "Claudia is *dead*?" he wheezes. "WAS IT BOTULISM??"

Playing dumb, huh? Well, this crossing guard wasn't born yesterday.

"Spare me the theatrics," I say.

He's not hyperventilating anymore, but he doesn't look guilty, either, just sort of confused. A criminal mastermind, no doubt.

"But. Why would I kill Cran? He was the one who was good at business. I hate this stuff."

"Because . . . okay, that's a fair question."

"And I literally just told you—Cran died of botulism. It's all right here." He reaches into his pocket, and reflexively, I punch him.

Except I've never punched anyone in my *life*, and my aim is terrible. I just barely clip his shoulder, but it still sends streaks of pain up through my elbow. He grabs his shoulder, looking more emotionally injured than physically. "Ow! Why the violence?" he says, handing me a folded-up piece of paper.

"Sorry," I say, shaking my punching arm. "I thought maybe you were pulling a weapon."

I unfold the official-looking paper. Sure enough—unless he forged this report on forged letterhead, Cran died of botulism.

Not murder. Damn.

Well, accidental poisoning could explain the slurring and stumbling Cran was doing before he died. Maybe the vomit deluge too. *Turns out Claudia was half-right when she suggested radium poisoning*, I think sadly.

Also, note to self: Check on symptoms of botulism in case it's something I should consider worrying about.

"But like for real, who the fuck is Benny?" Tond asks. "I'm telling you, I don't know this guy. And turn that damn thing off." He points at my phone.

I hesitate, then press pause because obviously my whole plan has been flushed down the crapper.

Once Tond sees I'm not recording, he leans in and whispers: "I had that conversation with *Merle* at the funeral."

Merle. Merle. Why do I know that name? "Who's Merle again?"

He looks appalled. "You don't know the name of your own alderman? Do you even vote?"

"Okay, I'm really not about to take civic responsibility lessons from a—" I stop as the full impact of what he's said hits me. Merle Carey. Not just *my* alderman. *Tasha*'s alderman.

Tond drunkenly bulldozes on. "And anyway, why would I give somebody bribe money and then simultaneously kill them? Does that make *any* sense to you?"

"Well, I guess not," I admit.

"Plus, if she's dead, her house goes to her next of kin . . . what a mess. Our company's going to hemorrhage money until it's out of probate. The red tape alone could bankrupt us." His face crumples in grief as he cries out, "I mean, *me*."

Oh.

God, I feel so stupid. There's clearly a whole lotta bribery going on, and political bribery no less—which, by the way, is already giving me a stomachache—but no murder. Just a couple of accidents.

Accidents happen all the time—they are, in fact, the fourth-leading cause of death.

And I've been so desperate to not feel like my life is in the toilet, I *may* have gotten a bit carried away. Getting carried away might be, maybe, possibly . . . a big problem for me.

I hand back the cause-of-death report.

Tond and Benny: officially not murderers.

And that's when I realize I've gotten poor, innocent Benny in some very serious trouble.

I flash back to the doorbell video, and it's like the whole thing comes into focus. He wasn't just dropping off an envelope of money. He was in the middle of *walking dogs*, and (oh god) I bet if I'd looked closely enough, one of them would have been mop-dog Charlie. Benny was just running an errand for Merle. He probably didn't even know what he was doing.

And if Rodney O'Malley IS right about what happens in Chicago holding cells?

The neighborhood's hottest dog walker is getting rolled and burged and whatever else Marlowe called it.

Because of me.

I need to find him and get him out of jail. Stat.

"Phew, well, glad we straightened that out," I say. "I've really got to run—"

"All we wanted was a stupid beautiful cash cow of a parking garage," Tond says, his blue eyes pleading. "I didn't *want* to bribe anyone."

"Uh-huh," I say, backing toward the door and snapping my fingers for the dogs. "Come on, guys."

"It's a classic Chicago move," Tond says, shaking his head and popping another pinch of sauerkraut. "It's why I'm so bad at business. I lose track of everybody I'm supposed to bribe."

I grab Jean in a full-body hug to pull him off what is probably his favorite sofa.

"Gotta bribe the old lady," Tond says, counting on his fingers. "Gotta quid pro quo the alderman. Gotta bribe the gas company."

"Good lord, dog," I mutter as the dog makes himself deadweight. "Come *on*, we've got to get a man out of jail."

But then I process what Tond just said.

He holds up three fingers. "Well, I guess that's just three bribes, but it feels like a lot when you're doing it."

"Tond," I say, going still. "You bribed the gas company?"

He shrugs. "We had to bribe the gas company to pass inspection on some seriously not-up-to-code stuff. Some cousin of Merle's wife. You didn't start recording again, did you?"

"Holy shit," I whisper.

"What?" he whispers back.

"Tond, Claudia died of a gas leak."

He slaps a hand over his mouth. "You don't think—"

There's a bang on the window, and both of us scream. Tond dives to the ground, and I swear like a (terrified) sailor. But just as quickly, I recognize the face pressed up against the glass and it's not a new, third murderer.

It's Marlowe.

I throw open the window, furious. "What did I tell you about tracking my phone? This is super dangerous! This guy could have been a murderer!"

"'Cept I'm not," Tond pouts, holding his funny bone gingerly.

I lean out of the window and see that she's balancing on the water meter. "You need to go home."

But Marlowe's eyes are wide. "Mo, I made a text autocorrect translation app."

"Of course you did. Can we talk about this tomorrow?"

"No, listen. I finally translated that text Claudia sent me the night she died."

Tond pads over to us and together we lean out of the window to look at Marlowe's phone screen. She holds it up.

Original text: Hells no apple the cat invite affluent odor

Translated text: Help mo solve the case, investigate alderman office

Tond drops the bottle of sherry, and it shatters.

Looks like there might have been a murder after all.

CHAPTER 26

The sherry pools at Tond's feet.

"I *told* you the text was bad news," Marlowe says as she pulls herself up and climbs through the window.

"I *hate* news," Tond says miserably. "It's *always* bad."

"Everybody stay calm," I say, mostly to myself. *I will not spiral.* "Let's look at the facts. What do we actually know?"

"What do we *know*?" Tond echoes, his voice getting shriller with each word. "This parking garage is cursed! Bad things happen to people involved with it!"

"Who is this guy again?" Marlowe asks me.

"I'm the guy who's *next*!" Tond cries.

His panic is contagious, and I can't hold back the spiraling any longer; my mind swirls with questions about how deep the conspiracy goes. Gas company hit men has to just be the tip of the iceberg, right? So many people are involved in this kind of deal! The neighborhood is clearly full of secret corruption. It's all around me. Anybody could be anybody, I don't know! Like, who is "Sheila," really? Is she actually

Roy's mom, or is she a plant keeping an eye on me? Is she on payroll? What's her deal?

"I DON'T DESERVE TO DIE!!!!!!!" cries Tond as he drops to his knees.

And just like that, I'm not spiraling anymore.

Because— Is that what I look like? That guy on his knees sweating and checking to make sure we're acknowledging his meltdown? Is that how Hannah sees me? And Eva? And my mom?

Woof. Okay. That is not what I want. Personal growth moment happening in real time here.

I need to take a step back. Like, seriously. While Tond weeps into a nearby houndstooth pashmina, I ask myself again: *What do I definitely know?*

Cran's death really was an accident, just not the accident it *looked* like. Check.

Which means Claudia was wrong—at least about it being murder. Check.

But—even though she was wrong about that, investigating Cran's *hypothetical* murder meant sticking her nose into some pretty dirty business dealings. And that's why she had to die.

The room goes topsy-turvy and I realize that if I'd managed to convince Claudia that Cran's death was an accident, *she'd be alive right now*. Oh god. I should have tried harder.

And then, because my body can't physically contain any more guilt, suddenly, I'm furious.

Claudia's only mistake was that she got too close to a bunch of crimes that were *actually* happening. The crimes of greedy, corrupt people who had no respect for human life and who would throw money and favors and *murder* around to get what they wanted.

Or maybe just one greedy, corrupt person. Someone who needed to hang on to his power no matter what it cost. Someone who's been in the background this whole time. Someone she warned us about as she was dying.

"Is it possible that Claudia was telling us who killed her?" I can barely whisper the words, but they tumble out of me. "Did *Alderman Merle Carey* murder her? I've been to his office, it didn't look murdery."

"Bro," says Marlowe with a shake of her head. "I saw him light the neighborhood Christmas tree-slash-giant menorah last year. You think you can trust a guy."

Tond leaps up and grabs me by my shoulders. "This is what I've been telling you," he cries. "*I'm* next! I need your help!"

He looks genuinely terrified, and, wow, I am SO out of my league here. From the very start, in fact.

Dead guy in a sinkhole, botulismed on his own pickles.

Death threat at a funeral.

Cops after me.

Neighbor murdered in cold blood.

Cutthroat political corruption.

And now this guy thinks *I* can save him?

NOPE NOPE NOPE. I am OUT. Out of this mess. Out of Chicago. Out of the country? I've got those three years of high school Latin, maybe I can hide out in . . . the Vatican?

"Take the dogs," I offer. "For protection."

Maybe a two birds situation?

But he ignores the offer and turns to Marlowe. "How about you, Nancy Drew? You're weirdly young looking, but you obviously have the investigative skills. Please, you gotta help me!" He lunges for her, and oh my god, *absolutely* the fuck not—I jump between them as the dogs leap up and flank me.

"Tond, she is not *weirdly young looking*, she is a *child*," I say firmly.

"Oops." He glances past me at Marlowe. "On the other hand, that's a good cover—"

I growl and Jean growls along with me.

Tond steps back.

"I swear to god," I say in my most terrifying voice. "This dog is always hungry, and he is *not* picky."

"It's just you two are clearly the only ones I can trust," Tond says as he backs off and sniffles pathetically. "*Come on*, secret girlfriend."

Oh. Right.

"I have a confession," I say.

"*You're* the murderer?" Tond asks, horrified.

"*No*," I say. "I wasn't Cran's secret girlfriend. I'm a crossing guard, and he was kind of a jerk to me."

"I knew it! Cran exclusively dates models. Usually from Slovakia." Tond leans in and whispers, "Never lets me meet them. On account of I've got too much game. Check out these abs."

He fumbles with his clothes, and Marlowe and I quickly look away, at literally *anything* else, as though Cran's decor has recently gotten very interesting.

And it turns out I actually *am* interested. In all the chaos, I missed the fact that the walls are, I mean, *covered* with ribbons and trophies and huge, blown-up glossy framed photos of the dogs at competitions. In some pictures they're leaping over tiny fences; in others they sit proudly next to Cran.

"Wait," I say. "The dogs are *show* dogs? That's why they can do all those tricks?"

"See?" Tond says, blessedly forgetting his abs. "You totally just detected that. You're great at figuring stuff out."

And you know what? I am. Because I spot mop-dog Charlie in one of the pictures, and a laugh bursts out of me as I realize that Tasha actually *meant* it when she said Charlie won awards for being a good boy. And thinking of Tasha just makes me more determined to get out of this mess. I want to be the kind of person Tasha could fall for, and I don't think that person is mixed up with cooking sherry–guzzling lunatics.

"Tond, listen," I say. "This has gotten way out of hand. Marlowe is in seventh grade; she needs to pass math. I am a *crossing guard*; I help kids like Marlowe cross the street. We suck at this. We've already gotten an innocent person arrested. Speaking of which, we need to go deal with that." I nod at Marlowe, who hustles toward the exit.

"Please??" he begs, slipping past Marlowe to plaster himself against the front door. "Stop me from being next?"

"Tond," I say, trying to wedge my arm between him and the knob. "We all need to forget about this. We need to walk away."

"I'm in too deep! I can't walk away!"

"And we can't help you with that. Marlowe, get the dogs."

"You're the only ones who can," he says, desperate. "And . . . and look! You're already on the case. You just have to infiltrate Merle's office, see if he might be wanting to kill me, and if so, keep me alive. That's it!" He opens his palms like the shrug emoji.

"Is that all," I mutter.

"That is *not* all. Because if you do this . . ." His eyebrows waggle at me. "I'll let you keep the money. From Claudia's house."

Oh. Shit.

That stops me. Eleven point five thousand dollars.

I really need that money.

Really, really.

It would, in fact, change everything.

I wouldn't have to worry about Sheila or how long it takes me to get rid of the dogs. I wouldn't have to worry about making rent. I could buy the good pepperoni. I could take Tasha to fancy restaurants.

Oh god. Am I actually going to do this?

Hang on. "Is this another bribe?" I ask suspiciously.

"No!" he says quickly. "It's a payment. For your services. But you only get it if you keep me alive."

"And *that's* how you leverage money," Marlowe points out.

"I can't promise to keep you alive." I grit my teeth. "But for 11.5K, I will *try*."

"YES!!" Tond pumps his fist. "I KNEW you'd cave—"

Buyer's remorse hits immediately with the reality of what I've signed on for. Am I going to barf? Maybe.

"I need a sec," I say and run back to the kitchen for a glass of water. What the hell am I doing?? Other than agreeing to something impossible and dangerous because I'm broke. Just like I *thought* Benny was doing. And, again, got him wrongfully arrested for.

I search all the cabinets for a glass, but they're all dirty and piled up in the sink. The only things to drink out of are the empty jars on the floor, but I don't do pickle water. I groan. Come *on*, is a glass of lead-infused Chicago sink water too much to ask??

And that's when I see Cran's okra-drenched calendar on the floor.

The pukey feeling dissipates.

Because—suddenly—I have an idea. I snatch the smelly calendar off the floor. Cran's handwriting looks cramped and easy to forg . . . erize. Forge? Easy to *forge*. Point is, maybe there's a meeting between Cran and Merle that just so *happens* to appear on this calendar, the week Cran died. And since I'm already boobs-deep in the alderman's office (thanks to Tasha), this soon-to-be-forged calendar is the boob in the door I need to compare with Merle's calendar and piece together his past movements and future plans. Plus, I've got plenty of Rodney O'Malley videos if I need help.

Maybe this *is* doable.

"Mo Ellery's on the case with a new growth mindset!" I hum a little bit of a cool theme song I've just made up and strike a detective pose.

"Mo . . . you okay?" Marlowe says, and I freeze mid theme song.

She and Tond are standing in the kitchen, watching me. Tond grabs a nearly empty pickle jar and sticks his fingers in.

"Tond," I say. "If I'm going to work this case, I need something from you. You have to tell the cops this Benny stuff was all a big misunderstanding. That he wasn't creeping around or murdering, he was just dropping off an envelope of real estate info for you."

Tond huffs. "You want *me* to *lie*? To the *police*? How dare you."

I give him what I hope is a stony expression. "Would it be better if I asked you to bribe them?"

He turns pale and looks away. Nice job, my face!

"But what if the cops find out the envelope was actually full of money?" he says.

I think of my hiding place in Claudia's basement. "They won't. Trust me."

"How do you know? How can you be sure?"

"You want me to poke around a murderous alderman's office or what?"

"Okay, okay I'll do it," he says. He pops a pickle in his mouth and then freezes midchew. "Oh god, the botulism. Do you guys think I have it? I want to live! Nancy Drew, call 911!"

Amateur.

"No way, you'll sit in the ER for hours," I say, hustling Marlowe and the dogs toward the door. "Urgent Care all the way. Tell Jessie I sent you."

CHAPTER 27

My confident feelings all ebb away as soon as I'm alone in my apartment, incapable of sleep, three hot poodles shoving me out of my own bed.

What if the calendar forging thing doesn't work? What if I get on Merle's list too? Is Benny okay? Benny is definitely not okay. And it's all my fault.

I called three different police stations (using an alias and disguising my voice, obviously), and every time, I got put on hold indefinitely or left voicemails for cops who were on vacation for the next two weeks.

The Cook County sheriff's online "inmate locator service" turned up nothing.

I desperately hope Tond got ahold of someone, but he's got botulism on the brain, and I forgot to get his phone number, which is like Detective 101. I doubt Rodney O'Malley has a video called MAKE SURE YOU CAN GET AHOLD OF PEOPLE. That's just a given.

Every hour, I come up with worse scenarios of what is happening to Benny. By 3 a.m., I'm at full-on medieval torture.

Get a grip, I tell myself. *Don't be like Tond.* But somehow, knowing I *shouldn't* spiral isn't actually keeping me from spiraling. What the hell, brain?

When I do finally doze off, I wake up thirty minutes before my alarm goes off, sweaty and confused from a nightmare about Benny being tortured by the poodles, who were secretly cops this whole time? I lie in bed and try to analyze *that* for a while, and by the time my alarm goes off, I'm somehow both exhausted AND jittery, which is a very bad combo for a crossing guard.

I *vaguely* remember a post Hannah forwarded me once about how cold plunges are better than coffee, so I turn on a freezing cold shower, hop in, scream so loud the dogs start howling, and then immediately stumble back out. They swarm my legs, leaving dog residue all over me, so okay—I may not be clean or smell any better, but it's true, I am awake and laser-focused.

I clamp a leash on each poodle and give myself a quick pep talk; I'll do one hour of staying awake enough to keep kids alive, a quick hop over to the alderman's office to keep him from murdering Tond, and then—nap.

Classic morning routine.

I'm hustling down the sidewalk, trying to untangle my neon vest, walk the dogs, and clock in on my phone at the same time, when I hear cheering and clapping coming from my corner.

I glance up and my steps get slower as my brain struggles to process what I'm seeing.

One Chicago Bears beach umbrella.

Two orange-and-blue-striped lawn chairs.

Three thousand percent of my recommended daily humiliation allowance.

"Mom? Dad? *But . . . WHY?*"

My mom takes off her sunglasses and waves hugely, like I haven't already seen her. "We wanted to support you at your new job! Save those kids!"

"And we brought mimosas!" Dad reaches into a cooler I hadn't noticed before and pulls out a travel cup that reads *Baby's Little Baby* on it. He offers it to me. "Want one?"

"Honey, why do you have three dogs?" Mom asks.

"Fresh-squeezed orange juice!" Dad says, shaking the cup at me.

"They're so fancy!" Mom says, reaching out to pet Louis, who is now yanking at my arm to get close to her.

"You can't be on this lawn!" I squawk.

"Oh, it's okay, sweetie," Mom says, taking the leashes from my hand. The dogs, of course, sit politely next to her. "We checked with the owner, Mr. Gonsalves, and he doesn't mind at all; also did you know his niece is married to that boy you went to preschool with—what was his name again?"

"Kevin," Dad says, sipping mimosa from a straw.

"You remember Kevin from preschool, don't you, Mo? I'm sure Mr. Gonsalves could tell him to come by and say hi."

The cold plunge is no longer working.

I look up to see if maybe there'll be a freak storm, during which I could be struck by lightning or maybe sucked up into a tornado.

The absolutely cloudless blue sky mocks me.

"So how do you usually stand?" my dad asks, peeling himself from the chair and taking a weird squat-stance, holding his mimosa cup like a stop sign. "Like this?"

Okay, I guess this is happening.

I pull on my neon vest, unable to care that it's still tangled.

"You won't even know we're here," my mom assures me, patting Louis, who I swear is giving me a smug smile.

The kids and parents start arriving, and I do my best to ignore my own parents. It gets harder when the mimosas take hold and they cheer each time I hold up the stop sign.

"Watch out!" cries a third grader as I step out in front of a car, refusing to hold up the sign. At this time, I prefer to be flattened than humiliated.

The kid tugs on my sleeve. "Want me to help you across?" Then, as the sidewalks fill up and I rush from one intersection to the other, my parents whip out Dad's custom foam fingers that say *MO IS #1* and wave them in the air. "YOU GOT THIS!" yells my dad.

"You're so lucky to have supportive parents," one of the PTA members says to me.

"I don't know those people," I say.

She hurries off.

I, meanwhile, zone out in the intersection for another second until a car honks. "Sorry, sorry," I mutter as I head back to the corner.

Not my best work. Certainly not #1 foam-finger-level work, but in my defense, no one has gotten flattened and no one has fallen into the sinkhole, which is currently at least a foot wider than the metal plate covering it. I make a mental note to call 311 and ask for a second metal plate.

If I survive this shift, anyway.

I see the bulging duffel bag that suggests Mom and Dad have even more humiliating accessories just waiting to be deployed in my final minutes, but then fate intervenes and actually does me a solid. "Look, Mo!" Mom cries. "Davey, pour another mimosa!"

"Roger that, sweetcheeks," Dad slurs.

And oh my god—like Venus emerging from her clam or whatever, Hannah climbs out of a rideshare holding a cardboard tray with two beautiful coffees.

I barely register the "sweetcheeks."

"Need some caffeine?" Hannah asks.

Am I crying? I think I'm crying.

Hannah looks behind me, where my mom is now talking to Mr. Gonsalves through his front window about Kevin. "Why are your parents here?" she whispers.

"I think I got cursed by a mummy and didn't realize it," I whisper back.

I reach for a coffee.

"So this coffee comes on one condition," Hannah says. "That you get another coffee with me. Can we chat after your shift?"

I take a sip and I am alive all over again. Sorry, cold plunge freaks. Coffee wins over cold shower any day.

"Mmm," I say. "This has a single pump of cinnamon syrup in it, doesn't it? You are my hero."

"So," Hannah says. "Chat?"

Jean is now yanking as hard as possible on his leash to see if there's food involved in our interaction. I let him sniff my cup and he practically rolls his eyes before going back to snuffling at Dad's cooler.

"You selling poodles now, Mr. Ellery?" Hannah calls.

Dad snorts. "Not scalable, too much overhead," he says. "You know me, I keep my operations lean and mean."

"They're mine," I say. Hannah's eyes widen. "I mean, they aren't real dogs, just temporary dogs. The dogs of a dead man, technically."

"I'm sorry I asked," Hannah says.

But that reminds me of my plan to make these dogs temporary. "Did you bring Eva's green screen?" I ask.

"Oh. Right," she says quietly. "I forgot."

"Then I have a great idea," I say. "I have to run an errand after my shift anyway, why don't you swing by home and get it, and text when you're on your way back? Then I'm all yours. Promise."

I hustle a few stragglers across the street, and my parents spend the last few minutes of my shift complimenting Hannah's dress and asking about her new campaigns.

And look, I didn't *love* it when they were waving foam fingers, but it's hard not to notice how completely they've stopped caring about my job. It's so stupid, but I feel a little jealous, and Hannah is honestly being kind of rude, giving one-word answers and checking her phone for her rideshare. Then the car shows up, Mom and Dad pack their things, I wave goodbye to everyone, and this long national nightmare is over.

I run home with the dogs, throw on clean(ish) clothes, check my hair and pits, and grab Cran's calendar. Time to earn that 11.5K and limit the body count in the neighborhood. And if I have to make out with Tasha to do that, well, that's a price I'm willing to pay.

My heart skips a beat. *Easy.*

I switch shirts a second time, to a black tee that shows off my clavicle. Then I think about Tasha running her lips along my clavicle, and *that* makes me have to put on a little extra deodorant. I keep the dogs with me, because for whatever weird reason, they make me feel more confident, like I have my own entourage. They don't smell fabulous, but they're still better than no entourage at all.

It's a sunny day, but it's breezy and not too hot or humid. As we make our way down the sidewalk, I realize I'm actually feeling optimistic about all this. Part of it might be the caffeine. And sure, I've made a couple missteps, some of them involving false arrest and imprisonment of an innocent man blah blah blah, but we all make mistakes. And I'm getting closer to fixing all that and finding the truth.

When we arrive, I see Tasha through the big window, talking into the phone with a serious face, but she brightens when she sees me and waves me inside. I point at the dogs, and she nods enthusiastically, so the four of us amble in and wait for her to finish the call.

It's still weird to me that the alderman's office is this janky storefront with buzzy, unflattering fluorescent lights—just one long room outfitted with those makeshift cubicle walls. It's even weirder now that I know it's all built on a house of cards of bribes. A house of bribe cards? Tasha can help me workshop that. Maybe while I kiss the soft skin of her thigh.

Mo. You are here on business.

But like, theoretically, why *couldn't* I be here for pleasure too? Maybe mixing business and pleasure is actually a *great* idea, like an Arnold Palmer or bacon on a donut. Or salty ice cream.

Now I'm horny *and* hungry.

I meander toward the cubicles, trying to look casual and distinctly *not* DTF, at least not immediately. I'm also checking to make sure Merle isn't around. There's a nameplate on the closed office door in back, announcing ALDERMAN CAREY, but I figure it's good investigative protocol to check the cubicles too.

Rodney O'Malley would be proud.

I've barely gotten past Tasha's desk when I get a text from Hannah asking if I'm home yet.

Crap. Spent too long on costume changes and haven't even begun detectiving yet.

I text her the address of the office and tell her to come here, figuring that this way, she can meet Tasha, too, which obviously she will love.

I've barely put my phone back in my pocket when mop-dog Charlie comes limping through the cubicles at a precariously high speed, making a beeline for the poodles, who start jumping and spinning.

And because they are all basically chaos muppets, one of the dogs *hip-checks me* into a flimsy cubicle wall, which topples over, and then acts like a huge domino and takes all the other walls down with floor-rattling thumps.

I cringe and freeze in place, as though no one is going to notice.

Spoiler: Everyone notices.

That includes (1) Tasha, who's spun around in her chair and got her hand over her mouth, trying not to laugh into the phone, (2–5) the dogs, who are delighted and chase one another through the ruins like mighty, fuzzy conquerors, and (6–7) at the back of the room, two people leaning over some documents on a table. They're frozen, heads up, gawking at me in surprise. I recognize one of them—it's the little old lady from the funeral with the bratwurst in her purse . . . Leslie? Does she live in the neighborhood? Small world. The other one I don't recognize. She's younger, wearing a beige pantsuit, and she shoots me a severe look of disapproval before turning back to her paperwork.

"Sorry, don't mind me," I whisper and start pulling up the closest cubicle wall, but there's nothing to attach it to, so I just kinda stand there holding it up, trying to look casual.

Once Tasha ends her call, she joins me in setting the walls back to their original positions. "Felt like remodeling the office, huh?"

"What can I say, I had a vision."

"Is your face normally that red?"

"Sunburn," I say. "Very recent."

"Well, don't sweat this." She lowers her voice. "My dedicated colleagues back there aren't currently saving Chicago or, even you know, *working*. They're collecting evidence to dispute some fancy dog show's decision that Charlie can't compete."

"I don't know, that sounds like exactly what an alderman's office should be doing."

"*Oh totally.*" She laughs quietly. "We're at the bleeding edge of government work."

Bleeding edge indeed.

"What's a dog show even like?" I whisper, trying to picture it as we lift another cubicle panel together. "Like a beauty contest? Do they all have talents? Because Charlie probably kills with his impression of a pile of rope."

Tasha shakes her head. "I've never been. But I think if he had his druthers, Charlie would love to retire. The old guy's got gas, hearing problems, arthritis—"

I laugh. Tasha doesn't.

"Oh, sorry," I say. "But you did just use the word 'druthers.' Should I be sympathetic? Do dogs actually get arthritis?"

"The fancier they are, the fancier their problems. And Charlie is a very fancy dog," Tasha adds with a shrug, and then she glances at her phone. "In fact, it's almost time for his shot, if you want a free lesson from Val. We're on the bleeding edge of dog arthritis treatment too, lucky us."

I shudder. "Thanks, but I don't really do needles. Keep the outside on the outside and the inside on the inside, I always say."

"That's a reasonable policy. And policy *is* my specialty."

She's doing that irresistible government flirting again. *Why* is it so hot? I step a little closer to her. "I'd say you have a couple of specialties."

"Tasha?" calls a deep voice, and I jump.

"Jumpy much?" she teases. "That's just Merle."

"He's here?" I'm instantly covered in goose bumps.

"Don't leave yet, I'll be right back," she says as she walks away. "I'm going to see what he wants."

It's all I can do to not pull her back toward me, to keep her here, and safe. Because I have a pretty good idea of what he wants. And what he's willing to do to get it.

While Tasha disappears into Merle's office in back, I go over to her desk, where all four dogs are cuddled up like nothing bad has ever happened. I find a spray bottle sitting next to her bedraggled plant and give myself a spritz right in the face, since I'm all out of coffee.

I'm here to find proof that Merle's a murderer. I didn't plan on him being here while I did it. But that's not going to stop me.

Flirting time is officially over.

CHAPTER 28

I don't breathe normally again until Tasha reemerges from the alderman's private office, all in one piece and holding a thick stack of official-looking documents. She gives me an apologetic smile as she plops them on the desk and sits. "I'm sorry, but I have to go through and notarize this whole pile. It's going to take forever. But thanks for coming by?"

"Anytime," I say, trying to sound breezy. "It was good to see you too. But also . . . I wonder if I could get your professional help? Before you start notarizing? Just for a second."

"For you?" She smiles, for real this time, and her voice curls around me. "I've got at least seven seconds."

"Dang, it is easier to get in your pants than get on your calendar." Even with a murderer in the next room, I cannot stop flirting with this woman. What is wrong with me?

She laughs, and it takes everything I've got, but I resist the urge to tell her the professional help I need most is to rip her clothes off in the office supply closet. I'm pretty proud that instead, I tell her the story I've been practicing.

"So you remember the guy who died at my intersection? Cran Johnston?"

She nods.

"I know this sounds sort of silly, but . . . his brother is trying to find out what his last words were. It's a whole grief thing." I pull out the okra-stained calendar and flip through the pages. "This is Cran's calendar, and it has this entry." I point to the morning of the accident. It says, *Meeting at Merle's.* I shake my head. "I couldn't believe it, but I told the brother I knew just who to ask."

I *could* believe it.

Because I wrote it there this morning.

Eat your heart out, Rodney O'Malley!

Except . . . I'm discovering in real time that lying to Tasha feels bad. Very bad. Much, much worse than I thought.

Just then, beige pantsuit lady—Val—walks through, a fat brown envelope in her arms. I think of the brown envelope in Benny's abs and get the shivers. "Running to the post office," she says to Tasha, and then wrinkles her nose. "Why does it smell like the butt end of a pickle jar in here?"

"Long story," I say, gesturing toward the calendar, as if that explains it all.

"Gross," Val says as she leaves.

Tasha shrugs in apology. "She grows on you."

"I'll take your word for it."

"So this thing says they had a meetup, huh?" Tasha slides into her chair and squints at Cran's calendar. "That's weird. I'll check Merle's calendar, but I honestly don't remember scheduling anything for them that week."

"That would be a huge help—I figure if anyone knows Merle's

every move, it's you!" I immediately bite my tongue, realizing that I'm drifting into "too much truth" territory.

Lie better, I scold myself.

Practice makes perfect, I snark back.

Look, it's not like I'm lying to get into her pants. And I'm not lying about *me*, or *us*, so maybe this isn't so bad? Even so, it still feels like I'm setting up a fuzzy gray cubicle wall of dishonesty between us. *I'll knock it down later*, I tell myself as she closes a document. *It's for 11.5K*, I think as she clicks into his calendar. *I can buy her so much Malört with that money.*

"I doubt it would have been Merle," Tasha says. She clicks around. "Yeah, according to his calendar, he and Cran Johnston met every other week, and the last time was eight days before his death."

I stare over her shoulder, scanning as quickly as possible. I'm not looking for a meeting the day he died. Obviously.

I'm looking for the day of the funeral . . . and . . . found it. Dang it. That day is blank.

But it's *completely* blank. No meetings whatsoever. Even the funeral isn't on there.

So maybe . . . Merle has a personal calendar? Where he keeps records of funerals and side hustle meetings with henchmen?

Hench*people*, I correct myself. The patriarchy can suck it.

Now that I think about it, that *would* make sense. If I was a murderer, I'd keep a secret calendar for my murdering to-dos instead of the official one my assistant manages. Damn. Wonder if I can somehow break into his back office . . .

Tasha catches the look on my face, thankfully misunderstands, and makes a sympathetic noise. "Sorry that didn't help with your mission."

"It's okay," I say, quickly. "I'll let the brother know. Thanks for your seven seconds." I meant it to come out flirty, but it sort of just sounds sad. All this lying, for what?

She's looking at me intently, and I'm *sure* she's seeing right through me, and I'm sweating right into my sleek fashion T-shirt that shows off my clavicle—but then she puts a hand on my arm and says gently, "You know, it's possible *you* were the one who heard his last words. Do you remember the last thing he said to you?"

And suddenly, I do remember. He was spitting venom about the fact that I'd stopped him from running over that kid, and the very last thing he said to me was that he was friends with the alderman.

And that the alderman knew where I lived.

It wasn't an idle threat.

Cran knew Merle could make people disappear.

The vibes just keep piling up! If only I could find some freaking *proof*.

I can feel Merle's presence at the back of the office, and as I reach out to grab the pickled okra calendar, I see that my hand is shaking. I'm not being as cool about all this as I planned.

And I'm not the only one who notices.

"Hey," Tasha says softly and turns my chin so we're forehead to forehead. "What's really going on, Mo?"

Shit.

I didn't mean for this to be a whole thing. It was just going to be a teeny tiny forgettable lie along with some light calendar forgery. But now I feel miserable, and that teeny tiny lie is taking up all the space between us. Not even the lie *itself*; it's the fact that I lied to her at all. If I want to actually date her, I have to stop lying.

And I do. I really want to date her. Desperately. Which is also kind of a revelation.

I have to fix this.

Time to bring the walls down for the second time today.

"Don't be mad," I say, keeping my voice quiet but talking fast, so

I don't chicken out. "I haven't been totally honest with you. I'm not here to find Cran's last words."

"Aha," she says softly. "I thought it might be—"

"I'm here because of *Claudia*, who is dead from legit murder."

Tasha blinks rapidly. "And Claudia is . . ."

"*Was.* Wait, let me back up real quick. Claudia was bribed and *then* murdered—but she never got the money. I have it. Temporarily. I put it inside a statue in Claudia's basement. But it's Tond's money—that's Cran's brother, Tond—and if I can keep Tond safe, I get to keep the money. As a payment, not a bribe. I'm not someone who takes bribes, that's one thing you should know about me."

I pause to make sure that sinks in, but it's hard to tell because Tasha's just frowning at me. I try to take things a little slower. "To keep Tond safe, I have to figure out who killed Claudia, which I know is *technically* outside the scope of my crossing guard duties, but it's also kind of a public service if you think about it that way? Especially since the gas company is apparently full of hit men, and . . ." I take a deep breath for this last bit. "All of the clues I've found are pointing to—I'm very sorry to say this—Merle."

She squints at me.

"What I'm saying," I whisper, "is that Merle merldered—uh, *murdered*—Claudia."

I feel like I laid it all out pretty well, but Tasha still looks confused.

"I . . . I-I thought . . ." she stammers. "I thought you wanted to talk about our relationship."

"Oh," I say. "OH."

"Yeah."

"Like a—"

"Like a 'what are we' or perhaps a 'do you have time for a relationship' type conversation."

"OH. Wow. Yes. You know what? Let's do that instead. We can circle back to murder."

"I'm at work, Mo."

I nod, deeply relieved that she's not dumping me, even though I lied a teensy bit. I totally made the right choice to tell the truth afterward. "We'll stick to murder for now. Relationship talk later."

"I don't want to be rude or anything," she says, "so I'm asking this in the least stigmatizing way I possibly can: Is it possible you have been prescribed a medication that you aren't taking?"

"I really hope we'll get to know each other better," I say, squeezing her arm tenderly, "so another fun fact about me is that I always take the full dose of any medication I'm ever prescribed."

"Ah."

"So back to the murder stuff: I know it's a lot to take in," I say.

"Mo," she says, not unkindly, "this isn't old-school Chicago. There aren't hit men at the gas company anymore. Actually, I'm not sure that was ever a thing. There are rules and laws and checks and balances. One of which is *me.* I know everything that happens in the office. I would have known if Merle was . . . killing people."

"You don't believe me," I say, my heart deflating in my chest.

She bites her lip, like she's wrestling with something for a minute, and then says, "I want you to have faith in city government, but I also want you to feel heard." She blushes a little bit and then clears her throat. "Truth is, Merle's a little out of it these days. Val and I are kind of picking up the slack." She puts her hand on my arm. "Only temporarily; I swear he's not always like this."

I shiver. "Like what?"

She holds up a finger and then calls, "Merle? I've got a constituent who wants to meet you."

"*Tasha!*" I squeak.

I know there's fight or flight, but is there also pee your pants a little?

Seriously, what is she doing?

"Oh goody!" calls a booming voice from the back. "Never miss the chance to meet a voter!"

And following that is about three solid, uncomfortable minutes of clanking, banging, and groaning noises. When Merle finally emerges from the back office, I see him for the first time: a small, rosy-cheeked, gray-haired man, who hobbles his way past the cubicles, leaning on crutches that he's using to accommodate, that's right, *the giant cast on his entire right leg.*

"Here, let me help," Tasha says.

"Now, Tasha, I'm not a feeble old man," he says, just as he catches one of the crutches on the floor and nearly goes down. "I have to figure this out by myself."

"What happened to you?" I ask. "Er, Your Honor."

He shakes his head. "I was at a funeral last weekend, and the stairs out front—woooowee. It's like they're trying to get more business, if you know what I mean!" He winks at me.

Tasha laughs awkwardly and then mimes popping a pill, nodding at Merle.

Holy cow, *what.* Merle does DRUGS? My mind is spinning a million miles a minute. This is bad. This means digging up dealers, sticking my nose into a seedy underbelly of the city I hadn't even considered—

Wait. She's miming *painkillers.* For the leg. Got it.

"So . . . you fell down the stairs at the funeral?" I ask, making absolutely sure I understand.

"Broke my leg in two places. I got the hardware to prove it!" He knocks on his cast and nearly topples over. Tasha helps prop him back up. "I got screws, nuts, bolts, the whole megillah!"

I echo what he said. "You broke your leg in two places."

He frowns. "Well, in one place. The funeral home."

"And the screws . . . you got those at the hospital?"

"Well, I didn't get 'em from Ace Hardware!" He guffaws at this and then squints at me. "Did I?"

I shake my head. "I think they're different screws."

He nods, then turns to Tasha. "What am I doing out here?"

"Meeting a voter," Tasha says. "This is Mo Ellery."

"Hi. So," I say. "Bear with me, I'm really interested in, um, how fast injuries heal—"

Merle's face lights up; it's like he just got new batteries. "Always a pleasure! Just ignore this cast. I was at a funeral last weekend, and the stairs of that place—woooowee. It's like they're trying to get more business, if you know what I mean!" He winks at me.

I open my mouth to tell him he already said all that, but then he starts the whole bit over *again*. Tasha elbows me and gives me a look.

Welp.

My dude is *out of it*.

The alderman rambles on while I do some quick mental calculations. The funeral and Merle's broken leg happened Saturday. Claudia's garbled text ("*investigate alderman office*") came in Sunday evening, when she was delirious from gas poisoning and too weak to do anything about her overaggressive autocorrect. And then, according to the first responder gas guys, she was dead within hours.

Merle couldn't have killed her *himself*, because he was in the hospital during the critical stretch of time—the two or three hours before her death. And I know Merle didn't tell *Tond* to kill her; that Funeral Deep Throat conversation was just about bribery.

So the other option is that Merle told someone *else*, a *different* henchman, to kill Claudia.

Seems risky, not to mention complicated, putting separate henchpeople on a murder operation and a bribery operation against the same person at the same time. But then again, I've never murdered before so what do I know.

The honest truth is, I'm grasping at straws here. I have precisely zero leads.

Nuts.

"Hey, Tasha," I whisper, "I should probably head out—"

"Oh, Merle, for chrissakes, listen to yourself—" A woman's voice snaps me out of my reverie.

"Lesliebear?" Merle says, breaking off from his leg-breaking story and blinking into the air. "Is that you?"

Leslie from the funeral comes around a cubicle wall—and wait, *Lesliebear*? Is that the drugs talking? Or is he one of those politicians who gives everyone a nickname? Can I suggest my own? I have thoughts.

Charlie extracts himself from the dogpile and limps over to her.

"Oh hello, Charlie," Merle says affectionately. "Have you met Charlie?"

I nod.

"He's a champ, yes, he is, aren't you, kiddo?" Merle tries to pet him, nearly losing his balance again. "I'm kind of the third wheel in this family," he says in a stage whisper.

Tasha steps in to help prop the alderman up.

"This is Leslie," Merle introduces us. "My wife."

Ohhhhh. *Wife.* Not a general nickname guy.

So much for picking my own nickname. I hardly knew ya, GeneralissiMo.

"I am *also* your chief of staff," Leslie reminds him before reaching into the giant fanny pack she's wearing and pulling out a dog treat that Charlie instantly scarfs up. Embarrassingly, the poodles also pop up and swarm her for their share.

"*Manners*," I hiss, but to my chagrin, they completely ignore me.

Leslie, meanwhile, holds a treat up in the air and all three of my guys sit obediently. She winks at me. "I guess my real job is Dog Mom Extraordinaire!"

"My job is more like Dog Mom Mediocre," I say sadly, pronouncing *mediocre* so it rhymes with *extraordinaire*. If I have to be humiliated, I want to be cute while I do it.

"Nonsense!" Leslie says, giving the poodles a nod of grandmotherly approval. "After everything they've gone through, these guys look *really* fat. In a happy way! You're doing such a good job." She puts a hand on my shoulder and smiles kindly. "Better than that Benny character ever did."

Well. That's nice. Finally, some appreciation.

"Are you *crying*?" Tasha whispers.

"*No*," I whisper back. It's not just Leslie. It's also the relief of the Merle-as-murderer theory turning into a dead end. Hopefully, Tond will still pay me.

I'm trying to figure out how to get Leslie to be my friend and give me more compliments *without* sounding needy, but I don't get the chance because just then, the front door creaks open, and my new bff, the Dog Mom Extraordinaire, starts screaming.

CHAPTER 29

HANNAH HAWKS!!!" Leslie screams.

Holy shit! My *old* bff! Two besties in one place! Let's gooooo!

The dogs all start barking, and Hannah, who has just pushed open the door, looks like she is about one second from turning on her heels and running in the opposite direction, green screen in hand.

"Hannah!" I say and dash over to pull her into the office. I'm about to introduce her to Tasha, when Leslie somehow manages to slip between us, enveloping Hannah in a huge hug.

Okay, but I kinda wanted that hug. From, like, both of them.

"Hi," Hannah says, glaring over Leslie's head at me like I maybe did this on purpose. I shake my head, but it's hard to convey complex topics like "I had no idea this was going to happen but trust me she's SO nice and also do you want to meet the girl I maybe possibly have a thing with?" from a head shake.

"You changed my life!" Leslie cries, clasping Hannah way too tightly.

"You're . . . welcome?" she manages.

I've known Hannah was internet famous, but this is the first time I've actually seen the evidence in front of me. It's pretty impressive how emotional Leslie is right now, and I try to push down my feelings of inadequacy.

And also, I can't help but notice Hannah's being a little bit rude again? Like how she was when my parents were gushing about her success earlier today? I would kill to have someone gush about how much I changed their life.

The only thing *my* great ideas and dedication got me was a low-wage crossing guard gig, a depressingly single life after a failed decade-long relationship, and a murder investigation that I've just realized I have no handle on whatsoever.

Then my eyes drift over to Tasha and I reconsider the "depressingly single" bit.

"Hannah, this is Leslie, Alderman Carey, and Tasha," I say, trying to put a little emphasis on "Tasha."

Leslie finally pulls away, and she is absolutely beaming.

"Leslie Carey, chief of staff," Leslie says to Hannah. "But my real job is Dog Mom Extraordinaire." She winks at Hannah, exactly like she did with me. It's silly, but that stings. "SO great to meet you IRL." She turns to Merle. "That means 'in real life.'"

For his part, Merle is starting to look like a man who's accidentally walked into a gynecologist's exam room. He glances back toward his office distractedly, and says, "I'm sure I've got some . . . paperwork back there. Stay safe, everyone. And don't forget to vote."

Then, crutches scraping against the floor, he makes the longest, most awkward exit I have ever seen.

While I watch Merle go, Leslie is regaling Hannah with all the ways Hannah's UPGRADE training has changed her life and helped her be her best, most assertive self, and when the alderman disappears into his office, I turn my full attention back to them, only to discover that Hannah's shooting me some pretty serious rescue-me looks. Which, I don't know, isn't having nice old lady fans gush over your work the whole point of being internet famous?

But Hannah did come all the way here for me, so I do my part. "I'm *so* sorry to interrupt, but we have some important business to attend to," I say to Tasha and Leslie, which I really hate because Hannah hasn't even gotten to talk to Tasha or, like, appreciate how hot she is.

"Do you have to?" Leslie asks, clearly crushed.

"Unfortunately," I say, collecting the dogs. "You know what they say—the internet never sleeps!"

Leslie nods solemnly. "They do say that, don't they?"

"Yep," Hannah and I reply at the same time.

Then she gives Hannah one last appreciative hug while I turn to Tasha.

"I'll text you," I say.

"Please do," Tasha says in a tone of voice I can't quite figure out. "Would love to . . . finish what we started."

I'm *really* hoping she means in a sexy way and not a "you're a paranoid weirdo, I'm done" way. Just because I was wrong about her boss doesn't mean I'm wrong about everything. I turn to wave as I walk out of the door, but she's already notarizing, absently pushing back the one strand of hair falling across her face. Dreamiest Notary Public in all the land. Sigh.

Out on the sidewalk, Hannah's walking quickly, and I have to jog to catch up. The three dogs trot along with me.

"You're so popular! So famous!" I say as Hannah speed walks ahead of me. "And isn't that lady nice? She told me I was doing a great job with the dogs—"

"What is the deal with these dogs, Mo?" she says curtly over her shoulder.

"I told you," I say. "They're just temporary."

She stops abruptly and turns to face me. "We need to talk."

"Yeah, fine. That's what we're doing," I say, and it comes out harshly because I'm annoyed, but I can't explain why except in a way that makes me sound like a jealous asshole. "What's up?"

"There," she says, waving toward Dickie's Tavern a few storefronts away.

"Maybe we should go to a park or something?" I say. "As you so astutely observed, I am the guardian of three dogs right now."

"Dogs are allowed," she says, pointing to a sign on the exterior that says *Doggos Welcome*. "And I need a drink."

We slide into a booth and the three dogs curl up under the table, surprisingly without any fuss. It's the same booth I sat in with Tasha, which makes me feel all warm and fuzzy and proprietary and excited to tell Hannah all about it. Finally I have something to report that will make her proud, and, more specifically, that isn't about murder.

We have beers in front of us—not the beers we ordered, of course, but Hannah doesn't seem to care because she's already housing her pint.

Now that I have a second to notice, it looks like she hasn't slept. Her eyes are puffy and her usually glossy brown hair is pulled back in a rough pony. Her vintage sundress looks stylish at first glance, but up close it's wrinkled like she's been sleeping in it, and her bra straps are sticking out awkwardly. They don't match the dress at all.

I realize with a start: My bff is rattled by something. And even though my first reaction is, *Guess she's not so perfect after all*, I obviously mean it in a *good* way. What's the point in keeping the bar so high that you can't even be a real person?

"You look terrible," I say approvingly.

"Um—"

"And I know you barely got to meet her, but that was Tasha! The hot chick with the glasses."

Hannah looks lost. "What?"

"Remember? The girl I maybe might have a thing with? My steamy government conquest? My spicy civil hookup? My risqué municipal bang?"

She just blinks and I'm not sure why she isn't giving me credit for this incredibly mature step I've taken of not just pining away for Chris nonstop. I thought this was what she wanted.

"I *told* you about her," I say. "She's super cool and smart and a ton of fun—"

"Your rebound." Hannah nods, glancing at her phone. "Right."

I feel like I've been slapped across the face. That's it? That's all she's got to say? What happened to the Hannah who demands every little detail? Who actually cares about my stuff and not just her own empire?

"What, got a new collab in your DMs? Too big-time to be happy for me?" I snap, regretting it almost instantly, but not willing to take it back either. Sometimes the truth sucks.

"Are you *kidding*?" she asks incredulously and then throws her hands in the air. "I wouldn't know what to be happy *for*. Do you realize we only ever talk when you need something from me? You've turned into a completely different person! A person with three dogs! Who does that?"

"I'm still the same person under all the dogs!" I say defensively. "And I told you, they're tempora—"

"Seriously, let's just look at the last twenty-four hours." She starts counting on her fingers. "Yesterday, you didn't call me when you said you would. This morning, when I *came to your corner with your favorite coffee*, you blew me off and made me run errands for you, made me lie to Eva about the green screen because you're too scared of her to just ask her yourself and then conveniently forget that I specifically asked you to make some time for me—"

"I'm here now, aren't I?"

Hannah shakes her head. "I've spent so much time trying to be a good friend to you, and you know what? I'm starting to think it's not worth it."

"Ouch, Han."

"I have *followers* who are better friends to me!" she says, her voice rising.

"Well, sucks to be them since clearly you don't give a shit about your fans," I say, my voice rising too. "You're just using them to enhance your brand."

She gasps. "I am not *using* anyone."

"Oh for *sure*," I say. "It's not selfish at all. Like Leslie just now, who's so sweet and clearly adores you, and you can't give her a second of your time? Even though she's clearly bought in to the whole stupid UPGRADE thing."

"Oh, my 'stupid UPGRADE thing' that got you a new life when you were fired and dumped on the same day?"

"I hate this new life!" I explode, letting go of all my frustration at trying to make my life, to make ME, more perfect, more like Hannah. "I did everything you said, and all it's done is ruin everything!"

We glare at each other for a second.

"Seriously, Mo? You don't need my help to ruin everything. It's kind of your whole vibe. Here," she says, tossing the folded-up green screen at me. "I *selfishly* spent like seventy-five bucks on rideshares today and *selfishly* stole this green screen and *selfishly* waited for you to finish flirting with your rebound girlie after I *told* you I needed to talk." Tears are running down her face, and she wipes her nose roughly. "I did all of that when I should've been taking care of myself and contacting the police about my stupid stalker." She slides across the booth, and I put my hand out to stop her.

"Wait, Hannah," I say. "You have a *stalker*? Like a real stalker? Are you okay?"

She blinks away tears. "I've tried to talk to you about this. You just didn't listen."

I rack my brain. Did she try to talk to me about this? I cannot remember. Am *I* the selfish one?

She shakes her arm free and scoots out of the booth, leaving me there to clutch the green screen and feel like maybe she was right. Maybe I am the worst possible friend.

No. I'm not letting her walk out like this, not for anything. I peel my thighs off the vinyl seats with a weak little cry and stand up.

"Hannah, stop," I say. And she does stop. She stops and turns to look at me, hand on hip.

I'm about to apologize for being a shitty, clueless friend. I'm about to beg her to please come back and sit with me, tell her I'll buy her another round, and we'll figure out what to do about her stalker, I really am. I'm just trying to figure out *how* to say it.

And that's precisely when the door to Dickie's opens, and Benny walks in.

BENNY.

Relief hits me like a tidal wave. I can't manage to say anything, not a word, but I do break into a *huge* smile, despite the fact that Benny is glaring daggers at me, which I definitely deserve.

Only when Hannah groans do I remember that I was about to be a good friend.

"Grow up, Mo," she says, looking between me and Benny. She blows past him with no idea who he is, because maybe she's right and I am a completely different person under all the dogs.

And then she's gone.

Benny claps a hand on my shoulder, and not in a friendly way.

"Hello there," he says. "Drinks on you."

CHAPTER 30

Benny orders a red wine. At Dickie's. Which, again—*dive bar.* But I suppose I'm not really in a position to give him shit about it. And maybe because he's a regular with a Polaroid on the wall, the bartender actually gives him the drink he orders, even if it is straight from the fridge. Meanwhile, I get a Coors Light by ordering a Guinness.

I feel sick about Hannah. I promise myself I'll make it up to her as soon as possible; I'll tell her everything. But first, I have to talk to Benny.

I can't stop staring at him, just to confirm he's actually safe. The dogs are equally thrilled to see their guy. Louis clambers up on the seat and rests his chin on Benny's shoulder with a contented sigh. Benny puts an arm around him like they're on a date, looks the dog over, and then frowns at me. He opens his mouth to say something, but I get there first.

"Let's just clear the air here," I say, palms up in a sign of defeat. "I'm sorry I got you arrested. But, on the bright side, I *also* figured out you were innocent and indirectly helped get you released."

"And you really think those two things balance each other out, huh?"

"You looked suspicious in that doorbell footage." My voice feels small, and I instinctively shrink back as Benny leans forward.

"Suspicious?" His voice is hard. "I was smelling *gas*. When I opened the mail slot, I knew something was wrong, and I had to get the dogs away and call 911. That's what you were seeing in the doorbell video. That's what you sent the cops."

"You know, *technically* Marlowe sent it to the cops."

"WHAT?"

Oops, no, I'm making this worse.

"I thought I was solving Claudia's murder."

"Claudia was my *friend*," Benny says.

"Exactly! If I'd been at the wrong place at the wrong time with an obscene amount of money you might have had me arrested too!"

He looks lost. Which, honestly, is better than angry. "What money?"

I quickly catch him up on the investigation. The money that was in the envelope he delivered. How I thought he was the murderer, then Tond, then Merle. How I have no idea who the murderer is anymore.

"But it definitely wasn't an accidental gas leak," I say as gently as I can. "She figured something out, and it got her killed, whatever it was." Something nags at the back of my mind, but I can't quite see it. Something I'm missing.

There's a long pause. I take a pull off my Coors Light while Benny processes all of this, and finally, he lets out a low whistle. "Holy shit."

"Yeah. It's a mess."

"If the murder got pinned on me, I'd have been so screwed." He gets a haunted, faraway look in his eyes. "Did you know, the toilet is just in the middle of the holding cell. And if you have to poop, everyone can see?"

"Did you? Have to poop?"

He turns a deep shade of red.

No more questions, Your Honor.

Benny shoots the rest of his wine and motions for me to get him another one. I suppose I owe him. When I return with his icy cold Merlot and slide back into the booth, he asks, "So who's left on your list of suspects?"

I wince. "My list is currently a little unimpressive." AKA nonexistent.

"Hit me."

"Well, if we're assuming Claudia's garbled text is right and the alderman's office is somehow involved, then I guess everybody who works there could be a suspect?"

He leans in, eyebrows raised.

"Except Tasha," I say quickly. "*Obviously.* And Leslie. I had high hopes for Merle, but it's not him either. So."

He gives me a look.

"I'm *working* on it, sheesh," I say, but I get his point. I'm chasing my tail right now. "How about . . . tell me everything you know about the alderman's office. Who else is generally around? I've only been there a couple times, but you walk Charlie, you must know things."

"Nothing useful. The assistants are the heart and soul of that place. Merle's been in office so long, he kinda phones it in, and Leslie, well . . . chief of staff in name only. She's only got eyes for Charlie." He shakes his head.

"We love her," I say firmly. I will not have two people shitting on my new friend Leslie, fellow Dog Mom Extraordinaire. Not today. "Anything else?"

"Okay. Well, Sunday morning, when I got there early to walk Charlie, Merle wasn't around. That lady gave me the envelope to drop off at Claudia's."

I look up from the dregs of my Coors Light. "What lady?"

"The one in the suit."

The *lady*? *In the suit?*

Val. Has to be.

"Beige suit?" I say.

He shrugs. "I don't remember, it's been kind of an intense couple of days."

I ignore the subtle burn. Val is not exactly a cuddly person, but HOW uncuddly is she? *Murder* uncuddly? Maybe. I try to recall every detail of my short encounter with her. Kind of snotty. Doesn't like pickles.

And, hang on—she was walking out the door *with a thick brown envelope*. Exactly the kind of brown envelope that some quote-unquote lady in a suit gave to Benny.

"What did she say when she gave it to you?" I ask.

He shrugs. "I think she said, 'here, take this.'"

"That's it? That's all you've got?"

"Once again: I've been very preoccupied getting myself out of jail," he says, sounding cranky.

"Could she maybe have said, 'take this *or else*'?" I ask. "Something sketchy like that?"

He chugs his second wine and pushes the empty glass over at me. "Why are you doing this?"

"Getting you bottomless refills?" I ask. "I'm hoping you'll forget I did a *Shawshank Redemption* to you."

"No, why are you investigating Claudia's murder?"

"Oh." That's a very fair question. I decide to leave out the part about Tond giving me the money—I don't think Benny would approve. And I also don't tell him that I'm haunted by the fact that I could have saved Claudia if I'd just convinced her to wait for Cran's autopsy before she went off the rails with a murder investigation. I should *also* leave out the bit about Mierzwiak and my possible status as dog thief. Yes, fine, I'm leaving out a lot. We're still getting to know each other!

"Well," I say, "I'm trying to do my civic duty. I've called the cops at every possible point—"

"I heard." Benny raises an eyebrow.

"—and it has never ever helped. In fact, it only made it worse." After a quick but vicious internal debate, I go ahead and tell him the reason I've only half admitted to myself this whole time. "I guess I feel like I owe it to Claudia. *Someone* has to find out what happened to her."

I don't want to see the look on his face, so I grab his empty glass and head back to the bar for the third time. And I think I need another beer too.

While I wait for the drinks, I force down the wave of guilt that was about to overtake me and review the facts: I now have exactly one lukewarm lead. Room-temperature lead, if I'm honest with myself. I suppose Val *is* semi-connected with the cursed construction site by virtue of working at Merle's office, but other than being a big B, she's got no real motive that I can see yet.

More kickbacks? Is it kickbacks all the way down?

A polite little bark makes me look back over to our booth, where I see Benny and Jacques engaged in a game of pattycake. Even when he's making dogs do tricks, Benny manages to look stupidly hot. Jean licks one of Benny's biceps and I realize I would also like to do that.

Stop.

I do not need any more complications in my life. Probably.

The bartender clears her throat and as I spin around, she gives me a judgmental look and pushes the drinks over to me, bumping against a bowl of matchbooks. I pick the drinks up and head back to the table, realizing there's something I've never cleared up.

"Can you think of a reason Cran might have come to Dickie's?" I say, sliding into the booth. "Doesn't seem like his kind of place."

"Yeah, he came here to fire me as the poodles' handler," Benny says bitterly. "Wouldn't tell me why, just that it was 'time to move into the twenty-first century.' I tried to tell him it has been the twenty-first century for a really long time already, but he wouldn't listen. Anyway, he wanted to meet in public, but somewhere no one knew him, in case I went berserk and/or embarrassed him. His words."

Damn. Well, that settles that, I guess. Why can't any of my loose ends lead somewhere good?

Benny gives Lou a scratch behind the ears and sighs. "Cran would roll over in his grave if he saw what you've done to these guys."

"By that do you mean caring for them and giving them a good home when no one else would?"

"They're filthy and their hair is all knotted, and they're getting fat. Are you still feeding them pepperoni?"

"They're fat *and happy*," I say defensively. "I've been told that's a good thing."

"They're *elite* competitors, Mo, not lapdogs. Jacques kills it in agility, Jean is, well, okay, Jean is more of a Miss Congeniality type, but Louis here had a real shot at winning *another* Best in Show at the Great American Dog Show this year, which could get him ranked nationally. They are a *B Fucking D*!"

"Well, I am not a *D Fucking T*," I say defensively. He stares at me, confused. "Dog Fucking Trainer. Actually, that sounds awful. Forget I said that. Look, you and Claudia *made* me take them, and I'm doing the best I can."

"Are you even trying to keep up with their grooming?" he asks.

"I can barely keep up with *my* grooming, Benny. I'm not spending my pepperoni money just to have a bunch of fashion dogs."

"It's not for fashion," he protests. "It's a *health* thing. They have to get professionally groomed."

"Right. And how much does a dog spa cost, out of curiosity?" I ask.

Benny grimaces. "Um, about a hundred bucks. Maybe one twenty-five."

"*Each??*"

"Plus tip."

I look at the green screen crumpled up on the seat next to me. I have *got* to get on those videos. Between Sheila and apology drinks and friggin' dog haircuts, I'll be broke by the end of the month if I don't get the eleven-point-five grand. God I need that money.

Literally a month ago, I had none of these kinds of problems. A surge of loss hits me as I realize how much I miss my old life.

Ah shit, now my eyes are burning, but there's no way in hell I'm going to cry in front of Benny. I rub my face like I'm just really tired and not crying and hope my eyes haven't already gotten puffy.

Benny doesn't notice. He's tipsy and getting nostalgic and starts reminiscing about Claudia. He's an artist, which is how he and Claudia met; he draws and paints portraits (*not* nudes, he assures me) and she, well, clearly loved *The Legend of Zelda*, and he happily modeled for her (again, *not* in the nude—"just topless," he says, blushing).

It's bittersweet—they're good stories, she was a fun, kooky old lady, and I wish I'd gotten a chance to know her better. But the thrill of Benny being out of jail has long since waned, and I can barely even fantasize about him posing topless. Now I'm just in a funk about the sad state of my broke-ass life, and really I just want to leave and crawl into bed and try to sleep for once this week.

Plus, there's that nagging feeling at the back of my head that I can't seem to shake. Probably just the reality of my inevitable SECOND eviction of the year.

That's when it occurs to me—I could take a *loan* on the eleven-point-five K. Just a teensy one? Like a payday advance. A down payment. Earnest money. That's a thing, right?

Because if I can't get through the month financially, then I can't solve this murder. I feel like Tond would understand that. And if I had his phone number, I would totally tell him.

I wrap up our conversation a little abruptly, but Benny is, at this point, many *many* cold red wines in and doesn't notice. We hug goodbye, so I guess we're friends now, and I feel my mood on an upswing as I head over to Claudia's with the dogs.

We sneak into her backyard through the alley, across the disheveled lawn, and creak open the bulkhead doors. The four of us trundle down the dusty concrete steps by the light of my phone, and I shine the beam over to the messed-up Benny statue—

—whose abs are open to the world.

No envelope in sight.

No eleven-and-a-half K.

Nothing.

Nada.

I give the chest cavity a good scour, sticking my hand in, and feeling up into the inside of messed-up Benny, behind his ribs all the way to his neck.

Nope.

It's gone.

My body goes hot and then cold. What. The. Fuck.

The dogs won't stay still, like they sense something.

"What do you smell?" I whisper, scouring the shadows.

They don't answer, and I can't breathe. And there are no paper bags anywhere.

All I wanted was a dang *loan*, and now I'm in a creepy basement with a possible lurking murderer. They could murder me right now.

How long will it take for anyone to notice I'm missing? Days?

How long would it be before someone found my body?

It is a depressing state of affairs that the person who will care most about my absence is definitely Sheila.

My only hope right now is that whoever was here has already left. Please *please* have already left.

"Is anyone there?" My voice sounds hollow in the darkness.

Nobody answers. I fumble for my phone, and the flashlight throws creepy shadows around the workspace, but no one's skulking in the dark. I wait for my heart rate to slow.

"All right, guys," I say to the dogs, trying to keep it upbeat for all our sakes. "What do you say we really quickly look for clues and then go eat a lot of ice cream to calm our nerves?"

Jean sits and offers to shake my hand.

Okay, so he does know a few tricks after all.

And since I, too, am motivated not just by my impending potential murder, but also by ice cream, I get on with my snooping.

But for what kind of clue, exactly?

I poke around as fast as I can, digging through filing cabinets and scoping out random papers on the workbench, but it's all drawings of grown-up Link from different angles (some of them in various states of undress: *very* imaginative, Claud). All her art supplies, already gathering dust.

I kneel down and shine my light sideways on the floor because I saw that on a show once, but the only footprints I see are ours.

I can feel myself getting more desperate. Nothing appears to have been moved since I was here last. Except the money, obviously.

The cellar is totally clue-less.

Just like me.

The poodles and I climb the stairs to the outside, where I shut the bulkhead doors carefully behind us. While the dogs romp through the yard, I flop down into the tall, buggy grass and try not to hyperventilate.

Who took the money? I have to open my mind to all possibilities.

So I picture Val in her beige suit sneaking down and grabbing the money.

Then I imagine the same with Merle, stumbling over his crutches.

Then Benny, snagging some oil paints on his way out.

Tond, sobbing the whole time.

But here's the problem—*nobody* knew where the money was.

Sweat prickles my forehead. My throat starts closing up. Is it hot out here?

Almost nobody.

There was one person I trusted. Someone who works closely with the alderman. Someone who works early and late and on SUNDAYS. Someone who knows everything that happens in the office. Someone friendly and smart. And sexy.

That lady gave me the envelope . . .

The one in the suit . . .

It feels like the ground beneath me falls away as I put the pieces together.

I didn't tell anyone where I hid the money.

Except for Tasha.

CHAPTER 31

Well, this suuuuuuucks.

Tasha took the money.

I've only just made the frankly *devastating* connection when something with the heft of an alley rat skitters across my ankles and I leap up, making a break for the back gate as if I need air, as if I'm not already outside, as if I can outrun this discovery. I start walking fast, and the dogs trot to keep up. I half-heartedly collect their leashes as I bombard myself with questions. Does that mean Tasha also killed Claudia? No, that can't be. Can it? Could she do that and also be so amazing?

My eyes blur.

This whole time, I thought she was the hero, the champion of the underdog, but damn, it sure seems like she's the villain.

I try to make it make sense. She is a total workaholic. She works on *weekends*.

Now that I think about it, the only times I see her are when I go to the alderman's office, or if she's coming from or going to work.

She loves her job and clearly props Merle up when he's struggling, sometimes literally. And it also tracks that she'd buy into a break-a-few-eggs-to-make-an-omelet philosophy.

Even if the omelet is a stupid parking garage?

Jean nudges my hand impatiently, and I give him a pat. "All right, yeah, ice cream."

Fifteen minutes later, we are the proud owners of a couple pints from the corner store. I've settled into my pink velour chair, a bowl full of slowly melting ice cream sitting next to me, while over in the designated "kitchen" area of my one room, the dogs are devouring their regular dry food with a tiny bit of ice cream on top. Hopefully, Benny can't get too mad about that.

I eat a spoonful of my fave—the peanut butter with jelly swirls—but I barely register its reassuring chemical tang.

Because I know what I have to do. I pull out my phone and type a quick message.

Me: Hey Tasha it's Mo. I mean, obviously, because my name came up. If I'm in your phone. Which I assume I am. Seeing as how you're in mine

Oh my god.

How am I so bad at this?

I try again.

Me: Wanna hang?

I almost hope I don't get a response. It would be easier.

But my phone pings immediately.

Tasha: Still at work, sorry!!! Crunch time

Me: Oh ha ha not like right now I meant tomorrow

Tasha: Oof tomorrow also a mess, what about weekend?

I know what'll get her to see me. Unfortunately, I don't want to do it any more than she does. My finger hovers over the text screen.

I've got to get that money back and figure out how Tasha is mixed up in all this.

Me: I think we need to have that what-are-we relationship chat. Sorry!!!

Ugh.

Tasha: Got it. Of course

Tasha: Will shuffle some things around. 6pm work? You name the place, I'll be there with bells on

Nope nope nope, don't think about Tasha wearing nothing but bells.

Crap.

Too late.

Okay, this has to happen somewhere I won't get distracted and try to jump her bones. And if I'm going to have the upper hand, I need to take her out of her element, out of the neighborhood. Somewhere no one knows her, where she might drop the act of dedicated public servant.

This is a job for the Petty Pig.

Memories flood my mind. The Pig is one of those rare coffee shops that stays open really late, so back in the good old days, when Chris had his overnight shifts, sometimes I'd play hooky from work and nap with him in the afternoon. We'd just lounge in bed, me wearing one of his old T-shirts, and then we'd throw on pants and go to the Petty Pig so he could get coffee and wake up for his shift at the hospital.

I hate remembering the good old days.

Especially when it seems like I've used all the good days up.

Petty Pig, South Loop? I text.

I pull the bowl of ice cream onto my lap, and, now that Hannah hates me and UPGRADE has ruined my life, I decide to look up my new inspirational guru.

I go to the Rodney O'Malley channel and open up the comments for the video titled, BEGGING THE QUESTION: EFFECTIVE INTERROGATION TECHNIQUES.

At precisely 6 p.m. the next day, Tasha peeks in through the door of the Petty Pig wearing a white V-neck tee, her hair in pigtails, and it takes every ounce of self-control I can muster to focus on the missing money and the possibility of her murdering Claudia. And specifically to *not* plaster my mouth all over her.

I wave at her from my place in line.

The Petty Pig, true to its name, reeks of stylish South Loop decor. White walls with one warm wood accent wall, vaguely industrial tables, and a few vine-y plants dotting the walls. But the baristas are chill, and the vibe is relaxed, and in the way back, there are several very private booths with tall seat backs and little plant canopies overhead, and tiny fountains and Zen rock gardens at each table. Each table is like your own mini spa, and—bonus!—the burbling of the fountain makes your conversation extra private. Not every coffee shop has a secluded nook where you can chat privately about corruption and murder.

I'm sweating so hard.

"This place is cool," Tasha says as she joins me in line.

What did she mean by that?

Does she know I know?

Why is my eye twitching?

"Oh yeah," I say vaguely. "I used to live around here."

The sexiest of her two eyebrows shoots up. "Ooh! You got a trust fund I don't know about?"

Oh no! Straight to money banter! According to the comments under the Rodney O'Malley video, any kind of friendly banter is good, because it can lead to a casual admission of guilt. But it's way too soon. I'm not ready! I'm one second from making a break for the door when the barista saves the day. "Can I help you?"

"Yes! Yes, *thank you*," I say, maybe a little too emphatically. "I'd like a chocolate croissant and a coffee and also a house red, please. And whatever she wants."

"Hey, thanks," Tasha says with a smile.

"No prob," I say. You can't investigate someone *and* ask them to pay for stuff. Even I know that.

We pick up our drinks and snacks from the counter (Tasha *also* gets a red wine—a good start to keep us both loose, perfect for interrogations I'm guessing, even though Rodney O'Malley didn't mention it), and we head straight for the hidden booths in back.

We're passing the first secluded booth when I hear a voice over the burbling of the table's personal fountain.

". . . *really* hard to do intermittent fasting when you're on call."

It's a familiar voice.

Really familiar.

"But on the plus side, there's no better appetite suppressant than two a.m. in the ER."

You have got to be kidding me.

Chris.

Perfect, of course he's here, right now. When I am also here.

This will be fine. I'll just stay the course. I am going to walk right by and pretend I never heard him. But then . . . there's a *second* familiar voice. Laughing at his dumb joke. And *that's* the one that stops me cold.

The wine glass sloshes in my hand, and suddenly I'm turning toward the booth. I really don't want to be doing this—stop doing this, Mo!—but I *can't* stop. And then, oh god, I'm roughly pushing aside the plant canopy to peek underneath.

I was right, obviously.

It's Kendra.

And she is not acting like the head of a marketing agency right now.

She has her fingers intertwined with Chris's.

She is wearing his faux vintage Bert & Ernie T-shirt from when they were remaking those like ten years ago, the one he sleeps in.

She is *feeding* him a piece of oatmeal raisin cookie, which, gross on *so many levels.*

I haven't seen her since I got fired. Actually, technically, I haven't seen her since I was butt naked on a Zoom call, exposing Chris's man meat to a bunch of tool execs.

Oh.

I get it.

That was their meet-cute. MEAT-cute.

WHAT THE ACTUAL FUCK!!

This all registers in the span of about a millisecond.

"Um, *hi*?" I say.

Chris squeaks in surprise.

"Mo, looks like this booth's taken," Tasha says with a frown.

"Ha ha, you're right," I say with an absolutely psychotic smile. "Pardon me, *strangers*."

I hustle Tasha to the farthest possible booth and try to hide us as comprehensively as possible beneath the greenery.

Focus focus focus.

This is not about Chris or Kendra. This is about corruption and murder and—

"I'm going to get some napkins," I say. "BRB!"

I duck out from under the canopy of vines before Tasha can say anything and slink back to Chris's table, looking over my shoulder to make sure she's not watching me.

I fling myself under their vine canopy again so I'm hovering over them with my ass sticking out the other side of the greenery.

"Oh! Hi! I guess it *was* Mo," Chris says to Kendra.

"Good to see you, good to see you, yeah great place for a hot date, I too am on a hot date," I blabber. "A KILLER date. Like—"

Don't do it, Mo. Don't—

I lick my finger and touch my hip with it and go *tssssssss* like my finger is putting out a fire.

Kendra coughs with embarrassment.

"You're on a date with *her*?" asks Chris, pointing in the direction of my table with Tasha, even though he can't see through the vines. He looks back at me, waggles his eyebrows, and then offers me a high five. "Nice! Way to aim high!"

Honestly, I was hoping for more regretful longing.

"Yeah," I say, bitterly finishing the high five. "It *is* nice. So. There's that."

I hover at the table for a second like a bisexual ghost of vengeance and then whisk away from whence I came.

Okay, that did not accomplish exactly what I was hoping for, which I guess was lots of apologies from both of them. Maybe a little coffee/red wine combo will help me come up with the perfect zinger. And in the meantime, back to the recon I've been prepping for.

"No napkins?" Tasha asks as I plop back down.

Shoot. Napkins.

"They're refilling the, ah, dispenser," I say. "So while that's happening, there's something I want to ask you."

She bites her bottom lip and I can't seem to look away. "Right. I'm ready."

"Remember when we were talking yesterday at your office?"

"Mm-hmm," she says.

"Well, I was just curious what you did after that."

There's a very long pause. She halfway smiles like she isn't sure, then tilts her head at me. "What?"

"You know." I try a casual laugh that accidentally sounds like a wild boar goring someone. "What did you get up to? Were you, like, around the neighborhood?"

"Yeah," she says slowly. "At work. As you know."

"Cool cool," I say. Rodney O'Malley's ease-in technique is harder than I expected.

"Why are you asking?" she asks.

"Becauuuuuse . . ." My brain goes blank and I forget the entire comments section I read last night, so I shoot my coffee and take a big bite of my croissant to buy time. It showers flakes all over me. "Mm."

"Listen, Mo," Tasha says, putting down her barely drunk wine. "I have an ex who was super jealous and controlling and hated that I loved my job, and I just—I can't do that again. Like, not ever. So if you need to know my whereabouts at all times, maybe it would be better if we just—"

"I'm not like that, I swear—" But then I interrupt myself, because this isn't *actually* a relationship negotiation and also more croissant is flaking out of my mouth. I should've gotten a muffin. "Thing is, I already know where you were."

"Right. At wo—"

"I know you took the money," I interrupt. "You're the only person, other than me, who knew where it was."

There. It's done.

Tasha does a double take. "The what?"

"The bribe money in Claudia's statue's abs," I clarify, my heart pounding. "The question I have now is, did you also kill Claudia?"

"Oh my god," she says slowly. "You're talking about murder again, aren't you? You catfished me here with a relationship talk. This isn't a *jealousy* thing, it's that after wrongly accusing my boss, now you're accusing *me*, the person who works for peanuts on purpose because she believes in the importance of helping people, of, what is it again? Stealing an envelope of bribe money from an old lady's basement, and—bonus round—possibly murdering her?"

Instead of answering right away, I take this opportunity to drink most of my wine. Because when she says it like that, a tiny little itsy-bitsy bit of doubt creeps in.

"That's the gist," I finally say.

"Mo—" She closes her eyes.

"The money is gone, and you're *the only person I told*. What am I supposed to think?"

"I don't know, maybe you could consider not getting tangled up in a fucking murder investigation! Mo, you are a crossing guard, not a secret agent. And playing at it, accusing innocent people of doing terrible things, is really, really shitty."

I wince because she's kind of yelling, and not in the hot date way I made it sound like to Chris. "You're the one who's always talking about civic responsibility!" I argue. "How is this different from what you do?"

"God, I take it back." She stands up. "I *wish* you were just a jealous girlfriend type. This is *so* much worse."

Her face is red and blotchy and she's about to cry. I really wish I'd gotten those napkins. And I guess I wish some other stuff too.

She levels a look at me and takes a ragged breath. "I didn't take the money. After you left, I was on a video call with the Chamber of Commerce for two hours. Go ahead and check my 'alibi' if you want." She grabs my phone and types a name and phone number in it, then thrusts it back to me. "I'm not a thief *or* a murderer, Mo, I'm a regular person trying to make this city better, and I thought you were too." She wipes her face roughly. "You know, I'm usually a pretty good judge of character. Guess I blew it this time." Tasha slides out of the booth, and then she's gone.

All the air goes with her.

I dig for my inhaler, cursing Chris for saying I don't need it. And even after I use it, my chest aches. This must be a record for me: only five minutes to lose the one good thing I had going. I want to chase after her, but what could I possibly say?

And—also pretty pressing—if she didn't take the money, who did? Maybe the gas company dropped in for another poke around? Maybe the murderer just casually came back to the scene of the crime and found it? *Or*—and I really hate this thought, almost as much as I hate myself for not thinking of it *before* accusing Tasha of stealing—*was the murderer watching me the whole time?*

Suddenly I'm not hungry for the rest of this croissant. My stomach revolts, and I very much regret housing both the wine and the coffee. I swing by the bathroom, and as I sit on the toilet, I run through the litany of possible fatal diseases that also cause a stomachache: Ebola (again, not in Chicago, not even when it was a thing in the US), sudden onset colon cancer (note to self: google this), food poisoning (unlikely because not usually fatal), oh and that new hotness: botulism.

I pause for a second.

Why would botulism only show up on my anxiety radar *now*? I mean, yes, the recent death notwithstanding, it seems like exactly the sort of condition I love to worry about. I sometimes stress about *leprosy* for crying out loud. But how did I never get around to worrying about botulism until somebody I knew died of it? I'm never usually this late to the game. I'm kind of a hypochondria vanguard, not to brag.

And then it hits me.

I run out of the stall and slam into Kendra who's on her way in. "Watch it," she says, before realizing it's me and blanching.

"I bet you'd like that," I say.

But it's good timing, because then I slide under the vines at Chris's booth and sit across from him. He flinches and then covers it with a smile. "Kendra just went to the—" he says feebly.

"Chris. I have a medical question for you," I say, all business. "How common is botulism?"

That takes him by surprise. "Botulism?"

"Yeah, you know. Terminal botulism."

"*Fatal.* Fatal botulism."

"Right. That's what I said. What are the chances of dying of botulism poisoning?"

"You're not going to get botulism, Mo." He sighs. "I thought we were done—"

"Spare me the lecture and answer the question. Please."

He cocks his head at me. "It's super rare. Like five cases a year, *maybe*."

"In Chicago?" I say.

"No, the whole country."

Whoa.

"Thanks." My whole body is buzzing as I run out of the Petty Pig.

What are the odds that an experienced canner and asshole perfectionist like Cran would make a mistake so *huge*? Well, the odds are five in however many people there are in the United States.

The odds are astronomically bad.

Which means that according to the odds, Cran almost certainly got murdered too.

Holy shit.

I walk down the sidewalk in a daze, threading my way through the suits and the corpos, the fashionistas and the yogis. As I climb the stairs to the train platform, every step up brings me closer to understanding.

It was always strange that Cran died in such a weird way. And heck, using botulism to murder somebody—contaminating Cran's beets or whatever—was genius, because *of course* it would look like an accident.

I suddenly remember what Tond said, that after the gas company delay went so long, his brother "almost gave up on the whole thing." If Cran backed out of the parking garage deal, then the deal was dead on arrival. DOA as they say. Just like Cran.

Interesting.

The train arrives and I step on, the door sliding shut behind me. At my seat, my phone dings with a new text from Chris. I'm ashamed that my heart does a little leap.

Chris: Just wanna say I think you look okay

Ah yes, the master of the compliment, that's Chris.

My phone pings again.

Chris: I mean, it might be a good idea to buy new makeup

Chris: Just like a product refresh

Chris: I don't think you need work yet. But Kendra has a groupon that's about to expire if you want it

Okay, what? Did I ask?? And it's not like Chris to neg so hard. I wonder if Kendra wrote the text.

I don't respond. Obviously.

But even that shitty text can't stop me from feeling the thrill/fear cocktail from this new break in the case.

YES!

Cran got murdered!

CHAPTER 32

Okay, that came out wrong.

It's not that I'm *thrilled* he got murdered, but I am SO pumped that I figured it out. I've got to tell somebody.

Me: Big news, Cran WAS murdered

I get an automated response.

Marlowe: By order of her tyrannical parents, Marlowe is currently not getting notifications. Will respond once workaround has been achieved.

Well, I guess it serves me right for having a sidekick capable of being grounded.

Good thing I have a backup sidekick.

Me: Drink? Dickie's?

Benny: Still hungover, can't afford to have you buy me more drinks

Me: Do I look like one of those rich crossing guards?

Benny: Also I'm sort of in the middle of something

Well, nuts.

But then my phone pings again.

Benny: You could come by here

Benny: Bring the dogs

Benny's place is only a few blocks from me, but it feels like a different world, and my jaw drops when he lets me into the largest studio I've ever seen, tucked away in a building that he says used to be a dance studio, and before that, a paint factory. It's got crumbly brick walls, tall ceilings, and dark wood beams overhead. One wall is a mirror with a bar running across it, which Benny says is great for when he's painting self-portraits.

The mirror *also* happens to be right across from the very sturdy-looking bed.

I mean, it's not on the ceiling *over* the bed, but . . . that could be hot.

WAIT A SEC, is it possible this is a booty call? I *am* a little tense. Sounds like just what the doctor ordered, honestly. A perfect way to make myself forget about how I ruined things with Tasha, so I can clear my mind and fully focus on the double murder aspect of things. I mean, if that's what it takes.

I decide to play it cool for now and spend the next moment focusing on the floor-to-ceiling windows that look out over the El tracks, as though it's a view I've always been deeply curious about. "Very nice, very nice," I say and keep moving around the room.

I guess it's a studio *and* a studio, so there's art and art supplies everywhere. Stacks of canvases lean against the walls. There are easels of all different sizes, including one that he seems to currently be working on right now, a sort of abstract cityscape that's dripping paint, but that's not the one I find myself in front of.

It's the half-finished painting of Claudia. I'm tearing up before I realize it.

Benny notices and comes to join me. "I know," he says softly. "I can't bear to put it away. Somehow if it stays in-progress, it's like she's not really gone."

I nod.

"So," I say, wiping my eyes. "What's your project tonight?"

"I'm in the middle of this one"—he points at the cityscape—"but sometimes it takes a while for an idea to really take shape in my head. I have to do a lot of staring, and I can sit around for days and not make much progress. That's why it's nice to walk dogs—I can still be in my head. But I figured if you came over, we could hang out and I could still be available for the muse."

"The *muse*?" I say, grinning.

"Don't worry, we're not monogamous," he jokes.

Helloooo I guess I don't need to play it *that* cool.

He is standing *really* close to me. I can practically feel those forearms flexing. But he doesn't make a move. I've never been part of a straight-up booty call before. Is there something *I* need to do, or is my showing up enough evidence that I'm interested?

"Cran got murdered," I blurt.

Nice, Mo. Very sexy.

He jerks back. "What?"

"Someone defiled his pickles," I say, trying really hard to thread that needle between murder investigation and possible hookup.

"Wow."

"Yup."

"I mean . . . really? *Wow.*"

Wow indeed. You could cut this sexual tension with . . . a really dull butter knife.

Oh well, now or never.

I step closer, slide my hand around the back of his neck, and lean in, lips first.

"Hang on, whoa!" he says, pulling away so fast I stumble and nearly headbutt him on the way down.

Ah. Not a booty call.

The humiliations pile up faster than bodies in this neighborhood, and that's saying a *lot.*

"Soooo you have a lot of art supplies," I say, staring at his shelves of paint and craft supplies so I don't have to look at him. "What's your, ah, favorite?"

"Mo," Benny says quietly. "I had no idea you were interested. I'm sorry if I led you on."

"No no," I say, my face hot enough to melt the ice cream I'm going to bury it in later. "My fault. I don't know why I did that. Force of habit, I guess."

"*Habit?*" Benny laughs. "Uh, thanks?"

It's true though. Since the moment Chris and I broke up, I've been on the prowl. I thought I was just massively horny but is that all it is? Holy crap, am I . . . afraid of being alone?

Dammit. I do *not* need more personal growth to think about right now.

I turn back and thrust out a hand. "Friends?"

"Yeah, obviously!" He hugs me. It feels good, actually, to not think of him that way. He pulls out of the hug and grins. "But if you don't start taking care of the dogs, I will call the cops on you."

He pats Jean's head, and I finally see what he's talking about. Their fur is gnarly and dirty and Jean has an actual pretzel stuck in there. Their legs are stubbly, and they look like they've gone feral.

I may be a hot mess, but they don't deserve to suffer for that.

Benny's shelves and shelves of art supplies aren't just paint—my eyes rest on a cubby of craft supplies, including wacky hair dyes, and a very bad idea hits me.

"Hey, does the muse allow you to do other projects while you're waiting on her feedback?"

It only took a little arguing before I got my way.

Turns out, Benny is a real pushover.

We're on the floor, on a tarp, and he's holding a pair of shears. I'm holding Louis XIV. Louis XIV is holding grudges.

There are puffs of dog hair all around us.

At first, Benny pointed out that he couldn't possibly give the dogs haircuts because he's "not a professional." We weren't going for conventional, I explained. We're going for punk.

I still had Cran's pickle-scented calendar in my bag, and since it features a month-by-month display of the poodles at the height of their well-groomed days, we propped it up as a basic guideline and then riffed. At this point, Jacques is already sporting a powder-blue

1950s pompadour. It looks great, and he knows it too. He's been posing in front of the mirror ever since.

Louis is a little less sold on the whole idea.

"Can you go any faster?" I ask as Lou squirms in my arms.

"No," Benny says with a grunt as he carefully applies the clippers to one of the dog's legs. "I cannot."

"Maybe you could just try?"

"Have *you* ever tried to give a dog a haircut?"

"No."

"Then take your Yelp review elsewhere."

We finish up Louis with a cotton-candy-pink undercut that I am frankly a little jealous of, and then pull out the calendar again before we start on Jean.

"He's going to be the real trouble," Benny says, switching out blades. "I'm not even sure we should try, honestly."

"Oh, I have a plan," I say and hop up to check out Benny's pantry. It's surprisingly well stocked, and I make a mental note to not let him see *my* pantry, which makes me look like an orphaned eleven-year-old.

Bingo. I hold the jar of creamy peanut butter in the air. "Ta-da!"

Benny waffles for a moment, and then he gives up with a shrug. "We're already in this deep, might as well go all the way."

I unscrew the lid, and Jean starts to hyperventilate with excitement—once I put the jar down, he flops to the floor, grabs it with two paws, and then nothing else exists for him. This is definitely going to work. "Okay, you start on his legs, and I'll have a plan by the time you're done."

I reach for the calendar, flipping to this month for reference. My eyes drift from the photo down to the individual entries for the month. A few days ago, I was so busy forging an entry of my own that I didn't appreciate how spooky it is to see everything Cran had planned for his alive self this month. Spooky and bittersweet. All the details of a life, crammed into each little box: exercise, heart rate stats, fasting—

Wait.

I reread the cramped, angular penmanship from the week Cran died.

Benny's talking to me, but I'm not hearing him.

My mind is reeling.

Whoever poisoned Cran—they didn't get to him through the pickles. He wasn't eating pickles, not that week.

He'd been fasting.

According to his own handwriting on his calendar, Cran was on a lemon juice fast the week he died. I know all about that! I squirted lemon water into Chris's eyes right before the Zoom penis debacle. When you do that fast, you don't eat. Nothing. Not a single pickle.

But the medical report wouldn't have been wrong, so how would Cran have gotten botulism if he wasn't eating? Is there another delivery method than pickles?

And that's when I belatedly put two very important pieces together.

BOTOX IS MADE OF BOTULISM. OBVIOUSLY. It's the same bacteria! Or whatever!

It's been such a whirlwind of murders and money and low-level government corruption that I somehow didn't make the connection.

But you know who did? CHRIS. So when I asked him about fatal botulism rates, he thought I was thinking about getting Botox, and he figured, in classic me fashion, I was panicking about dying from it. That's why he sent me the texts about makeup and Kendra's Groupon after we talked at the Petty Pig—he wasn't trying to be a *dick*, he was trying to be *supportive.*

I mean, he was also kind of being a dick.

Oh shit.

I don't realize I actually said it out loud until I hear Benny ask, "What's up?"

Cran was obsessed with his appearance. *He* probably got Botox. So WHAT IF someone paid off Cran's aesthetician or dermatologist or whatever to inject him with too much Botox? And that's how he died? It's the perfect crime! Even better than a gas leak!

I frantically flip back and forth through the months. I just need to find the appointment.

"*What?*" Benny says again.

Shit. Nothing. No doctor appointments. No Botox.

Okay, Mo. Breathe. Don't be a Tond. Don't spiral. Don't jump to conclusions, because that just makes people mad at you.

I have to be okay with not having all the pieces of the story just yet. Even if I hate it.

"Never mind," I say, trying not to be frustrated.

Benny's still staring at me.

"It's the Cran murder thing," I admit. "For a beautiful moment, I thought I figured it all out."

"Ah," he says, sitting back. "Well, as long as it doesn't end up with me being in jail, I'd love to hear all about it."

I explain my theory about the Botox as we give Jean a mohawk and dye it plum purple, and just as we're finishing, I think of another possible suspect. "Hey, did you ever meet any of Cran's model girlfriends?"

If they were models, they might know about Botox.

Might even have their own stashes. Is that a thing? Is my suspect list about to get longer?

But Benny smashes that idea to pieces. "Honestly? I think he just photoshopped random models into his vacation photos. Pretty sure the girlfriends were fake."

The revelation bums me out, not only because it's another dead-end theory and evidence that I'm still completely in the weeds with this investigation despite adding another murder to it, but also because it's hard to hate someone who was just a lonely dog dad who did too much CrossFit.

"Also, why would the model girlfriend have killed Claudia?" he asks, and I shrug.

"It was a dumb idea," I say. It's like the harder I try, the further from the truth I get.

"Maybe." Benny squeezes my shoulder. "But this poodle haircut idea was awesome, Mo. They're not going to win the Great American Dog Show like this, but they do look pretty badass. You're a pretty good dog mom, you know?"

Hey, that's two good reviews of my dog momming in one week.

"I actually kind of needed to hear that," I say. "Thanks."

"Man, I miss these dorks," he says, ruffling Jean's mohawk as we start cleaning up. "Still don't really understand why Cran fired me. He always seemed happy with my work. Now I can't even use him as a reference."

Even with the second dog compliment still humming in my heart, I spot an opening. "Do you want the dogs now?" I ask hopefully, but he shakes his head.

"I've got a 'no pets' clause in my lease."

"Yeah, that *is* a problem, isn't it?" I say, punching him on the shoulder.

We say our goodbyes and I start to make my way home with the freshly coiffed punk rock dogs. It's a slow journey, what with all the peeing and smelling, and I'm running through the case again when a really bad thought occurs to me: If Cran was murdered, then Tond really *could* be in imminent danger. And maybe *has* been this whole time. I should call him—but dang it, I don't have his phone number.

I mean, I don't really want it. I don't want *him* calling *me*. But this is still pretty inconvenient right now.

I'll have to go to Cran's house and just hope that he's hanging out there.

I turn left instead of right and head to the block with the ugly modern house.

When I get there, I don't notice anything unusual from the sidewalk. We climb the front stairs and I bang on the door. Tond doesn't answer.

Maybe he's not here, which would be fine.

Or maybe he's dead inside.

I circle the house, sniffing for a gas leak until it makes me dizzy. The dogs, who already sniff everything anyway, are *also* doing a lot of sniffing, and as a group, we aren't exactly keeping a low profile. I stand up from shoving my nose into the crack of the front doorjamb and I catch one of the neighbors watching me from her porch. I wave.

And thankfully, I don't smell anything.

Except wait, you can smell a gas leak, but *carbon monoxide* is odorless, right? Oh god, does this mean Cran's house is full of carbon monoxide?

Take a breath, Mo. Panicking is 100 percent not working as a detective method.

I pull out my phone and find the Johnston Bros Real Estate phone number online, kicking myself for not thinking of this before. No one answers so I leave a voicemail.

"Hi, this is Mo Ellery calling with an important message for Tond. Can you please call me back as soon as possible? It's regarding our . . ."

Our what? I guess I'll just try to sound like a normal businessperson calling about business. Nothing suspicious or creepy.

"Our . . . *deal.*"

I really need to make the time to watch Rodney O'Malley's videos instead of just scrubbing through and reading the comments.

My legs feel like lead when I finally get home. I try to convince myself that Tond is okay, and I don't need to panic. But I can feel my mind spinning off in a thousand directions. Is Tond already dead? Does the killer know I'm getting closer? Are they watching me, and from where, what if they're in the apartment building, how well do I actually know Sheila? She's *clearly* money motivated. What if she's not Roy's mom at all??

I catch myself.

Mo.

No.

Seriously, why is not spiraling so much work?

I should email Rodney O'Malley and ask him to do a special video on talking yourself down during an investigation. Because I need some coping strategies here, yeesh. No one is watching me. No one is after me. Sheila and Roy are the same kind of weirdo with the exact same face. They are definitely related. And I need to stay calm if I'm going to solve this.

Because yes, I've figured out a lot in the last few hours, but the murderer doesn't know that.

Whoever they are.

Okay, sure, I haven't figured out the most important part.

But I will.

CHAPTER 33

The moment I wake up the next morning, I check to see if Tond has called.

He has not.

Dang it.

It's a school day, so the dogs and I head over to my corner, and thankfully, they are a huge hit with their new haircuts. The kids and parents are delighted and charmed by the glow-ups and it's just the distraction I need to hide that I myself am extremely distracted.

Distracted by murder.

There's still something I'm missing. I mean, yes, obviously—the murderer. But what I really mean is, I can *almost* see it. I have this very distinct feeling that I know something I don't know I know.

Isn't this what therapists are for?

Maybe I need a therapist who can help me solve murders.

Is that a category of therapist? I wonder.

I'm in the middle of this thought, kneeling in a scrum of kids and dogs, when the dogs start barking, and something above me blocks out the sun. I blink up at the tall, rumpled shape backlit against the sky.

Is that . . . Tond?

It's Tond!

He's alive!

His face is drawn, his hair is greasy-floppy, and the dark shadows under his eyes look ghoulish, giving him a decidedly unhinged-adult-man-standing-outside-a-grade-school look.

"Oh thank god!" I say, breaking up the poodle petting zoo situation and ushering the kids along to school. "I was worried about you."

"Mo," Tond whispers urgently, grabbing my elbow. "You promised to keep me alive and then you just vanished, and I haven't heard from you in days. I could've been murdered so many times already."

"Well, you didn't give me your number," I hiss. "I went to your house—"

"THAT'S CRAN'S HOUSE!" he whisper-yells. "I HAVE MY OWN, DIFFERENT HOUSE!"

"I called your office—"

"YOU CALLED THE OFFICE???"

"Yes, and I left my number there and then *you* didn't call *me*."

His eyes widen. "You left a message? Are you crazy? Tell me you didn't say anything—"

"Point is, I've been doing things. *Detective things*," I say under my breath, and when I can see that he's about to interrupt me, I beat him to it. "Cran was murdered!"

He freezes.

"Sorry! I meant to say that more sympathetically, but you were really getting on my nerves."

"That's impossible." He shakes his head. "No, he died of botulism."

"Your brother was botulismed *by someone else*," I say emphatically, before pausing to walk a group of kids across the street. When I get back, I lay out all the evidence I found. The calendar, the fasting, the general availability of Botox, via Groupon and what have you. The fact that Tond, despite eating a tremendous amount of Cran's pickles, did not, himself, die.

"Don't remind me of pickle night," he says, looking a little green. "And if that's true, who killed him? And why? And also . . . how?"

"Yes, those are good questions. Great questions. In fact, they are exactly the ones I'm trying to answer."

"It was Merle," he says, panicked. "Had to be. There's nobody else that powerful in this neighborhood. He must have been putting on an act when you saw him. Pretending to be old and helpless, when he's really a power-hungry government shark!"

"Take a breath," I say, not unkindly. "It was not Merle. I've looked into it already. And I'm not spiraling with you just because it's uncomfortable not to know things."

If I had a murder therapist, I bet she would be so proud of me right now.

Tond apparently is not. "Uncomfortable not to know things? What are you talking about! *This is murder!* I'm *paying* you to know! Okay, here's the deal," he says, decidedly *not* taking a breath with me. "You suck at this, so I'm taking my money back."

"Um, you're what?"

"I want my money back."

Shiiiit.

"I want to trust you, but this is *my life* we're talking about. I need leverage in case someone comes for me. Maybe I can pay Merle off with our bribe money. And if I'm miraculously still alive at the end of all this"—he knocks on the brick wall of the school and then winces as it scrapes his knuckles—"we can *talk* about whether you did enough to deserve any of it."

Think, Mo, think fast.

Think like the wind.

"That's an awful lot of back-and-forth," I say. "I mean, phew, what a hassle for you."

"That's very thoughtful," he says, "but I don't mind. I'll just come with you to get the money after you're done here."

"Right. That makes sense." My brain scrambles to buy me some time. My shift ends in ten minutes. Ten minutes to come up with an excuse not to take Tond where the money isn't. "Together, you and I will get your money, just as soon as my shift—"

My feeble excuse is interrupted by Tond screaming with his mouth shut. He slaps his hands on my shoulders and ducks behind me. I can't imagine this is working well, since I'm significantly shorter than he is, but he's giving it a go anyway.

"*What?*" I ask.

"There!" He sticks his arm out from under my armpit, so it looks like I have a hairy third arm pointing at the unmarked van that's pulling up to the curb half a block away.

"It's a van," I say.

"Unmarked," he whispers.

"There's nothing inherently criminal about an unmarked van," I say, trying to sound reassuring for both our sakes. I will not spiral, *so help me*. "The world is full of totally innocent unmarked vans."

As the door slides open, I feel Tond clench himself even smaller behind me so that his head is getting a little uncomfortably close to my anus. I'm clenching a bit, too, also in the anus department.

But then, a couple of awkward guys around my age in work khakis and neon vests hop out of the van. They unload some equipment, and within a few minutes they've got one of those surveyor tripods up and they're scoping out my intersection. I let out a sigh of relief.

Behind me, Tond squeaks, "They have a telescope. Probably with a laser. Possibly snipers."

"OR," I say, "they're fixing the sinkhole."

"What sinkhole?" Tond asks.

I point to the incredibly huge and obvious sinkhole several feet away from us yawning out from under the metal plate. "The one your brother died in?"

"They didn't have time to botulism me, so they're just going to *push* me in the hole," he says, pulling me closer to him, which is not physically possible.

I wave at the small crew and they wave back. I shake myself free of koala-Tond's grip. "Actually, they're city workers who are going to fix the sinkhole."

"But—"

"Watch. I'll confirm it." I pull out my phone to message Tasha, brushing off the pangs of regret that suddenly swamp me. "Just real quick, sending a text to my . . . road fixing connection."

Me: I'm really sorry, again, about what I said. I understand if you don't want to talk, just . . . thanks for sending surveyors to fix the sinkhole

Me: You make this city a better place

There's no answer for a few minutes.

"What did they say?" whisper-shrieks Tond, still squatting behind me.

Finally, Tasha gives the second message a thumbs-up.

It's not exactly romance-level forgiveness, but at least she isn't ghosting me as a human being.

"Yep," I say to Tond, ignoring the pinch in my chest. "It's for the sinkhole."

He visibly relaxes. "This is what I want more of from you, you know? Asking questions, sleuthing stuff."

"I can't be around you all the time, Tond. Go about your business like normal, but you know, stay aware of stranger danger. Be alert. If you see something, say something."

I sound so confident! If only I *felt* confident. Maybe I need a hat.

"Okay," he says reluctantly, and then he wiggles a finger between me and the surveyors. "But even if you can't be glued to me, I want to see more of *this*. You detecting."

Perfect—an opportunity to save my own ass for a little longer. I glance at my phone with a frown. "My shift is almost over, and we *could* go get that money right now. *But* . . . that's just more time away from my important detective work." I shrug. "Your call."

He squints at me, and I try to seem both confident and annoyed that he's bothering me with things like the measly eleven-and-a-half grand that I have lost.

"Fine," he says. He makes sure we've got each other's phone numbers, and then he tries to look stern. "Get it to me by the end of the week."

"Consider it done."

After the shift ends, I run all the way home, which the dogs think is a blast. It's not for them, though—I don't want to be anywhere near the corner if Tond changes his mind. As usual, running does not agree with me, so I'm sweaty and out of breath when I let us all into the mailroom. I unlock my mailbox and pull out an envelope (a new bill *already*?), a package from my parents because they've never gotten over sending me care packages even though we live in the same city, and a crumpled-up note.

A murderer might leave something like a crumpled-up note, wouldn't they? My hands tremble as I uncrumple it.

Sent you a Venmo request, please pay promptly. Love, Sheila

God.

Read the room, Sheila.

Though to be fair, this does officially strike her from the suspect list. She wouldn't ask for my Venmo if she had Tond's money. Once we're inside my apartment, I turn the dogs loose, remembering how it felt to have all those hundred-dollar bills spread out across the floor. I miss them so much.

Seriously, what is with this neighborhood and its high-profile criming??

I should have moved to the neighborhood that smells like chocolate.

That thought sends me into the kitchen where I help myself to a spoonful of peanut butter and chocolate chips. It helps a little.

Because no matter what, this is not an imaginary world populated by chaos and monsters. Underneath it all, flawed humans are involved, and there's a *logic*, and I'm going to figure out what it is.

Chocolate peanut butter spoon still in my mouth, I crack open the package from my parents, hoping it's more chocolate.

It is not. It is a tiny canister of pepper spray and a whistle, both of them SpongeBob SquarePants themed. Plus a note:

Stay safe out there!!!!!! Xoxo Mom

Hey kiddo. Just got these from a warehouse liquidation sale. Hoping you'll be my first product tester. Your corner is perfect for a test run. Dad

I refuse to puzzle over whether he's expecting me to pepper spray children.

I push the "gift" aside, and that's when I take a closer look at the other piece of mail. Maybe it's not a bill after all? There's no return address. My name and address are typed on a sticker. I open it.

Inside is a single folded piece of paper with four typed words:

STOP OR YOU'RE NEXT

CHAPTER 34

The murderer did not send a crumpled note. They sent a very nicely folded letter in an envelope. I think that freaks me out more.

I go sit in the tub with the pepper spray and the whistle.

I don't turn the faucet on, I just sit there and take slow breaths to calm my heart rate down.

After about five minutes, Louis comes in to check on me, and within a few seconds all three dogs are sitting in the tub with me. It's not a very big tub, but I'll admit there's something comforting about the three of them being crammed in with me, like I have a weighted blanket of punk rock dogs.

I lean my head back against the cool tile wall.

The murderer can't want to kill me, or I'd be dead already.

Right?

I'm just gonna go with that.

So if they don't want to kill me, and I just do what the note says—if I just STOP—I'll be okay?

I can just be a regular crossing guard or even get a *new* job. I don't have to avenge anyone's death or find missing bribe money. I don't have to do *anything*. I can go back to having a normal life.

But what does normal even mean? There's no Chris. No Hannah. Not even Tasha.

Does it just mean a life without murder? Because that is a low-ass bar.

As I contemplate how incredibly low the bar is, Jean drives it home, ripping the worst fart *I have ever experienced*. It takes me so long to escape from underneath the three dogs that it's verging on violating the Geneva Conventions, and the moment I'm out of the tub, I don't even pause to think about it.

I reach for the green screen.

My first step to normalcy, whatever that looks like, is getting Sheila off my back and giving these adorable fart bags to someone who can appreciate them.

A breeze wafts out of the bathroom and I gag.

It's time to make some videos.

Past time.

An hour later, the apartment has fully aired out and I have some great material. Turns out punk rock dogs who can do tricks are excellent video subjects. Marlowe was really on to something.

I cleverly cut the ten minutes of Jacques ignoring me, Jean eating my shoe, and Louis XIV dragging his butt on my kitchen mat, and with a few special effects—BOOM. I have some very compelling adoption videos of three cuddly, well-behaved poodles.

As I fold Eva's stolen green screen, I can't help but think how much fun Hannah and I would have had doing this together. We've never had a fight this big, but it can't be the end of the friendship. Right? Maybe it's time I come clean, tell her about the murders, bribery, etc.? Let her know what I've been up to lately?

Nope. I can't drag her into this shit show. I definitely wish Claudia had never dragged *me* into it.

And I especially don't want Hannah to think *I'm* just using *her* for advice. Not after I accused her of using other people. I won't tell her about the murders. I'll just see how she's doing. Is that so hard?

I pull out my phone.

> **Me:** Hey so I was a dick, and I'm really really sorry. You're right. I've been super self-involved, and not at all present for you. I want to make it up to you. Can we meet up and talk? Name the time and place

I hit send and wait, but there's no activity on her end. I probably deserve that. After a minute of waiting pathetically, just watching my lock screen, I toss it on my chair and roll up the green screen to keep it from wrinkling.

And then the phone rings.

It's a video call from Hannah, and when I swipe to accept, I see that she's crying. "Are you okay? What happened?"

"Can you . . . get a drink right now?" she asks through tears, wiping a hand across her face.

I probably shouldn't drink before my afternoon shift, but this is clearly an emergency, and I need to prove to Hannah (and myself) that I can do better.

Time to get my priorities straight.

"Absolutely. Where?"

"Not out here—somewhere near you," she says, her voice catching.

We plan to meet up at Dickie's, which is maybe becoming my place, against all odds.

I don't want to bring the dogs along and annoy Hannah any more than I already have. But they're all hyped up from shooting the videos (and all the snack bribes I gave them) and can't be left alone for that long. Too much temptation to do something terrible to my poop-free floors.

I text their favorite human and get a response right away.

Benny: Do you think I sit around all day waiting for dogs to hang out with

Me: Not only that, I think you have a picture of the poodles as my avatar on your phone

Benny: Guilty as charged

Benny: I reluctantly agreed to train Charlie today, buuuuuut

Me: ???

Benny: I'll reschedule

A few minutes later, we meet at the dog park by the school for the handoff.

"Thanks for doing this," I say. "You're gonna have to put it on my tab though. My dog handler budget is pretty tapped out."

"Don't worry, I actually turned down a PAID gig to do this," he says. "This one's pro bono."

"Wow, must be nice to turn down work," I say with a smirk.

"Some dogs are more important than money," he says, ruffling their punk poofs.

God, I wish he would just adopt them.

"Text you in a bit?" I ask. "After you wear them out?"

"We'll be here when you're done," he says, and as I slip through the dog park gate, I glance back to see that he's already got the guys running an agility course around the place. He truly is a dog wizard.

Meanwhile, *I* am going to be a life wizard.

By which I mean, I'm not *only* making up with Hannah—I'm also determined to get as far away from that cursed construction site as possible. That's right: Baby's getting herself a new job. As I walk to the bar, I pop into every single store and restaurant and coffee shop and check if they're hiring.

Tragically, by the time I mustered up enough humility to call that guy from LookShopNow, they were done setting up interviews. And I'm clearly not getting the magical 11.5K infusion that I hoped I would. So if I'm going to quit being a crossing guard, I need a new job pronto, or I'll have to move back in with my folks, which is obviously not happening.

#thankssheila

I'm only a little sweaty by the time I get to Dickie's. It's cool in there and the lights are low, as usual, and Hannah's already there, sitting in the booth farthest from the door.

She looks worse than I've ever seen her.

She's also already got two beers at the table, so I don't waste time at the bar and just slide in across from her.

"I've ruined everything," she says, before I even get a chance to ask.

It takes me a second to understand what she's said, because Hannah's not the ruiner. That's me.

She's the perfect one.

"What do you mean?" I ask gently. "You don't mean *us*, right? We were both in a weird mood, we said dumb things—"

"No, not us," she says, waving a hand dismissively as she chokes back a dry sob. "With Kenji and Reuben and Eva. Eva found out that I borrowed her green screen and just lost it at me. Which is fair. I should've asked."

Oh boy. "Just blame me," I say. "It's my fault and she hates me anyway."

She shakes her head. "That's small potatoes compared to the arguments with Reuben and Kenji. Kenji says I spend more of my time online than with him. And Reuben just thinks I'm doing everything wrong with my business, so I can't talk to any of them about—" She kind of chokes and then blows her nose on a napkin.

Here's me being honest: Yeah, fine, I've been jealous of Hannah's setup. I always joke about how her polycule seems way more complicated than fun, but at the end of the day, she's got so many people who care about her . . . it honestly makes me feel like she doesn't really need *me*. Which sucks.

But the fact that they're making it work and are in love and romantically humping—it's inspiring. It makes me think it could happen for me again someday. So as much as the comparison game can creep up on me, I want those crazy kids to make it. I want love to be real, even when it looks like a dodecahedron. I don't want my friend to be as heartbroken as I am.

I reach out and squeeze her hand. "I'm here for you," I say. "No matter what."

She takes a deep breath. "Mo, they don't believe me."

Did I miss something? I missed something. "About what?"

"The Instagram stalker."

"The stalker you tried to tell me about?"

Hannah sniffles. "That one."

"And I didn't listen?"

"And you didn't listen. But at least you believed me. And I just—I feel so alone, and I'm a little scared, Mo. I need help."

"Let me see," I say, holding out my hand. "The messages."

She hesitates. "I haven't shown anyone these."

"Why not?"

"You heard Eva and Reuben and Kenji when you came by. They say I'm too online and don't protect myself. And these messages prove they're right. But I need *help*, not fucking scolding."

That would explain why they were all so weirdly upset with me when I came over thinking I had a stalker. They were upset with Hannah and taking it out on me.

Okay, that is not cool. They should be supporting her and helping her through this. And I suddenly see that I *am* still important. Even three romantic partners can't take care of all your needs. Sometimes you still need a best friend.

"I know it's scary, but you have to show them, Hannah," I say gently. "And right now, you have to show me."

Especially a best friend who accidentally sort of has a lot of experience at detective work.

Hannah hands me her phone.

And as I scroll through her DMs, I can see just how many people Hannah's reached. How public her life really is. How many people think they know her. It isn't as cool as I imagined.

Then Hannah points out her thread with the stalker.

And holy shit, it's intense. The person isn't just spamming her, they're obsessed. They know way too much about her.

Like . . . why is there a photo of the house Hannah grew up in? Facing Hannah's old bedroom window?

I feel sick.

"That's just the latest thread," Hannah explains. "I've blocked them five times and they just open new accounts. But the words they use— It's clearly all the same person."

"Did you tell anyone that?"

She shakes her head. "I was so freaked out, I didn't really want to believe it, myself. I told Kenji I've been getting weird messages, and he says I'm bound to have a few people who have a 'parasocial relationship' with me." She shakes her head. "But you're right—I need to *show* him the messages. This is *way* beyond just parasocial. Let me show you another one."

She takes the phone back, and I feel mine buzz in my pocket, but I leave it alone. Right now, Han deserves my full attention.

I slide in next to her so she can show me more easily.

My phone buzzes again, and I ignore it again.

A lot of the messages in her DMs are about how much Hannah has made people's lives better, but she's right—all the stalkery ones are clearly the same person. Not just a fan. Not just a try-hard. There's a forcefulness that's unsettling. Hannah shows me a message where the person says they wish they could be inside her actual skin so they could make things happen the way she does.

Which, aside from being *super* icky, honestly feels like a threat.

The different avatars all lead to accounts with no pictures. None of them follow anyone else, and they have no followers of their own.

"You're right," I say. "This is really upsetting."

"You believe me," Hannah says, relief flooding her face as she starts crying.

"I'm sorry it took me this long," I say, handing the phone back.

"I felt paranoid, but it's so stressful, and it just doesn't *stop*. Every time I block an account, a new one springs up." She wipes her eyes, mascara smudging, and then scrolls again. "Here's the latest message."

I'm getting yet another text, and I subtly shove my shirttail in my back pocket to mute the buzzing while Hannah hands me her phone and slides out of the booth. "I need to wash my face."

As she heads for the bathroom, I read the message on her screen and promptly forget how to breathe.

The message in the bubble reads:

HANNAH HAWKS YOU ARE MY HERO I NEED TO HIRE YOU FOR PERSONAL COACHING I'LL GIVE YOU $11,500.

It was sent *yesterday*.

What are the chances that I'd lose $11,500, and then some stalkery rando would offer Hannah *a different* $11,500 on the same day? I'm no math genius, but I'd say NOT GREAT.

Holy shit.

The Benny statue ab thief and Hannah's stalker are *the same person*.

So who is it? I squeeze my eyes shut and think back to the only time I mentioned the money—that moment in the alderman's office when I told Tasha where I'd stashed it.

I remember spritzing myself in the face with the plant spray, and I do that again, mentally, to make my brain focus harder. I'm missing something. Something so obvious, it keeps slipping out of sight. And then it hits me.

We *weren't* alone.

Merle was in his office, but his door was definitely shut.

However, on the other side of those flimsy, definitely *not* soundproof cubicle walls was the sound of a copy machine.

An image of Val pops into my head, brown envelope tucked under her beige arm, scowl on her face. No, wait. She left for the post office *before* I told Tasha about the money.

But Leslie was still there.

Leslie, who seems to be slightly obsessed with Hannah and UPGRADE.

No, no, no, not my new bff! She's too sweet. She's who I want to be when I grow up. She's not a big creepo.

I think about the charming way she winked at me. The way she seemed so confident about being a great dog mom and then made me feel confident about *my* dog mommery. Why would a big creepo do that?

Unless. No way.

Did Leslie Carey friggin' *UPGRADE* me into liking her? Did I actually fall for an UPGRADE?? She wasn't seeing some buried truth about me and my dog parenting—she told me the lie I wanted to hear. Because it's undeniable. I am *not* a good dog mom, like, empirically. I know this! It's why I'm trying to get the dogs adopted by someone who is!

Damn, Hannah is *good*.

But hang on—Leslie wouldn't have done that for shits and giggles. Han created UPGRADE as a tool you use to get what you want. So what did Leslie want from me? Statue ab money? Clearly. Access to Hannah? Well . . . no, actually. She had already UPGRADEd me *before* Hannah burst into the office.

So if she didn't know Hannah was my bestie . . . what could she possibly want from *me*? And why would she try to get it by making me feel confident about the poodles?

Okay. Leslie definitely loves dogs, that's for sure. It's like Benny said, she doesn't care about the parking garage or Claudia's house or the bribing or any of that alderman stuff Merle cares about. She's only got eyes for Charlie.

I even hear Leslie's voice in my head. *My real job is Dog Mom Extraordinaire!*

And Merle: *I'm kind of the third wheel in this family.*

Oh my god. Wait.

Now my mind is going a million miles a minute, but not in a spiral to nowhere. It's driving *toward* something in a fancy, expensive car kind of way.

Yeah, I admit it—I fell for Leslie's UPGRADE because I wanted to feel confident about being a dog mom. But what did she actually *say*?

That the poodles were fat and happy.

The same poodles SHE was wantonly feeding fattening "purse dogs" at Cran's funeral, while giggling inappropriately.

The same poodles who, under Cran's parentage and Benny's tutelage, were lean, mean, dog show–winning machines.

And the same poodles who—before their "fat and happy" makeover under my care—were Charlie's biggest competition at the Great American Dog Show, according to Benny.

What if Leslie needed me to keep the poodles in pepperoni so there's no way they could compete? And then what if she needed Hannah's help to UPGRADE the dog show judges into, say, *letting Charlie win*. How far would she go to secure Charlie's future as dog king?

I think she might go all the way.

Which means I have to ask: Is *Leslie* the murderer?

Because other than a bribe and an UPGRADE, the only way aging, arthritic, possibly past-his-prime Charlie could win was if the poodles and their handler were, let's just say, "handled."

Slow down, Mo. Take a breath. Don't be a Tond. Just because Leslie loves dogs doesn't mean she killed Claudia and Cran. Because if Leslie WAS the murderer, she would be after Benny for spending all this time with the poodles instead of Charlie.

Hannah strolls back to the booth, patting her eyes dry with a paper towel. "Your face is making so many faces right now," she says. "What's going on?"

My phone buzzes and I jump up, thighs ripping painfully off the vinyl booth for the millionth time.

I pull out my phone, hands shaking.

It's the latest in a series of approximately a zillion texts from Benny.

Benny: Nursery

Benny: Nursery

Benny: DUCK

"Where's Marlowe's autocorrect translation app when you need it," I mutter, heart pounding.

Benny: MURDERER

Shitballs.

CHAPTER 35

I start running.

Through the door and down the sidewalk; I can't get there fast enough.

Hannah chases behind, calling after me, "Mo, I'm coming with you! Just—what's going on? Bullet points are fine. Why are we running?"

"It's a little complicated," I yell back. "There's been some new developments!"

"Since I went to the bathroom?"

"I know who your stalker is!"

"*What? How?*"

"I'm kind of a detective now," I call over my shoulder, simultaneously dodging a mailman.

"You solve mysteries?" she asks incredulously. "Does that come with health insurance?"

God, it's nice to be seen.

"Still don't really understand why we're running, though!" she adds.

"I think my dogsitter might be in danger!"

After that, we run in silence, punctuated only by the very loud sound of me trying to continue breathing while also being athletic. I'm guessing Hannah's processing all this new info, but I'm so out of breath, I couldn't explain anything else even if she needed me to.

I don't know what's waiting for us, but Benny said he'd stay at the dog park, so that's where I'm going. I don't know if Leslie is trying to kill Benny or the poodles or all four of them at once. I also don't have any weapons to stop her unless you count the one crappy chef's knife I got on sale from Target, which is back in my kitchen anyway.

But I can't do *nothing*.

As I turn and close in on my corner, I start to hear yelling, but . . . it's not coming from the dog park.

It's coming from the parking garage construction site.

And this is where things start to get a little weird.

Tond is there. He's the one yelling. He's also wearing a hard hat and sort of jousting with an orange traffic cone.

The person he's yelling at is *Merle*, who's on his crutches and appears to be very confused.

I run past them to look inside the dog park gate. No one is in there.

Meanwhile, behind Tond and Merle, Tond's neon-yellow Ford Fiesta has clearly plowed through and toppled the fence around the construction site. The car is currently banged up and smoking in the middle of everything, looking really out of place among the piles of cement bags and assorted equipment.

What the hell is going on?

Where's Benny?

And Leslie?

And the dogs?

I slow to a stop and Hannah pulls up next to me, panting. She swipes her forehead with her cap sleeve and then points at the altercation in front of us.

"Hey, isn't that the alderman?" she whispers, eyes wide. "Who's the construction site avenger with the hard hat?"

Merle looks over and sees us, his eyes pleading. My heart races, and I reflexively shove Hannah behind me. "Call 911," he says. "Hurry!"

"She's on my side, you fiend!" Tond declares, holding the cone upside down above his head, where it stays rigid for a second and then flops over.

"Tond, what the hell?" I shout. "Stop attacking him! Have either of you seen Benny?"

"Who's Benny again?" Tond asks.

"We already had this conversation, Tond!"

"Well, I was probably drunk on cooking sherry!"

He's not wrong. But I don't have time to deal with . . . whatever this is, and I need to find Benny before it's too late. Merle, meanwhile, has opted to make a slow hobbling break for it.

"Nice try!" Tond lunges and jabs at him with the traffic cone, knocking him off-balance. Merle crumples to the sidewalk and cries out in pain. His crutches clatter to the side, and Tond grabs one, planting it at Merle's solar plexus like the flag on the moon.

"Benny is the dog walker, you dumbass!" Merle moans. "God, I wish your brother was here."

"Oh no, you're not gonna murder old Tond too!" Tond says, laughing maniacally. "Not today, not ever!" He turns to me and grins. "Got him! I got him before he got me!"

"Murder? I can't even *stand*!" Merle yells. He turns his head toward us. "Girls, help! Help me! Stop this lunatic!"

"First of all," Hannah says, pulling out her phone, "we are women."

"Hold on," Merle says, his voice shifting in surprise, as he registers

Hannah. "You have *got* to be kidding me. Why is Hannah Hawks here?"

Hannah waves uncomfortably from behind my shoulder.

And that's when Merle *really* loses it. "YOU STAY AWAY FROM MY WIFE!"

"Can everyone shut up for a second?" I say, looking up and down the block frantically. "BENNY! BENNY!"

"I, er, haven't done anything to your wife," Hannah says, confusion splashed across her face.

"I should sue you!" Merle calls out, despite still being held down by one of his own crutches. "You brainwashed her!"

I cup my hands to make a megaphone. "BENNY!"

"I don't brainwash people," Hannah says. "I help people get what they want!"

"BENNY!" I listen hard over the sound of Tond jumping in to ask follow-up questions about who's brainwashing who—but it's just regular neighborhood sounds, no cries for help or anything. This isn't working. What if he's already dead? In desperation, I try something else. "JACQUES!"

And from behind the school, I hear a familiar howl. Two other dog voices join it.

It's not a howl that says *we need to pee* or *let's rip the duvet to shreds.*

This is a *we-might-be-fancy-show-dogs-but-we-used-to-be-literal-wolves* howl.

"Hold on, Benny," I plead as I take off sprinting toward the spot where the dog park curves around behind the school, a small patch of grass that's just out of sight from the sidewalk.

And I know this is definitely NOT the right moment to celebrate—but HOLY COW I THINK I WAS RIGHT ABOUT THE DOG MOTIVE THING? I transformed my anxiety into creativity and solved the case??

The round of high fives I so desperately deserve will have to wait.

As I turn the corner, they all come into view: Jacques and Louis are leaping and pawing at a woman's hunched back. Jean is delicately but firmly tugging on the hem of a silk blouse with his teeth. Charlie is pawing and barking at Jean.

Balls.

That's Leslie, all right. There's officially no doubt—she's a killer/stalker/thief and all-around creepazoid.

I need better role models.

Leslie's kneeling on the ground, and she's got on one of those tote bags that parents put baby toys in, the wide strap diagonal across her back. She hasn't seen me yet.

There's a pair of legs with sneakers sticking out horizontally from under her, and they're not really moving.

I know those calves.

Benny.

I throw myself through the dogs, ignoring the growling and snapping teeth all around, and grab the bag strap, yanking Leslie as hard as I can off Benny. She topples backward and skids across the ground on her butt.

Benny's lying on his back, panting, his face beet red and his hands pulling at something around his neck. It's a dog's choker collar. The metal kind with prongs sticking into his neck—basically a spiky noose.

Oh my god.

I straddle his body and try to help him loosen the collar, seeing the bruising and pinpricks of blood on the skin of his neck where Leslie jerked it hard enough to cut off his airflow.

Behind me, Leslie screams bloody murder (*Literally!* I think, unhelpfully), and I feel her slam into my back, trying to wrestle me off him. She's tiny, but terrifying, and as her bony hands grab for my hair and my face, all I can think is that I need to keep her off Benny until he's okay and I'm sure he can breathe. I don't know how to body-slam somebody, but maybe now's the time to try?

But then everything turns into a freaking animal channel movie of the week, and *the dogs actually come to my rescue.* Or at least it feels that way. Jacques throws himself at Leslie, shoving her a little off-balance. Then Jean gooses me, which is super weird but really does boost me up, and Louis—well, Lou sneezes in my face, but I know it's out of love this time.

I'm up, I'm on my feet, but when I whip around to hold off Leslie's next attack, I see that she's pulled an actual *syringe* out of her tote bag and is pointing the business end right at me.

"Benny!" I yell, kicking out at Leslie to give us a little distance from that death needle. Benny's still red and gasping, and he's not ready for this, but it doesn't matter anymore. I yank him to his feet and we start running for the gate.

The poodles follow us, and Charlie chases them, nipping at their heels. They all seem to be having a great time, but there's Leslie right behind, racing after us with a syringe of . . . cyanide? I don't know, arsenic? What are poisonous things that go in a syringe? And why does she have one??

We race out of the dog park onto the street and then it's, like, do we just keep running? Benny's injured, Leslie's not exactly in her prime, and I'm really not in good enough shape for all this running and kicking and whatnot. This is, frankly, a pretty agonizing chase. But what are we supposed to do? *Stop* running and face off with a geriatric murderer-slash-stalker holding a syringe full of deadly stuff?

I don't love that either.

That's when I see Tond and Merle and Hannah all standing next to the sinkhole, remarkably calm. Hannah's planted between the two men and taking notes on her phone. Oh my god, she is

"UPGRADE"ing them. I feel a pang of guilt, again, at how I treated her. It really is amazing to see her at work. She could be an incredible diplomat. She can do *anything.*

Just not right now.

I wave my arms frantically.

"Hannah!" I call out, and we approach, our slow murderous entourage and dog pack, and as Hannah turns to face us, I realize I've just led her stalker, the one she is absolutely terrified of and came to me for protection from, straight to her.

"HANNAH HAWKS!!!" Leslie screams. Then her voice lowers dramatically like in those demon possession movies. "This is your fault, you bitch! None of this would've happened if you'd just responded to my messages!"

Boy, those fangirls will really turn on you.

And with that, Leslie gets another wind, sprints past the dogs, past me and Benny, and makes a beeline for Hannah, murderous syringe aloft. Hannah's eyes widen.

Tond leaps out of the way and lands face down on the parkway, protecting himself with the orange cone over his head.

"Lesliebear?" Merle says feebly.

And suddenly I get the full picture. Maybe too late.

One time, I had a twinge of knee pain and was convinced it was osteoarthritis. I searched for treatments for days, went down a surprisingly intense rabbit hole, and became very attached to an experimental new treatment. You could only get it if you were part of some study. By the time I emerged from said rabbit hole, my knee was fine again, and I completely forgot.

The "bleeding edge" of experimental arthritis treatment is *Botox.*

Of *course* Leslie would pull out all the stops for Charlie's dog arthritis. And I would bet approximately 11.5 grand that the syringe Leslie is currently wielding is filled with Botox, AKA BOTULISM.

This revelation happens in slow motion. In my mind, I mean. In real life it happens at top speed.

Benny breaks away from me, running toward Hannah.

But he's not going to be able to get to her first. Leslie is too fast. She's the fastest old lady in the world.

Hannah is frozen in place.

Benny leaps into the air, full-on horizontal, arms outstretched, like he's going to tackle Hannah. He's too far away, but somehow it's still just enough. His palms just *barely* reach Hannah's knees. He pushes her backward onto the curb.

Leslie's momentum betrays her, and she stabs the syringe into the air where Hannah's neck used to be, stumbling over Hannah's legs, and smashing face-first into the hood of a parked car.

The car alarm goes off, and I'm having flashbacks to Cran's Kia in the sinkhole all over again.

Benny slides across the metal plate covering the sinkhole.

Benny keeps sliding.

Benny slides right into the sinkhole.

CHAPTER 36

"Benny?" I squeak, peeking over the hole.

Nothing. Infinite darkness.

Finally, one sexy forearm emerges and grips the metal panel. A matching one follows. Down below, his feet are balanced precariously on a slippery-looking pipe of some kind.

"Don't panic, Benny!" I say, panicking. "Just hold on for a few minutes. You're probably safer down there anyway."

"What?" he groans.

I glance up and see a dazed Leslie trying to shake off the impact of hitting the car. "Just gotta take care of this murderer thing real quick. BRB."

Right. The murderer thing. How to take care of it.

"Leslie," I say evenly, forcing myself to be a confident grown-up. "It's over. You can't kill all five of us."

She blinks at me, wiping a stray hair out of her face, but instead of politely agreeing and handing over the syringe, she grabs Hannah.

In the blink of an eye, that old woman is holding the syringe to my best friend's neck.

Hannah struggles to free herself, but Leslie is like a damn boa constrictor, and Hannah's struggling just brings the syringe closer to her jugular.

My whole body goes numb.

"Everybody throw your phones in the sinkhole," Leslie says, sticking Hannah with the tip of the needle, just enough to make a thin trail of blood run down her neck. "*NOW.*"

Tond is first, and throws it quickly, almost eagerly, like he wants to be the best hostage. It hits Benny on the way in.

"*OUCH,*" Benny echoes from below.

"Oops," Tond says, by way of apology.

I reluctantly take my phone out and drop it over the edge, while Hannah, bent awkwardly to accommodate Leslie, blindly reaches for her phone and drops it in front of her, so that Leslie can kick it in.

Merle holds his out, like he's about to follow suit, when his wife stops him. "Not yours. There's some pictures of Charlie I want."

He dutifully slips it back into his pocket.

"Leslie, please don't do this," I say, hoping that the phone thing has appeased her enough. "Let's quit while we're ahead."

"UPGRADERS never quit," Leslie says. "Right, Hannah? I am UPGRADING MYSELF."

"The acronym doesn't really support that conjugation," Hannah whispers and then cringes, clearly realizing you don't correct someone about your branding when they're holding you hostage.

And sure enough, that just makes Leslie madder, and she actually shoves the needle *into* Hannah's neck.

"Acronym *this*!" Leslie cackles.

"Mo!" Hannah screams.

"Hannah!" I cry.

"Boo-bear!" Merle pleads.

"Everybody SHUT UP." Leslie looks around frantically. "And . . . um . . . now *you* get in the sinkhole."

"Not a lot of room down here," Benny calls up.

"Shoes on or off?" Tond asks, confused. The man is such a total chaos hostage, I don't know whether to thank him or kick him.

"On. No, off. Wait, give me a second," Leslie mumbles, unsure and frustrated.

Tond nods, sympathetically. "First time?"

Meanwhile, I can't stop looking at the syringe. She hasn't pushed in the plunger yet, but that doesn't mean she won't.

Okay, stay calm. Leslie is desperate to feel competent and impressive. So that's what I'll help her do.

What I *really* want to do is blurt what I figured out about the case, but this isn't about me and my ego. Not yet. Right now, it's about keeping Hannah safe. So I play dumb.

"I'm dying to know how you pulled all this off," I say. "You couldn't have—no, it's *too* clever."

Leslie narrows her eyes at me. "You don't think I'm clever?"

Shit shit shit.

"No way, dude, I think you're *too* clever!" I say, loudly. "This is how you killed Cran, right? The Botox for Charlie's arthritis? I *never* could have come up with that."

Leslie laughs. "No, you couldn't have. But I figured it out right away. That idiot, always drinking out of that stupid water backpack. He left it in the front of the office during a meeting with Merle and I just pumped it full of everything I had."

Well, damn. Why didn't I think of that? He was sucking on that thing on my corner the day before he died.

"That's a *super* creative way to murder someone," I say, warmly.

"*Thank* you," she says, shooting Merle a hard look. "Nice of *some* people to notice."

"Leslie, what do you say we take the syringe out and talk like adults, hmm?" I say gently. "This isn't a Cran-style murder situation is the thing. Bit less of a creative approach this time, unfortunately. Since we're all watching you do this."

Leslie grunts and twists the syringe.

"MO!" Hannah cries. "You *think* you're helping, but you're not helping."

She's right. I need to pivot, and fast.

But before I can, Tond has clearly decided this is his chance to escape. We all watch in disbelief as he sprints across the street, clambers over the wrecked fence, leaps into the neon-yellow Ford Fiesta, and guns it, taking down the fence in the *back* of the parking lot site this time so the entire construction area is open and exposed with all its sharp and pointy dangers.

Tond disappears down the alley.

But most importantly, it distracts Leslie from pumping Hannah full of Botox and gives me an idea.

Merle still has his phone. Right now, he's probably desperate to call 911. And he wouldn't even need to pick up the phone and say anything because they'll have his location immediately.

So all *I* need to do is whip up another distraction, and he can make the call.

Whew, Hannah's not going to like this, but it's what we've got right now. I take a deep breath.

"You don't have any more syringes or other weapons in that baby bag, do you, Leslie?" I say.

Leslie narrows her eyes. "Why?"

I shrug. "It's just that, well, one syringe of Botox isn't gonna take down all three of us. And once you push that plunger . . . it's three against one."

Hannah widens her eyes at me and mouths something sweary.

"Four," calls Benny. "Just as soon as one of you can give me a hand."

I can see Leslie realizing it's true. She's got the advantage right up until she empties that Botox into Hannah.

And then she's got nothing.

"It's too bad for you that this whole showdown didn't happen over there." I jerk a thumb toward the construction site. "You know, where there's drills and metal pipes and all kinds of stuff. Tools for the serious, self-actualized murderer."

Leslie takes the bait.

"I am VERY self-actualized," she says defiantly. "I am a POWERHOUSE."

"If you say so," I say with a shrug.

"I DO say so." Leslie squints over at the site, presumably trying to spot the drills and metal pipes. While she does, I throw a quick thumbs-up at Merle, and then cough and clear my throat, but *of course* he's not looking at me. He's still gaping at Leslie.

Come on, Merle.

Leslie gestures at me. "Go get me a self-actualized murderer tool," she demands.

I point to myself and pretend to look surprised.

"You heard me," she says.

"What's going on up there, guys?" Benny calls from the sinkhole. "Sounds pretty bad, actually!"

"Shut up, I can't think when you're whining," Leslie says, kicking a pebble into the sinkhole.

While she's briefly distracted, I open my eyes real wide at Merle, who opens *his* eyes wide back at *me*. I mime dialing a phone, but he just looks confused. I mouth *call 911*, and he mouths back something that looks like *I am a hamburger*.

Am *I* crazy? How is *call for help* not his primary goal?

Who voted for this guy?

I carefully pick my way over to the fence Tond mowed down and give it a good once-over.

"Just a lot of cement so far!" I update Leslie, giving a thumbs-down.

"Keep looking," she says.

I hold up a shovel. "How about this?"

"Nice try," she says. "That's an amateur murder tool."

"How about you, *Merle*?" I ask. With me over here, Merle's out of his wife's line of sight. He could *so* dial 911 right now and be a national goddamn hero.

So I throw him a bone—"Merle, what's YOUR CALL? NINE pieces of cement or ONE . . . ONE shovel?"

He shrugs. "Whatever the TWO of you think is best."

I scowl, mentally giving him the award for worst hostage, and I realize his reluctance to actually DO anything reminds me of Chris. Maybe I really am better off without him.

"Hurry up," Leslie yells again.

Not that I'll ever get to tell him that if I can't stop this self-empowered murderer.

After poking around, I find a crowbar next, and in a sort of Hail Mary, I hoist it up to my ear as if it's a phone.

"What is that?" Leslie asks.

"A . . . crowbar," I say. "I was joking around, *pretending it was a phone*."

Merle just blinks.

"That'll do," Leslie says and waves me back over.

And my dumb idea has officially backfired. Instead of providing a distraction while Merle called for help, now I'm just literally handing weapons to Leslie.

Unless *I* hit *her* with the crowbar first, I guess? But my aim isn't great and I might hurt Hannah. If only Leslie would just get that needle out of her neck.

Time for Plan B.

By which I mean, time to come up with Plan B.

I'm almost back to the sinkhole when the whole situation sinks to an even lower ring of hell. Across the street from us, the school bell blares, announcing the end of the school day—and the imminent arrival of a whole bunch of innocent children I have sworn to protect.

Shitballs.

Leslie spins around as kids start to trickle out of the building, and Hannah shrieks as the needle goes a bit deeper.

"*Leslie*," I call, trying to sound stern. She's too jittery now, too on edge, I need her to keep the syringe hand calm and balanced. What calms her down, other than looking smart?

Charlie.

Who is currently sniffing some bushes where the poodles just peed.

Here we go. The moment has come. Here's where we bring down the hammer of justice.

"Your Charlie really is such a spectacular specimen of dogdom," I say, hoping *dogdom* is a word.

Leslie's face softens, and she looks past me for a moment as the dogs frolic. Attagirl. "Those stupid poodles are such *showboats*," she says, "but Charlie—he's subtle, he's *understated*. Deep down, he's the one who really has the goods. He's a champ. I've known it since he was a puppy."

I shake my head. "You had me convinced that Cran's murder was about the parking garage. But it wasn't."

"*That* eyesore?" Leslie scoffs. "Obviously not."

"It was all about being Dog Mom Extraordinaire, wasn't it?" I say, pausing for dramatic effect. "The Great American Dog Show wouldn't let Charlie compete because of his age and arthritis. They wouldn't listen to reason. And *you* couldn't stand the idea of those poodles winning *again*. So you had no choice. You had to get Cran out of the way to keep the poodles from competing."

I look around to see if anyone is impressed at my sleuthing.

They are not.

They're all watching Leslie's syringe hand. No gasps or "wow"s or anything. I realize we're in a tense moment, but come on.

"Hello!" I say. "I figured it out. Hannah, can you believe it? I'm good at this!"

Hannah gives a shaky thumbs-up.

Even Leslie isn't impressed. "You make it sound so *gauche*. I tried the civilized way first. I used Hannah's UPGRADE method. I did every one of those stupid letters. All the way from U to E."

"Oh god," Hannah whispers. "I shouldn't have said E was for 'execute.'"

Leslie shoots her an irritated look. "No, you were right, Cran had to die. It was the only way to get the poodles off the board. I tried to deal: I paid my cousin to make sure the construction site failed the gas inspection. Then I met with Cran and told him if he fired Benny as the poodles' handler, I'd clear things up with the gas company."

"Should've gone with E for 'enact,'" Hannah rasps. "Or 'effectuate'?"

"You bribed the gas company?" Merle asks from his spot on the grass.

"*You* got me fired?" Benny asks from inside the hole.

"Would you all please stop interrupting!" Leslie is clearly on the verge of a tantrum. "*I* needed Benny. He's practically a dog wizard."

Dog wizard! That's what I said!

"But that *asshole* refused to be Charlie's handler for the dog show and only *deigned* to do some basic training. He said—" A cry escapes her throat. "He said—my wittew baby Charwie is too *old*. And then he *cheated on me* with those awful poodles."

"Charlie's a great dog, but his show days are over," Benny calls up. "Also, Mo, I'm definitely slipping here."

"Good!" Leslie snaps vindictively.

Meanwhile, a veritable tsunami of children has begun to flow out of the school across the street, and parents have started to turn the corner, and everyone is drinking in the scene.

Cool.

Cool cool cool.

CHAPTER 37

"Should we be waiting for you, Mo?" calls one of the parents, clearly not recognizing the urgency of the situation that is a murderer and a whole bunch of hostages standing around a sinkhole.

"Yes, please," I yell back. "Just a little traffic jam!"

But wait. These parents, and some of the kids—they have PHONES. They can call 911. Forget Merle. I just need to telegraph to them that they should call but make it subtle . . .

"But *none* of this icky violence would have been necessary if it hadn't been for Hannah ignoring my Insta messages," Leslie says. "And when E for Execute didn't work, what was I supposed to do?"

Hannah grimaces, and as she speaks, I can't help but notice how hoarse she's become. "I never meant to hurt anyone."

"Yeah, well, that's why your stupid program doesn't work. I killed Cran and still had problems. So I upgraded UPGRADE," Leslie says, her pitch escalating. "To POWERHOUSE. P is for Pick your Weapon, O is for—"

No, no, this is getting away from me—Leslie is way too angry at

Hannah, and I don't like the sound of this POWERHOUSE. I need to get her to focus on *me*. And I need to catch the eyes of one of the parents, which should be easy because they're all gaping at me.

"I'm going to put your crowbar down for you," I say, trying to maneuver my body to face the parents. I catch the eye of one mom and sort of nod at her in a way that I hope says *call 911 but don't announce it.*

"So you started POWERHOUSE, which sounds really interesting by the way," I say.

The mom pulls out her phone. Yes!

"Thank you," Leslie says. "Took me a long time to figure out the acronym."

"And once you got Cran out of the picture, next step was to kill Claudia?" I ask as curiously as I can.

The mom lifts her phone high in the air and yells, "I'm calling 911!"

Oh come *on*.

But Leslie doesn't seem to notice the crowd we're amassing anymore. She's too wrapped up in herself.

There's a lesson in here somewhere for me. Not that I *like* getting my life lessons from murderers.

Leslie barks a laugh. "That was Claudia's own fault for snooping. She was on to me from the beginning. Like you said at the funeral, she was getting close."

That's Leslie for you, always lurking, always listening. Meek, forgettable, and murdery. I suddenly remember her peeling out of the funeral home parking lot. She probably made a beeline right for Claudia's house and the gas line.

I retch at the confirmation that my big mouth got Claudia killed. *I'm so sorry*, I think.

I can practically hear Claudia's voice in my head: *I'm gonna haunt the shit out of you for this.*

But now isn't the time to get waylaid by regret. "How'd you do it?" I ask.

"Psht. I went in the same way you did, in back. Turned on the gas in the basement. Made it look like a leak. Easy peasy."

"And the money?" I ask.

"An unexpected bonus," she says, patting the bag around her body.

Oh shit. She's got it on her *right now.*

Time to shut this whole thing down once and for all. But how? UPGRADE? POWERHOUSE? Rodney O'Malley?

I'm going to have to wing this, Mo Ellery style.

"That money isn't going to help you," I say kindly, and then gesture to the entire school standing around outside, watching rapt. "There's too many witnesses."

Leslie suddenly notices the crowd around us. She narrows her eyes at me. "And what would you suggest I do, *crossing guard*?"

Okay, she's being snarky, but I think she's feeling the squeeze.

Before I can say anything, Merle pipes up out of the blue. "Sugarcube, maybe take the needle out of the nice girl—"

Shut UP, Merle. This guy has the worst timing.

Leslie whirls around and Hannah squeals a bit. "For ONCE could you just put me and my needs first," Leslie hisses. "Make yourself useful and grab that crowbar."

I shake my head at Merle, but he's already hobbling toward the crowbar. Shit shit shit.

What is taking the cops so long?

Leslie keeps talking as she backs away holding Hannah, toward the curb, over the edge of the metal plate where only Benny's wrists and hands are visible. "Merle, you are useless. I am sick and tired of dealing with the messes you make. I bet you haven't even noticed the FBI rolling past the office in their unmarked windowless vans. You know who did? ME!"

Huh. Well, that's an interesting development.

"So on top of everything else I do for you, *now* I've got to shred—"

At that moment, Leslie trips on Benny's forearms, he screams, and Leslie screams and stumbles, and Hannah screams as the syringe gets yanked from her neck, which has apparently gone straight into her jugular, and not in a careful way, because a thin but very steady stream of blood starts spurting out.

This is suddenly a very different kind of mess.

I race over to where Hannah's crumpled to the ground and dive next to her, pressing my hand firmly to her neck as she stares up at me, wild-eyed. The blood is slicking her neck and my hand, and making it impossible to keep the pressure on, and (oh god) I can feel her heart beating, pumping the blood through my fingers. There's so much blood. NOT HANNAH, my whole body screams as I push down on her neck. *Where is that ambulance?*

And the kids seem to realize it, too, that this is not the fun after-school entertainment they'd thought it was. One of them starts screaming, and almost immediately, all of them are screaming. Half the parents are trying to drag their kids away, and the other half are now taking video. Very helpful, everybody, thanks for the assist.

Meanwhile, Leslie has fallen to her knees, and *that's* when we all hear the sirens approaching. She scrambles up, glances at the ambulance and cop car skidding around the corner, and starts to run.

I can't leave Hannah, and clearly Leslie is faster than me anyway, but there is no *way* I'm letting this woman get away.

Suddenly, my mind clears. I don't have to chase her. I know exactly what to do. I take a huge breath and holler at the top of my lungs.

"JEAN VALJEAN!" I yell, pulling one hand from Hannah's neck to point at Leslie. "TREATS!"

And just as I knew he would, that dog bounds over at top speed, following where I point, and leaps onto Leslie, grabbing her baby bag in his jaws. As he rips it open searching for the treats, hundred-dollar bills start to flutter out. Leslie swats and tries to spin out of his grasp, but she's wrapped up in the strap. She whips around, and Jean clearly thinks this is a fun game because now he jumps and bats at her arm.

The one with the syringe in it.

The syringe goes into her face, right under her eyebrow. Jean noses in at exactly the wrong moment, and the plunger goes down.

Leslie screams and collapses under a pile of dogs.

EMTs rush over with their gear and pull me gently off Hannah.

I am covered in my best friend's blood.

I watch as they start fixing her up, but she looks so, so pale. Her eyes are fluttering open and closed.

After an agonizing, endless moment, one of the EMTs looks up at me and smiles. "You did a good job," she says. "She'll be fine."

Relief washes over me for exactly one second before I hear Benny calling out from underground, the strain clear in his voice. "A hand anybody? I can't do this much longer!"

I whip around to the sinkhole and those sexy, but—for me—platonic forearms, and despite the slippery blood coating my arms and the knowledge that I am a bona fide weakling, I'm about to lie on my belly and try to pull him up, when I hear a familiar voice behind me. "We've got this."

It's Marlowe. With a firefighter.

She shrugs. "He offered to help."

"I didn't offer to help, kid," the firefighter points out. "You dragged me over here."

However he got here, he's got a massive ladder and I am so relieved when he lowers it into the hole.

The ladder clunks to solid ground . . . approximately five inches below the pipe that Benny's slipping off.

"Oh," Benny's voice echoes from the hole. "Well, that's embarrassing."

He climbs out of the hole.

That's it. Everybody's safe. My whole body is shaking, and I flop down onto the dirty-ass street, right in the middle of the intersection.

Marlowe hovers over me. "I can't believe you started all this without me," she grumbles.

"Next time I'll give you a heads-up," I say.

Except no freaking way will there be a next time. My sleuthing days are so over. One and done, as they say. I think I might just stay here, spread-eagle in the middle of the street, in fact.

Behind my head, I hear a guy scream-whispering at someone about how much trouble they're going to be in for "missing the whole thing."

I squint up and because I'm looking at them upside down, it takes me a second to recognize the two young guys, one of whom is holding a Dickie's Tavern pizza box.

They're not wearing the vests, but I know a neon vest wearer when I see one.

They did the same thing I did when I was pretending to be the gas company. Everyone respects a neon vest. Shoot, a neon vest is basically a Rodney O'Malley confidence hat.

"Well, I'm SORRY I'm not a ROBOT who doesn't need to eat LUNCH," the other whispers back angrily.

It's the fake surveyors. AKA the FBI.

CHAPTER 38

Not gonna lie, I feel pretty proud of myself for putting that part together too.

As soon as Leslie mentioned the unmarked windowless van, I remembered the one that showed up at my corner. The one that made Tond so scared he hid up my butt crack.

The surveyors weren't surveyors, and they weren't hit men after him or me, they were FBI guys scoping out dirty dealings at the construction site. Honestly, I'm relieved that I'm not the only one concerned about the goings-on at ol' man Merle's Corruption Emporium.

Not far off, Leslie's being handcuffed, which, *yay*. Her face is furious and swollen around the eyes, but she's giving up without a fight. A very bloody Hannah gives me a weak thumbs-up as she's being loaded onto a stretcher. Benny's sitting on the curb, getting his forearm wrapped up from where Leslie stomped on it. Leslie's bag of cash has been tossed onto the parkway, semi-hidden behind a tree where Jean dragged and then abandoned it when he discovered its lack of treats (note to self: Make it up to him later).

The bag is surrounded by a halo of green bills, and I see Marlowe edging toward it. She catches me watching, so I shake my head a little, sending the telepathic message *Not yet*, hoping she can hear it.

But where is Merle? I didn't see them take him away. Did I miss it? I crane my head a little more and see him surrounded by a crowd of . . . admirers?

Merle is literally shaking the hands of the cops and the EMTs and a couple of parents who dared to venture over.

I'm sorry, WHAT?

I scramble to my feet and brush off my shirt as though the blood there is just a little dust and not a whole-ass gore fest. "Pardon me," I say to the FBI guy holding the pizza box. "Hi. Concerned citizen here. Shouldn't you be arresting that guy? He's the alderman, mucho corruption, if you know what I mean."

The FBI guy does not respond. He kind of squints and looks through me, as though thinking about important FBI stuff through my torso. Like he can just *will* me into not existing. I'll admit it is very disconcerting. So I take a page out of Claudia's book and snap my fingers in his face. He sort of jumps, but then goes back to his pretending-I'm-not-here schtick.

I probably shouldn't try the slap.

Meanwhile, the other guy is still taking in the scene with a panicked look on his face. I'd bet a baby bag full of Tond's money that these guys are low-level interns who did not expect to see *any* action at the sinkhole and then missed alllll of the action. And because I'm a nice guy, I'm about to save their asses and give them the scoop of a lifetime on Merle.

But before I can say a single juicy word, the panicked one steps in, whispers to the staring one, and they brush past me, speed walk toward the bag of cash, stuff the escaped bills back into the bag, hop in their windowless van with something resembling relief, and drive away.

Marlowe's jaw drops.

My soul escapes through my anus.

Welp.

That money is gone for good.

A couple yards away, the EMTs call out to the firefighters, and I realize they're finishing up. The ambulance is about to shut its doors, so this is my chance to be a good friend. Last time I fumbled. This time, I take it.

I hop in the back of the ambulance, ignoring the EMTs' protests, and give Hannah a big, gentle hug.

"Thanks for keeping my blood mostly on the inside," Hannah says. "I know outside blood isn't really your deal."

Honestly, I hadn't thought about it for one hot second. I did it because I had to.

"Text me when you get home, okay?" I say.

She gives me another thumbs-up, and I edge around the bag of saline, hop out of the ambulance, and watch it drive away. Then I join Benny and Marlowe on the curb, all three of us totally exhausted and absentmindedly petting the dogs as they stretch out around us.

"Is Leslie going to die?" Marlowe asks. After missing most of the fireworks, Marlowe seems to be determined to get every detail out of us.

I shake my head. "The EMT said she wouldn't be able to lower her right eyebrow for a few months, but otherwise, she'll be fine. Turns out there wasn't nearly enough Botox in that syringe to actually do any damage. Which I wish I had known like thirty minutes ago."

"This is all my fault," Benny says, holding his head in his hands. "I should've just said yes when she asked me to be Charlie's handler for the dog show. And I definitely should *not* have told her I was taking the poodles to the dog park instead of training Charlie today."

Apparently, when he told this to Leslie, that was the last straw for her. The straw that pushed her from carefully plotting one murder at a time to committing many, many crimes of passion all at once.

"I'm the one who asked you to take the poodles," I say. "And anyway, we had no idea she was an unhinged murderer." But I understand how he feels, because I don't think I'll ever shake the feeling that I failed Claudia. I put my hand on his good arm and he winces. "Sorry."

"She stomped on both of them," he says.

"Well, I hope you get those arms in tip-top shape for dog walking soon," I say. "These poodles aren't going to walk themselves . . . and neither am I!"

"Pro bono, I assume," he says, grinning.

"You know it."

Marlowe has been picking leaves out of Jacques's pompadour, and she abruptly changes the subject. "Hey, Mo, did you finish those adoption videos?"

"Sure did," I say.

"How come you haven't sent them to me yet?" Marlowe says impatiently, tapping her phone.

"I've been solving murders, hello? A little busy?"

Marlowe rolls her eyes. "Yeah, and I had a math test. It's called MULTITASKING."

"Okay okay," I say, sending her the files on my phone.

Yeah, I still can't wait to get rid of the poodles, but as Jean nudges me for another scritch, I know I'm really going to miss them. Without them, it'll be like none of this ever happened.

At least I'll still have my seventh-grade sidekick. And hopefully Benny. And even more hopefully, Tasha—

Shit.

I leap up. "I have to go tell Tasha that things are about to get very complicated at her job." I point at Benny. "Can you watch the dogs real quick?"

When I burst into the alderman's office, Tasha is perched on the edge of the desk, staring blankly at the floor. She looks up when I enter and sort of grimaces at me.

Okay, with murder on the brain, I did neglect to take into consideration potential romantic awkwardness between us after the whole "accusing her of theft and possibly murder" thing. We'll just have to push through. Couples have been through worse, right?

Then she hops off the desk and runs into my arms, and I feel my whole body relax.

"Tasha, I am so *so* sorry about the other night at the coffee shop. I should've never accused you of murder."

"Apology accepted. I'm just glad you're okay!" she says. "Did you get my texts?"

I pull out of the hug and look at my phone, full of unread notifications from her.

"Mo, listen, those weren't real surveyors at your corner," she says breathlessly. "No one put in an order to fix the sinkhole. And once I started digging into it, there's so much weird stuff—bribes, kickbacks, favors, extra books! Old-school Chicago shit! That parking garage looks problematic in a thousand different ways. *And* there have been a bunch of weird people milling around outside the office, in *khakis*. Just today, we've gotten a *ton* of hang-up calls . . ."

"It's cool, it's cool," I say, rubbing her shoulders. "It's just the FBI."

"I'm sorry—the what?" she says, stiffening.

"They've been investigating Merle."

Her eyes widen. "Are you sure?"

"Yep. But just for fraud! And maybe tax stuff!"

"Why do you sound so excited about it?"

"Oh, because he's not the murderer. *Leslie's* the murderer!" I have a feeling I still sound too excited, so as a little coda, I give my best serious face.

She closes her eyes. "This is sort of a lot."

"Yeah," I say. "Guess you might want to think about giving your two weeks."

"Damn," she breathes. She bites her lip and looks at me. She's in that stupid bow tie again and it's driving me crazy. Is it possible that the massive amount of adrenaline coursing through my body after stopping a murderer is being chemically converted to horniness? Could be. This is the absolute *worst* timing, what with the FBI running around and everything, but I nibble her ear and whisper, "Let's hop over to my place, I don't think we should be here right now."

"I can't leave the office unattended. But I *also* probably shouldn't do any more work until I know what's going on." She nods at the cubicle next door. "So . . . I have a better idea."

Moments later, we're on top of the actual conference table, hidden by that flimsy cubicle wall. And as hot as it is to bang on a folding table with federal danger nipping at our heels, I can't stop myself from wondering how much of our relationship is going to take place in a government office.

I'm in socks and not much else, and her skirt's hiked up, shirt open, when the sound of screeching cars fills the air, followed by a polite—but loud—knocking.

She's buttoned back up in a flash, but I seem to have lost my shirt, which is just *great.* I'm still hunting under the conference table when she unlocks and opens the front door.

"Mo?" she calls back to me. "It's the FBI."

Of course it is.

There are eight of them this time, but (ugh) not the interns with my cash. These guys are in dark suits and skirts, like it's opening night for an FBI musical or something. They briefly question Tasha and me in separate rooms, and maybe it's the fact that I'm not wearing a *shirt*, but they're easily convinced that we were making out and not shredding important documents.

I'm still a little salty, though. Those jerks take my money, interrupt my quality time, and then have the nerve to question me in my bra??

The team efficiently loads up dollies of boxes and computer towers while I stand there trying to look like I meant to be shirtless. They can't be there for longer than about ten minutes, and then they disappear out the door. The last one to go hands me my shirt, all neatly folded and creased, which feels like a violation of my privacy for reasons I can't articulate.

I put it back on, and as Tasha walks me to the door, I give her a kiss on the cheek.

"That was wild," she says. "It all happened so fast, I can't believe it was real."

"I need a second job anyway," I say, "so maybe we can job hunt together. How romantic, huh?"

"What do you mean?" she asks, with a frown.

"We'll sit in coffee shops and look at LinkedIn and maybe even be each other's references. Don't tell them about my sweet sex moves, though, that's what got me fired from my last gig."

She shakes her head sweetly and nods back toward her desk. "But I don't *need* a new job. I have a job."

I blink at her, waiting for the punch line.

"Merle's gonna go *to jail*, Tasha."

She smiles brightly. "No, the FBI lady I just talked to said it looked like it was *all* Leslie. The extra books and the corruption and everything. Merle told them everything when the cops arrested her."

"But you know that's not true," I say quietly. "It was on his computer. You *know* he was being dodgy about the construction. He was definitely bribing people. And that's probably the tip of the iceberg."

"Or *maybe*," she says, pulling me close again, "it was just a slip-up. Maybe it was more pressure from Leslie. I thought he was a *murderer*, Mo. But he's a flawed and decent guy who loves this complicated city. He just needs to be reminded of that."

Is she right? Am I being too judgy? I think about how he was going to hand the murder crowbar to Leslie.

No, I am absolutely not being too judgy.

Merle's a coward, sure, but he's a coward with a *lot* of power. And worse—entitlement. If he wants to be corrupt, to get what he wants, then that's what he'll do. Tasha wants to believe in a new Chicago, but she's not willing to admit that the old bribey Chicago is still in operation, right under her nose. She's too relieved that her boss isn't a murderer.

"No way. I'm not buying it," I say. "He may not be a murderer, but he's definitely corrupt. Which is a bad look for a politician."

"This is a huge opportunity for me, Mo. With Leslie gone, I could be chief of staff."

"You *want* to be Merle's chief of staff?"

"I can help people," she adds. "And I can keep an eye on Merle."

I bite my lip.

"What?" she demands. "Come on, Mo. I supported you during your hijinks."

"*Hijinks?* I solved a double murder!"

"This is my *career*. I've only ever wanted to be a good guy in politics."

"Well, Tasha," I say, "you'll make a hell of a splash as Merle's Number One Henchperson."

Her beautiful, nerdy, lovable face goes on lockdown.

"Why do you care so much about my job anyway," she says stonily. "You didn't even know what an alderman was a month ago."

Honestly, fair point. Why *am* I so upset about Merle's dirty dealings? And do I really care that much about aldermanic office politics??

I pause for a second to actually feel my feelings. "You work *so much*," I say, finally. "You can only ever squeeze me in between meetings and projects, and only if I visit you here." I wave my hand at the conference table that so recently hosted us.

"That's not fair," she says. "We went to Dickie's that one time, and I met you at that cool coffee shop in the South Loop where you accused me of murder."

I roll my eyes. "God, let it go already. It's not always just about you, if you're keeping track, I accused *every*body of murder."

We grin at each other.

"I'll make more time for you, I promise," Tasha says. "Here, I'll prove it to you. Let's have a date, a real date." She pulls out her phone and scrolls through her calendar, and I cuddle up next to her.

"Um, are you free October third?"

Oh. Nuts. She's serious, isn't she.

"That's like a month from now," I say softly.

"I'm sorry, Mo, it's an election year, things are about to get crazy and I want to make sure we win—"

I lean in and give her one last long kiss.

"I should go," I say. And then I walk away without looking back.

Because if I look back, I'll see what *I* want.

And I know I'm not getting it.

CHAPTER 39

The corner still needs guarding, so somehow I manage to get up the next few mornings.

On the job, rumors are flying.

The FBI told us all to keep our traps shut until Leslie's trial is over, so the official explanation for what happened is just "public disturbance." Still, I've heard the whispers as I walk kids and their parents across the street. Some of them think I'm a secret agent. Some of them think I'm a mob boss. Some of them think I'm being paid by the mayor to take out people who haven't paid their parking tickets.

The effect, though, is that everyone crosses the street when I tell them to.

It's making work a lot easier.

AND WHEN *Block Club* posts their write-up of the whole affair a few days later, I can't help but read it. It's as close as I get to Tasha these days.

Leslie Carey, wife of north side alderman Merle Carey, was arrested Sunday on charges of murder, racketeering, bribery, and extortion, abusing her position as the spouse of an elected official to solicit and extort private legal work and other benefits from companies and individuals with business before the city, one of which went south and led to the horrific murders.

"I am shocked and horrified," said Ald. Carey, via a statement released by his new chief of staff, Tasha Moore. "I had no idea Leslie was running around committing these heinous crimes in my name. I will do whatever it takes to regain the trust of Chicagoans and restore the good name of Carey. My office has always, always operated with integrity and lawfulness, ask anyone! And we will continue to run our ward with honesty to be an example for the city."

Tasha and I haven't communicated at all since the breakup, and I don't know how we would start.

I really miss her. I miss having something to look forward to. Somebody to get to know better. But a lot would have to change for our relationship to work. And I can't hang on and wait for her to fit me in her schedule.

Even good things can be not good for you, I guess. Like having ice cream with every meal, including breakfast. Which I should probably stop doing, I think, as I house a pint of ice cream while waiting for my frozen mac and cheese to cook in the microwave.

Eh, it's dinnertime, so it's okay. I'm just having dessert first.

My pocket buzzes. It's a text from Marlowe.

Marlowe: Come to school now and bring the dogs

I think about ignoring her, but recently, Marlowe has adopted

Claudia's tone of texting, and it's hard to say no. I stop the microwave, put the pint back in the freezer, and go. And like she asks, I bring the dogs, who are super pumped to get an extra walk in.

Marlowe, meanwhile, brings her moms. Mom #1 looks very lawyery in a sleek gray suit—she's definitely Shoshanna, the one who yelled at me over the phone. Mom #2 has a curly undercut with blue streaks in it. I can see how this combo might result in a Marlowe.

"Mo!" Marlowe runs over and hugs me, talking under her breath so her moms don't hear. "Don't mention my involvement in the case, okay? We'll debrief later. Your place?"

I don't get to answer because Marlowe shoves me toward her moms. "Mo, this is Shoshanna and Alexis."

"Hi, Mo," says Shoshanna. "Thanks for looking out for our little troublemaker."

"That's the job," I say. "The crossing guard job, I mean. If you've heard any rumors, they aren't true. About murder. Or whatever."

"We saw the adoption videos you made," Shoshanna says, thankfully changing the subject. "For the dogs."

Wait. I swivel to look at Marlowe, and she's grinning at me. The little sneak. She made me make the videos FOR HER.

"I'm a pediatric surgeon," Alexis says, "and we were thinking, with training, the poodles could be great therapy dogs for kids at the hospital. So—"

"YES," I say, a little too eagerly, and Alexis looks startled. "I mean, yes, please take the dogs. They would make *great* therapy dogs."

"Thank you," says Alexis, beaming.

"Thank youuuuuu," says Marlowe, who's already hugging all three of the dogs at the same time.

WE GO BACK to my place, I put everything I've gotten for the dogs in a trash bag for them to carry home, and then they leave.

My apartment is quieter than I think it's ever been. No dogs, no bribery from Sheila, no panicked hiding of piles of cash in the bathtub.

This sounds bad, but I feel a little . . . *lost* without the chaos? So I pull out my phone to text Hannah or Benny or even watch some haircut videos to distract myself, but then after a moment I put it back in my pocket.

Because honestly? It's kinda nice to be quiet for a hot second.

Cran's calendar is still rolled up stinkily on my one table, and I unroll it, carefully rip out the best photo of the dogs (April), and Scotch tape it to the wall. I take a step back to admire it, my first wall hanging.

It's a start. And now I'm feeling motivated to actually live this new life I keep talking about.

So I grab a pile of résumés and do this the old-fashioned way. I stop at every store on the main drag. I chat with the bearded guys at the record store and get talked into buying a used grunge album (I resolve to someday get a record player). I stop in Urgent Care, and sure, Jessie's not glad to see me, but I eventually make her laugh, and when I hand her my résumé, she doesn't immediately crumple it up. I pop into the YMMV Car Repair in case they need a receptionist or, I don't know, someone to wash tires? I even drop into Dickie's and meet the actual Dickie (!) who is a middle-aged lady (!!).

Honestly, I'm having a great time. Even though I'm alone, I don't feel lonely at all.

I'm all out of résumés and am about to head home when a storefront I've never seen before stops me in my tracks.

Jack n' Dils, it's called.

There's a banner that says GRAND OPENING, COME MAKE YOUR OPENINGS GRAND! and in the window, festively arranged and gorgeously lit, are the most spectacular sex toys I've ever seen.

Every color of the rainbow. Shapes I never imagined in my wildest dreams.

It's like looking in the window of a candy store.

Back in my Chris era, I *never* would've been brave enough to actually go inside a store like this. Chris wanted to keep our sex life "natural," so the only dildo I ever bought came from the internet and was, let's just say, *not the right size*. I briefly used it as a doorstop, but Chris didn't like that either.

I walk in, kind of proud of myself but also super nervous? It's embarrassing, I'm a grown-up, I should be totally unfazed by shelves packed with sparkly dongs.

Because *everything* is on display in here. You know exactly the size of the toy you're getting, that's for sure. And there are no shadowy, creepy corners, no lurking dudes. It's all well-lit and weirdly . . . cozy?

I have no idea how to behave. Act cool, Mo.

So I make a selfie duckface as I sashay across the store, and then immediately realize that was the wrong call.

I look up to see if anyone saw me and the person at the counter is smiling at me, so I think the answer is yes, they saw me.

Oh god, I'm going to have to buy something now.

I pass the shelves of lube and a table of fishnet things and realize that the vibrator display is calling to me. They're all out of their packaging so you can see what they feel like and turn them on and everything.

I've stumbled into a sex toy petting zoo.

Bullets and dick-shaped things, sleek aerodynamic shapes, lots of things with bunny ears and rotating shafts and and and . . .

Yes, okay, I *am* overthinking this, but at heart, I'm just a girl standing in front of a wall of vibrators asking one of them to love me.

The question is, *which* one?

The counter person sidles up next to me and straightens out the vibrators that I've just flung around willy-nilly, but they're not being judgy or anything. Actually, their presence is sort of calming.

"Let me know if I can help," they say with a sweet smile.

I think about saying no thanks, I got this, but after several weeks of pretending to be an expert in a thing I know nothing about, I'm ready for some expert advice.

"Actually," I say, "I never knew there were so many options. I'd love some help."

They talk me through all the differences using words like *rumble* and *zing*, and honestly this feels like some Willy Wonka shit. I love it.

In the end, I decide to go with a basic model for my first outing. It doesn't look like an actual penis, it's just a hot pink hard plastic wand. A hot pink wand that will, with a couple AAA batteries, rock my world, at least according to the packaging.

As I pay for the wand and some lube, pretending not to think about my rapidly draining bank account, I spot a sign on the cork-board behind the counter.

Now hiring.

"You should apply," the vibrator expert says when I ask about the sign. They hand me a business card. "Just shoot over your résumé and a short cover letter."

I don't even wait to get home—I type up a cover letter quickly while standing on the sidewalk. It's possibly too honest? About how up till now, I've relied on the people I'm dating way too much for my happiness, and how coming to the store made me realize I have to take my happiness into my own hands.

Literally.

In the sex department.

The horny arena.

The boning bureau.

The randy division.

I delete those last bits and add in that I'm currently helping kids during the day as a crossing guard and would love to help adults at night as a sex toy guard.

So stupid, but I leave it in, attach my résumé, and hit send.

And now it's ME TIME.

AFTER, UM, *seducing* myself several times, I pass out, sleeping better than I have in *weeks*. No poodles to beg me for food or walks, no demands for Venmo bribes, and because it's the weekend, no need to throw on any neon vests.

I wake up to my phone buzzing, and my first thought is *Who could possibly be calling me at this hour?* Then I blink my eyes open and look at the time. Holy cow, it's almost eleven a.m.

"Hello?" I answer blearily.

"Is this Mo Ellery?" a voice asks. "This is Alex from Jack n' Dils—not to gush but we *loved* your cover letter, which is maybe the first time that sentence has ever been uttered out loud."

I laugh, and so does Alex.

"Anyway, we'd like to set up an interview if you're still interested?"

Oh *shit*.

I finally got one.

"Absolutely," I say, and then catch myself. "It's not . . . a video chat, is it?"

Not that I'd make the same mistake twice. Probably. But better safe than sorry. We set a time for the very IRL interview, and then hang up.

I text Hannah: I think I might get a job at a sex toy store!

She responds with the "!!" emoji and then replies TELL ME EVERYTHING.

Me: Dickie's? Later tonight?

I get a thumbs-up.

But first—I reach over to my bedside table.

Just need to do a little more research.

You know.

For the job.

ACKNOWLEDGMENTS

In January 2024, we each hit a rough patch. In writing, in life, in *waves hands at world.* Around that time, the Green Post—a classically British-style pub with a killer egg sandwich, Malört shots aplenty, and an abundance of cozy writing nooks—opened in our neighborhood.

We decided to meet at the Green Post a few times a week and write a murder mystery set against Eden's day job of the moment: Chicago crossing guard. We removed all pressure. Our one goal was to make each other laugh. Lo and behold, it helped. Writing this together has been unspeakably fun.

So first of all, we want to acknowledge each other, and how the joy of writing for a friend led to a fully grown book of its own.

Lucky for us, a LOT of other friends contributed along the way: early on, Joshua Mark met with us to talk us through the procedures and dynamics of aldermanic offices and Chicago zoning laws, and we are so grateful for his very patient responses while we bombarded him with increasingly bonkers scenarios about how the office could be corrupted. Thank you for being incorruptible, Joshua.

Dan Garguilo and Ben Clark answered some crucial building structure and emergency services questions, while Sarah Rosenberg-Scott and Andrew Scott offered some incredibly valuable medical insight. Thanks also to Rory, Sassy, Diogenes, and Razelus Carlisle. Any inaccuracies about first responders, various bodily symptoms and treatments, or poodles are ours.

We're grateful to beta readers Jessica Hilt, Rachel Hylton, and Marianna Baer for reading that rough-around-the-edges first draft, and we'd like to thank all of our wonderful friends who listened to us read chapters at assorted gatherings and told us we were deranged (complimentary).

We want to thank Chicago Public Schools and the city's crossing guards: Good job, everybody out there who keeps watch over the kids of Chicago in the face of Poodle Dudes and other antagonists. We also want to thank Chicago itself: All of the real neighborhoods that we lightly disguised, as well as all of the neighborhoods that we didn't disguise at all. We're lucky to have you, Chicago, in all your moods.

Cameron McClure agented the bejesus out of this book, guiding it with a sure hand and reining us in when necessary (look, it was *always* necessary). Dylan Haston (riding shotgun) gave us phenomenal notes throughout the process. We could not have possibly imagined more ardent advocates for Mo and her shenanigans, and we also just think you're both so darn cool.

We are outrageously, like *tub-full-of-hundos* lucky that Mo landed at William Morrow. Nate Lanman and Tessa James have absolutely been the editors of our dreams, and every single person who's worked on the book has made it sexier (is that weird to say?

Welp, too late). Thank you also to the whole Mo team at William Morrow for their time and incredible talents: Yeon Kim, Amanda Hudson, Jen McGuire, Chris Connolly, Laurie McGee, and Lisa Glover.

And finally, we'd like to thank our families, especially Kyle and Jorin. We'd help you two nerds cross the street any day of the week.

ABOUT THE AUTHOR

BIRDIE HORNE IS the combined pen name of former enemies Eden Robins and MW Garguilo. Over the years, they have been love rivals, co-godmothers, and neighbors across an alley in Chicago. Separately, they have published more than twenty books, and together they have a résumé full of the kinds of jobs that genuinely worry their parents. One of them was nominated for—and lost—Chicago Crossing Guard of the Year. This is their first outing as Birdie Horne.